IX

0006795

Sting of the Bee

STING
OF THE
BEE

Seth Rolbein

A
Joan
Kahn
BOOK

St. Martin's Press
NEW YORK

Copyeditor: Elaine Chubb

A Joan Kahn Book

Library of Congress Cataloging-in-Publication Data

Rolbein, Seth.
  Sting of the bee.

  "A Joan Kahn book."
  I. Title.
PS3568.0533S7   1987   813'.54   87-4409
ISBN 0-312-00688-8

First Edition
10   9   8   7   6   5   4   3   2   1

This book is dedicated to everyone who has helped me and taught me so much. But most of all, to Kathy.

Sting of the Bee

CHAPTER ONE

"**D**ECLARE yourself."

"What?"

"Decleear yahrself, mahn," the customs agent repeated, relaxing out of rigid tourist talk, seeing from the passport that Martinson Sanders had been born in Jamaica.

"Declare myself, is that what you're trying to say? What do you mean?"

"Coome, mahn, dere are tourist waiting and tourist them no like to wait. Yah got any divin knife, or fresh thing from States like fruit?"

Marty Sanders shook his head like shaking a bee out of his hair. Yeah, that's the sound; lazy, like Mom said, but lilting too. "No, no nothing like that."

"Well, all right, den, walk on, mahn, walk on. Step lively."

It's the heat, he told himself, it's the heat makes everything so strange.

The lady in the Hawaiian shirt who'd sat next to him on the flight from Boston waved a pink hand good-bye. "Have a good visit home," she called, "and I hope your father is all right."

Why the hell did I even talk to her to begin with, he wondered. Maybe nerves, or the beer, or the ease of airplane anonymity . . .

Before he found the answer he found company. A Jamaican dressed in an airport uniform, maybe the guy who connects the fuel hose to the engines, had fallen in step.

"Takin care ah biz, mahn?" and a pair of brown eyes shot through with red veins peered at Marty Sanders with a sleepy intensity that put him off.

"What?"

"Takin care ah biz, mahn, bizness, mahn?"

"No way, brother, I'm taking care of my father," and Marty chuckled at his private joke, at how apt his comment had been.

The sleepy eyes were not put off. "I tell you true, true as sun in sky. Is *me* load dat cargo, mahn. Is *me* can get ah bundle of ganja onto dat plane like nothing, mahn. Me know yah got good connection in States. Everyone got good connection dat coome Jamaica. What say we do some biz, mahn, some good bizness?"

And so the hustle begins, thought Marty. Doesn't take long, does it?

"Fella, I don't know what the hell you're talking about, but it doesn't sound straight. So back off, all right?"

"Yessir, yessir." The man smiled, his accent suddenly changing and his mouth open to show a gold tooth up front. "No problem, everything just cool as can be," and he dropped away.

2

Down the whitewashed corridor of the Montego Bay airport Marty Sanders paced, quickly and purposefully, none of this bullshit jive walk so many so-called brothers resorted to back home. His pinstriped shirt was buttoned and so was his collar, his slacks had a crease in them, and his sneakers were running shoes. Big gold-rimmed glasses with a habit of slipping down the bridge of his nose, especially when he was reading or working at the library, were bothering him because both hands were full up with luggage and they were doing their slow slide and he didn't want to stop because he just wanted to get this damn trip over with and the flight had been delayed and it's just like this country to have everybody and his sister coming on to you within two minutes of arrival and he very nearly bowled over a table that had been set up with dozens of plastic cups half-filled with some kind of red drink.

As if he was their cue, a dozen young women dressed in colorful flowing costumes suddenly burst into song, swaying in time:

> *Coome coome to Jamaica,*
> *and see what we done*
> *we live by our motto*
> *Out of Many Peoples, One.*

Even Marty Sanders, as intent and preoccupied as he was, just had to stop and admire. He took a plastic cup, smelled strong rum, and sipped gingerly. The women smiled, but they looked tired and didn't really try to conceal it. His heart went out to them. "Thank you, thank you very much," he announced, as the rest of his plane's passengers caught up and swarmed around.

Through the final swinging doors and again the wall of heat made him feel as if the air was liquid and he was swimming. Clustered in front of him, jostling for first contact, were fifty people who had been waiting two hours for the money this jet represented.

"TAXI TAXI TAXI," yelled many voices at once.

"What you need, mahn? I got it," one man with giant reflector sunglasses told him, grabbing an elbow.

"No no, not him. ME, mahn, make it ME," yelled another, cigarettes behind both ears, sweat staining his bright red shirt. "Him thief you, you let him."

"ME tief? Take ah tief know ah tief," yelled the first, giving the second a shove.

Yet another driver slid over, whispering, "Leave dem fight and coome dis way. Best music and ganja in me own car—guaranteed or mooney back, mahn, mooney back."

"Forget it," Marty mumbled, "all of you can just forget it." He picked out a man who wasn't among the throng pressing toward the door and stumbled to him. "You got a taxi?"

"Yah mahn."

"Would you like to take me about fifteen miles outside the city? I know the way, if I can remember it right."

"Sure, mahn, dat what me here for."

His first view of his native country after thirteen years, after prep school and college and a U.S. citizenship, was framed in the rear window of a rattletrap Chevy taxi. That made sense, that seemed right, everything contained within his private made-in-America movie screen. Even the sound track was there, but it was definitely made-in-Jamaica—reggae music blaring out of the front seat, the dominant bass line buzzing like a thousand bees through a blown speaker propped on the dash. And so Marty could sit, removed from the spectacle, window rolled down, and watch his past merge into the present.

The streets of Montego Bay were smaller and dirtier and

more crowded than he remembered—everywhere there was pressure and movement. At each turn, at each honk of the taxi's horn, someone was selling something. A boy pushing a wooden wheelbarrow carried a block of ice wrapped in black plastic; quickly he grated off some slivers into a cup and added syrup before the sun could melt his money away. "Move it, move it, silly pickney," yelled Marty's driver, hanging out the window. Green coconuts lined a curb and an old woman with her legs spread wide sat among them, packs of cigarettes in the lap of her dress. "Give me one," yelled Marty's driver, gesturing to the smokes. She ignored him, looking instead at young girls who balanced straw baskets filled with mangoes and oranges and tangerines on their heads as they swayed past the station where the big old buses still waited; Marty looked for the one named King Alphanso with a lion's head painted on the front, wondering if it still left a trail of blue smoke as it chugged along the coast road toward Falmouth filled to overflowing with people hanging on to their seats, their packages, maybe even their live roosters, for dear life.

"Wallassss," yelled the taxi driver over the syncopated reggae back beat.

"What?" Seems every other word out of my damn mouth is What?

"Me name Wallassss."

"Oh, Wallace, yes. My name's Marty."

The square in the center of town still gleamed too white to look at and banks formed the corners of the plaza, pillars of the city, as if everything would collapse if they weren't there, façades holding back the Jamaican countryside of corrugated tin and tiny shacks that otherwise would creep like vines into the square itself. Boys hawked the *Gleaner* and the *Mirror* side by side. Police with

5

ramrod backbones dressed in uniforms that still smacked of England stepped lively through a shaded archway, moving slouchers with the light touch of one black boot. At the side of the square a grandstand like a high school football stadium had been erected, as though people would pay money to sit and watch the doings at the center of town.

"What dat for?" asked Marty. He slapped his thigh as soon as the words were out: Speak English, man, English.

"Oh, it boolshit, mahn, boolshit! Queen coome last year, dem spend more on her den dem spend on real peoples for work or food. Boolshit, me say. And den when she coome, she not even dressed up in a gown or crown. Nothing at all, just sitting dere like any tourist. Cha! Dem build dem seats like it a big show: Watch Queen Sit Down! One thing good, at least dem pay a wage to build dem damn thing."

The side streets and back streets were jammed with sign after sign, bars wide open blaring more reggae, dark little hardware stores and bakeries where old men sat in corners away from the sun, most of the bigger markets named Chin or Chen or Chang, runty dogs nosing streaming murky water in the gutter. Schoolboys dressed in khaki and schoolgirls in blue and white bounced through it all, their black faces gleaming and glad to be out. Fashionable secretaries sashaying back to work from a late lunch ignored the guffaws and whistles of appreciation punctuating the reggae. Men clustered around the front of a used appliance store in animated argument, all standing, faces inches apart, looking like they were on the verge of some serious violence. Wallace let go with another blast of his horn and they all stopped, waved, yelled a greeting—and picked up the argument with just as much heat as ever.

"Palateeks." Wallace laughed.

Past the town park, vendors had set up a line of wares to

attract tourists. There were bits of black coral, black knit caps with rings of red and green and yellow, and always wood carvings—of heads covered with dreadlocks, or birds with arching necks. Strolling casually among them were couples, men in Bermuda shorts and women in tank tops, their skin pink and red as rare meat, browsing and shaking off hawkers and hustlers. Marty just had to laugh; they looked like glowing neon signs, calling attention to themselves. And then there were some fashionable homes rising up on the side of rock hills, Montego Bay's suburbs, metal gates between stone pillars protecting long driveways lined with banana and coconut trees. He caught a glimpse of a woman sitting on a balcony high above the hustle of the street; her hair was straightened and her black skin made a sheer blouse look even whiter. She was a black-and-white photograph framed by more color and movement than any film could ever capture. Then she was gone, out of the frame.

"Me not see many black tourist, mahn," said Wallace.

"I'm not a tourist. Well, I take that back, maybe I am a tourist, but I'm going to see my father."

"Where him live?"

"Off the road to Falmouth, past Still Valley and Bishopgate. You know the road?"

"You call dat ah road? Dat no road up dere. If me know you're going dere, me no take you. Ruin me cab, mahn, ruin it."

"No no, Wallace, you're thinking of the wrong place. The roads up there are good. Hell, I remember as a kid I could ride my bicycle from the house into MoBay in less than an hour, and it's got to be a good fifteen, twenty miles."

"When you been dere last time?"

7

"Thirteen years, I figured it out on the plane. Half a lifetime ago."

"And why you coome back now?"

"Well, my old man says he's dying and he wants to see me."

Wallace turned to look at the customer in the backseat who had just announced in such a matter-of-fact way that his father was getting ready for a cedar box. "Not seen him all dat time?"

"No." Marty thought of the last time he saw his father. He had been a boy standing on the balcony at the back of his parents' bedroom, overlooking rolling fields where the cows and goats grazed. It was late in the afternoon and the sun was turning everything to gold. Behind him his mother was hustling around the house, putting the last few things into their bags, hurrying. He wasn't helping, and for some reason she didn't expect him to help. It was unusual for her to leave him alone and let him stand on the balcony and do nothing but look. Then, out of the woods, Father appeared; the simple tan cloth cap like the hat of a baseball player without a team and the tan short-sleeve shirt and the tan pants and the leather boots and the long black rifle, always pointed down when walking, wedged under one arm where it belonged. He emerged out of the mahogany and lagwood trees with his long slow strides, as if one of the trees had decided to take a walk across the field, two brown dogs circling his heels like roots shaking off dirt.

"Here coome Father," he had murmured.

"Come on, Marty, we must go right now," she had said with urgency and fear. They raced down the stairs carrying whatever they could, letting things fall behind if they would, past Cora, who stood near the front door in her apron without condemning them or wishing them well. The little truck started and they were gone.

"Him be mighty mighty glad to see you, mahn," said Wallace.

"I hope so."

"No hopin about it! Listen to me clear: You be glad to see him, him be mighty mighty glad see you. Dat true speech."

"Yes, I suppose it is."

"Cha!" Wallace was getting exasperated with this young man's haziness. "Den tell me dis: Why you not see him all dis time? Everyone go to States who can, get chance at good livin, dat make sense. But not *one* visit? Not one? You strike out over dere, mahn, yah got no money coome home till now?"

"Hey," Marty flared, "I've done far from striking out. I got a good education and a good job and good friends and I'm making decent pay. Frankly, my personal affairs are not much of your business."

Wallace settled back; didn't take much to figure this boy out. "All right, mahn, cool, mahn."

Montego Bay had thinned away to nothing, and the blacktop of the coast road shimmered. On one side the sea played turquoise tricks, calm like a postcard. But on the other side the mountain ridge rose straight up, mimicking the shore as it met the sky, gray and mysterious. That was where he had to go and that was where he was scared of going. What was there to be scared of? The White Witch of Lyman Hall? He laughed as the gleaming plantation house appeared in the window of Wallace's Chevy. No kid would go near there within hours of sunset. Even grown men preferred stopping by in the morning lest the black magic power of Obeah make them sick. At midnight with a full moon, blood spilt long ago on the front hall steps was supposed to shine like black ice. A big hotel loomed on the oceanside, built since Marty had left. He craned to see its name; "Lyman Hall Holiday Inn," he read. "Wonder if there's blood on those steps."

"Not as much as at dat old slave plantation, and I don't mean no White Witch neither."

This Wallace is pretty sharp, thought Marty, pretty aware. "I don't know about that, Wallace. Seems like the tourist industry is doing its share of exploitation. Not to mention the International Monetary Fund—"

"IMF muthafookah!" Wallace exploded. "Dem drive Michael Manley from office, put squeeze on evreeting till Jamaicans say, Forget it, mahn, got to eat. So vote Seaga. Den here coome Seaga, him got teeth like rat fang and dat what him, fookin rat!"

This was the kind of talk Marty liked, politics and how people were getting repressed and who was putting the squeeze on whom, the big picture, nothing too personal, but before he could really explore it they had come to the bus stop where King Alphanso waited (cement bench now, with corrugated zinc to hold off the rain—quite an improvement). And then the turnoff, the beginning of the beginning and the beginning of the end, the place he'd often dreamed about the past thirteen years, the place where he and his mother sat for such a long long time, truck engine throbbing, her head on the steering wheel, sobbing more from exhaustion than grief, waiting forever and ever and ever until finally the huge diesel engine with no muffler could be heard and King Alphanso's gold lion face with a trail of blue smoke ground to a halt. She left the keys in the truck because everyone knew whose truck it was, so no one could get away with stealing it, and then she asked the driver if he would be willing to take them to the airport even though it was a little out of the way. In the dreams sometimes the driver turned into his father, or sometimes the gold lion's face became his father's face, but always he took them to the airport, and always the two of them flew away.

"Turn, mahn, turn," Marty shouted, as if Wallace hadn't already put on his blinker. The Chevy hit a deep hole in the last crumbling remains of blacktop before the road turned to dirt.

"Me break taxi axle, you pay for it."

Barefoot pickneys, as Marty knew they were called, came scampering to watch a major event. "Car coome, car coome," they shouted, running alongside, able to keep up. They made Marty feel as if he was in one of those old film clips of army generals riding through a mountain village after liberation, acknowledging the grateful cheers of the populace. They also made him feel rich, and he didn't like either of those feelings.

"What a damn shame," he cried. "These roads have been here for three hundred years, did you know that? Three hundred years, and now they've come to this. They used to carry enough sugarcane out of here to make London's coffee sweet and London's lords drunk. Now it's fit for a donkey."

"Dat what happen when IMF squeeze. No money for road in bush."

They bounced along, chatter from kids broadcasting their arrival, reggae turned down. It was good for Martinson Sanders that they were going slowly; so much was flooding through him that the crawl of the taxi was a kind of decompression, giving the bubbles of memories in his brain a chance to work themselves out to the surface and fizzle instead of exploding inside. The open pastureland, remains of the original plantation, still had the same old footpath shortcut across the long loop of the road, a snake in the grass worn to dust by many bare feet. But there was a pair of parallel tracks across the trail—if he didn't know better, Marty would have said they were the marks of some kind of primitive airstrip. Then came banana trees old and uncultivated, more useful for shade than food, overgrown far beyond the last vestige of the straight lines of their planting. There were coconuts, towering as usual, with their green and yellow nuts nestled under the crown waiting for some monkey of a kid to shinny up and cut them down. He used to be able to get up one of those in no time with a machete dangling at his belt—no big thing, because if a kid couldn't do that he might as well not show his face in Still Valley. He could still feel the sting and hear the taunt of the village kids after his mother saw him at the top of a tall coconut one day and screamed, for all to hear, "Be careful, Martinson, for God's sake be careful." Months later, whenever he walked the road, from behind a wall or bush would come the mimicking voices, "Keerful, Martinsoon, fahr Gawd's sake keerful, little bwai."

The cluster of shacks that was Still Valley had changed little except that now there were utility poles lining the dirt road. Electricity had reached the district. It seemed odd that the modern world would string its line here when everything else had fallen into deep disrepair; even the rusting sign advertising Cold Red Stripe Beer in red and white hung crookedly over the dark doorway to the little bar that he had never dared enter. An outdoor porch with open sides, nothing more than a corrugated metal awning above a dirt floor, still housed worn wooden benches and tables where the men slammed down dominoes so hard that the wooden posts holding up the roof would shake. A naked light bulb had replaced kerosene lanterns, that was the only change, and as Wallace drove slowly past, the men leaned against the building and stared with the same impassive scrutiny they had always applied to any passerby.

Next door the little post office was closed as usual and

the slot in the door to drop mail was ringed black from year after year of hands rubbing against it as they left their special messages. That Still Valley had its own post office was a matter of pride, even if it often took weeks for a letter to make its way twenty-odd miles from Montego Bay. Marty wondered if people still told the story about the day his father returned from the city with a government man dressed all in blue with shiny brass buttons, Father armed with statistics and cogent, convincing arguments in favor of the establishment of a postal operation to service a fast-growing district. In the end the man in blue tossed off a shot of overproof rum under the metal awning and made it clear that such a thing would happen only if he had something to gain from it—just a small contribution from each household that stood to gain so much from this valuable service would suffice. Everyone had expected something like this, but not so insulting, not so blatant. Goodwill in the bush meant sharing your goat or your rum or your roof, but it was all done in good time and meant more because the return of a favor was unexpected when it arrived, so sweeter. It certainly didn't mean passing money in the middle of the day after barely having met.

So Martin Sanders stood up, donned his tan cap with the long visor, returned his black rifle to the crook of his arm with the barrel pointed not quite as straight down as usual, and informed the postal representative that he was a disgrace to his country and an embarrassment to his host in the district—who was now informing him that he had better walk quickly down the center of the road and return to Montego Bay directly. That way he might have a chance to keep his skin intact, as well as get in his side of the story before his host reached Long River's telegraph office. He might then be able to refute the wired report of his attempted bribe that would be sent to Martin Sanders's old school chum, who due to his long-standing personal relationship with Norman Manley now had a sinecure of seniority in the Ministry of Interior, which oversees the postal department. Marty never found out if any of that ever happened, but the post office had been established within weeks.

"Much farther, mahn?"

"Do I think much about my father?"

"No no, how much farther? Me tires and rim getting worn t'shit, mahn."

"Not much more, hang in there." But that was a lie and Marty knew it. They had barely started to climb. They had to pass over the big culvert which let Black River sluice under the road into a tumbling waterfall that used to be so strong you couldn't stand under it, but an earthquake had shifted the bed so it wasn't much more than a trickle during the hot months. Sure, and there was the water collection system the government had installed just months before he and his mother left, the biggest thing to happen in a long, long time because now a sloping hill of concrete fed into a big cistern and tropical rains were caught and saved for the village. Women had begun to gather around with their wash and pickneys to gossip before hoisting a big jug full of water onto their heads and returning home, and sure enough the day of Marty's arrival was no different—they were out with colorful cloths wrapped around their hair, laughing and scolding as they pounded their clothes on some rocks until they saw the car, stopped everything to see what would become the big news of the night, and as Marty leaned out the Chevy window, finally pushing through his movie screen, an old woman straightened up completely, threw a pointed finger, and shouted, "Martinson! Him Martinson big and wearin eyeglasses." He had no idea who she was.

They had been reduced to a bare crawl, with Wallace stopping every hundred yards to examine the terrain in front of him like a soldier trying to slip through a minefield. Marty didn't even notice. He didn't want to get out of that Chevy, he didn't want the movie to end and real life to begin, he wanted to keep sitting there watching the lagwood trees that made the honey so sweet and clear on the ridge over Dagi the beekeeper's house. He wanted to see the funny little old truck that Dagi loaded to move his bottles to market, bottles that used to hold whiskey, not nearly as proper and antiseptic as his father's honey bottles. God, the truck was still there, though it looked as if it hadn't moved in all thirteen years, now more a help to clinging vines. Knowing Dagi—clever and compact and light brown from his Indian ancestry, a symbol of when the British Empire mingled people from around the world—in a true moment of need the little truck would pull out of the yard as smoothly as a cat, as smoothly as Dagi himself moved, with cousin Bomba shouting jokes and tossing bits of honey candy to the kids running behind.

But the luxury of his passive detachment had to end. The moment came at Big Turn, where the road swung past a tiny church manned by a thumping evangelist full of missionary fire and Caribbean beat. It was the last, steepest switchback before climbing to the top of Rose Hill and then down the other side to the Sanderses' property. Hard rains had scoured the road and washed away the last semblance of smoothness, leaving nothing but rocks that would not erode.

"End dah road, mahn," said Wallace.

"I still have a mile and a half to go," Marty protested.

"Yah got two legs as well. Pay me and give thanks yah got dis far. Thirty U.S., or one-fifty Jamaican."

Marty gave Wallace thirty-five dollars because truly it had been a long haul.

"Appreciate it, mahn, truly. Cool runnings, all right?"

"Yes, Wallace, thanks." He hoisted his two leather suitcases, wondered about the old family donkey Desmond, pushed his drooping glasses back as well as he could, and started the long walk up and down the road.

"Forget yahr failure, mahn, forget de past which is gone," Wallace called after him. "Present tense is what matter now, and dat true sight from me to you."

And an explanation of why you're wrong, an explanation of thirteen years, would take forever, thought Marty. Anyway, the man is only the taxi driver and not worth arguing with.

Instead he concentrated on the trek before him. Fifteen years ago he would have skipped past the soursop tree and around the cluster of bananas, chucking a rock at a coconut, but now the heat and the luggage, the prospects of what he had to face and the belly he had grown sitting at a desk all day, weighed him down. He kept his head bowed to the middle of the path, taking a grim straight line to save energy, one step at a time, one more one more one more. Dark stains pooled out under his armpits, ruining his shirt, and sweat dripped into his glasses and made his eyes sting. A voice was chattering, laughing "Hee hee hee," and he had the dim idea his name was mentioned but it sounded like the jungle, he couldn't figure out what was being said, he tried to nod his head politely but it was all he could do just to keep stumbling on. That must be Miss Ethel, a deeper part of himself whispered, and he remembered her toothless and sagging in her tiny shop halfway between Big Turn and the gateway to his house, willing to argue for an hour that if you wanted to buy a pound of rice from her you were going to have to buy a can of beans too because no one was buying beans but everyone wanted rice.

The voice receded and soon his head was filled with a low hum, a constant unchanging buzz as if the island itself had begun to chant. He knew what it was. He was passing the cluster of boxes where his father's bees made their home and honeycombs. They filled the air with their sound until it seemed to seep into his bones. Several circled his head, patrols for the hive, and when he tried to shake them off without letting go of his suitcases one landed on his neck and buried a stinger as deep as it could go.

The pain forced him to stop. He swatted at the bee and it fell to his feet, curling into its death wriggle. "A welcome-home present from my father," Marty announced sarcastically, but even as he said it he remembered the Jamaican belief that a bee sting was a sure omen of good luck to come. "With good luck like this, who needs bad?" he muttered, confused and exhausted.

But the pain, strangely enough, cleared the haze out of his head and allowed him to see the last stone wall clearly, to turn off at the big red birch with the kind face in the bark of the trunk, to throw the latch of the metal gate that creaked more than ever, to shut the gate behind as must be done without fail every time, to see the big house at the back of the field, to walk past the old stable and the remains of the slave quarters and the cistern and well that had dried up after the earthquake and the grapefruit tree planted at his birth, which was loaded down with huge yellow globes like Christmas decorations as if to honor his arrival, and the generator that gave them light before anyone else had light and the barrels of rainwater collected from gutters carefully attached to the roof and the concrete steps to the porch and the yellow tile inlaid on the porch itself and the sunlight shining through the blue plastic awning and the wooden door carved in geometric patterns intricate enough to hypnotize in the fading light of an evening and the brass doorknob and the cool air inside always welcome and Cora standing in the doorway, wearing her apron.

"Welcoome home, Martinson," she said gently, her eyes warm, but no reaching out to hug or help him.

"My name is Marty now, and this is no longer my home," he told the housekeeper, but with little of the bitterness he had practiced night after night from the time he knew this moment must happen.

He walked upstairs slowly and carried his things into his old room. It felt very familiar. Without delay, because he worried that if he stopped he might lose his will, he moved down the corridor to the bedroom, expecting to find his father propped up in bed, wan and bloated. The bed was empty.

"Where is he?" asked Marty. The thought was in him that it was already over.

"He's walking the land," said Cora. "He's worried that thieves keep chopping down the mahogany trees and soon none will be left."

"You mean he can still tromp around?" Marty demanded angrily. "I thought he was dying. I thought that was why I left my job at the library to come back here."

"When him no walk dat land," said Cora softly, reverting to dialect, "den him ready for funeral."

Marty opened the glass door and stepped onto the balcony, overlooking rolling fields where the cows and goats grazed. It was late in the afternoon and the sun was turning everything to gold. Behind him Cora stepped away so he could be alone. He stood for a long time, waiting.

Only when it happened did he realize what he had been

waiting for: Out of the woods Father appeared; the simple tan cloth cap like the hat of a baseball player without a team and the tan short-sleeve shirt and the tan pants and the leather boots and the long black rifle, always pointed down when walking, wedged under one arm where it belonged. He emerged out of the mahogany and lagwood trees with his long slow strides, as if one of the trees had decided to take a walk across the field, two brown dogs circling his heels like roots shaking off dirt. Then he stopped, put the rifle butt in the ground (something Martinson had never seen him do), and stood still for a time. Marty realized that he was resting, using the rifle as a cane.

"Here comes Father," he murmured.

CHAPTER
TWO

"**H**oi hoi hoi!"

Horace pick up rock, chuck it well front of Starwhite, name Horace-sister Dawn give she-goat with white patch like star on forehead. Starwhite with two little ones don't like pen. Horace laugh, throw another rock head her off, circle into bush, force her back to yard. Running easy on rock and thorn in bare feet, him round up last of herd but one. Them safe in roundup of stick and wire him build.

"Starwhite want eat all de peas in garden, but Momma work too too hard for 'em go in yahr belly." Him laugh again, show wide space where front teeth be before sugarcane rot them away.

Horace crouch beside big rock, think about problem for the day. One goat still free in bush. Could try and chase her down but might take all day—she cunning cunning cunning. Could take bag with him, round up akee from ripe trees, star apple, lime, so Dawn have something take to MoBay market and sell, but that mean all day shinny up trees while Papa and brother Kozmo work at seaside. Horace lift head, sense wind. Men be coming in now, over reef to shallow. No one go out again until later when sun stop beat beat beat down so hard and wind fall quiet. Him want to be there while them sit and clean bait, tell stories and quarrel to pass time. That where men belong, and him get be men now. Seaside, yes. Bush, no. Seaside mean music and cold beer, electricity, men's talk, and later on a visit to friend Clinton wood-carver. Who knows, maybe Papa got snapper or longjaw or even barracuda sell Miss Ella at Neptune Café where tourists shoot pool. No no, and Horace tap him forehead with finger, she want goat. Miss Ella ready for another goat. And him laugh.

"Seaside," Horace call up to house.

"Yes," answer Momma from inside cooking shed. "All goat all right?"

"Yah mahn, all but one."

"Where him, near garden?"

"No, him to Marse Martin land." Garden toward seaside, Marse Martin land away from seaside. Horace know Marse Martin land because him take shortcut go to school one year, through mahogany that Clinton love to carve, then run run past big house. Better for goat go there than trail to seaside because no garden there. Better too because no one thief him Marse Martin side but plenty thief him seaside side.

"All right, Horace, cool runnings," call Momma. Horace throw rock near shed so she know him move on.

Horace think to take district road for a while even though it longer that way. Him want walk past big water collect spot see what girls out this morning. Papa say him eighteen and Momma say him nineteen but either way him reaching prime, strong and well built like all men paddle dugout canoe against waves, then walk long trail up tall Rose Hill. Him come to where they sit washing clothes. Walk tall.

"Sexy feelin dis mornin, Horace?" call one voice, and all the others laugh like birds in tree.

"Belle be here little later, you want t'wait?" call another, and that one even make Horace laugh. No secrets round district, that for sure. When the women look up again him already gone, slip onto trail to seaside.

Horace walk trail so many time, so many different ways carrying different thoughts in him brain, different things in him arms, with different people day and night, hungry and full both, loving it and hating it, that it just part of him. Him know it like him own house. When rain come up quick, him know where stay dry. When him hungry, him know where mango best or where orange ripe right now. When him burnt by fire, him know where aloe plant grow. When him rise up long before sunrise and carry gas lantern to seaside so him and Koz have light for night fishing, no need to waste gas on trail. Him know old plantation road, too rough for cars so so long no one alive can remember when it not just good wide part of trail. Him even know where line of red ants pass to their nest in dead red birch so him don't step there and them don't sting up him ankles make him feet numb. Fifteen beats of heart after red ants, if him want check on Papa's tobacco plants him can turn off and duck under cedar plank carve with two big X's. Between X's true writing which Horace know say Manley Wynne, Papa name. Or him can go another fifteen beats, turn to heart side past baby lime to rock ledge, tend to ganja plants him very self plant from seed.

Horace smoke tobacco but not smoke ganj, it make him brain too fuzzy and fussy. But Papa can sell tobacco to man with truck who bundle it up with plenty more and Horace can sell ganja to man with donkeys who bundle it up with plenty more.

At tree with branch like machete can go straight to fishing at seaside or on side trail to Shire Hall and Neptune. Horace go to side because him want talk Miss Ella about goat. Him reach wide open pasture of Shire Hall where plenty slave once work. Big house still stand but now that house full of people living there, plenty family can fit in such big place. Papa say it right that plenty Jamaican live there now because plenty Jamaican build up that place. Wheel take long time but it always turn, say Papa. Goat and donkey and cattle graze nice flat land. Man with donkeys keep them there, and him keep one stretch clean of rock so when plane set down it be smooth. Them can take plenty ganja and no roads go there for police come shoot them dead. Other landing strip along district road longer, good for plane, but police can come there. Then look out, best thing get to sea or deep in bush because even if you know you do nothing wrong them just take you away or shoot you prove they serious dangerous.

Past great Shire Hall come water system they use long ago keep sugar green. Plenty water still collect but no cover and goat fall in. Make water bad, too bad even if boil real good. But that all right. Plenty rain fall in barrels off roof and not so far find big old pond good enough to drink. Pond so big it have good turtles. Some days Horace go to pond, find spot in tall grass where him can sit with just head above water, and if him become brown log real real quiet real real long time them turtles come around close. If one big enough, catch him for turtle soup and sell shell at market. Horace catch plenty, but plenty get away too because just when them around and ready be grab Horace feel laugh come up from deep inside and nothing can stop that laugh. It just bubble up the water so him grab right then, little before him really ready. Big ones paddle away and Horace laugh some more.

Trail get small and steep in deep bush past rusty old drum so big Horace can fit inside through blowout on side. Papa say it a boiler, explode and fly like bomb into bush, kill plenty workers. Good spot hide things before seaside if Horace not want anyone to know what him carry.

More house come now. Getting near MoBay–Falmouth road. Goats jump on stiff legs and pickneys chase chickens about yard. Burning smell from where some men make charcoal in fire pits, smoke and burn green wood long long time. Rooster crow all day. Tin can heap build up around useless car. Spot once clear by whathimname for new house before him get sick. Now everything grow tall again. Three trail meet and then nothing but flat open field to road where Neptune Café and Miss Ella wait. Horace see pipe them sneak off waterline at seaside. Pipe still bust, spit water into ground every minute every day. Something bad happen from that waste. Papa say it, Horace know it. Got to be bad because nothing good can happen from it and something must always always happen. That the rule of everything.

Big hog sniffle at him feet on path behind Neptune. "Hoi, Horace," call Kenrai. Him work MoBay.

"Hoi."

"Whappenin?"

"Cool."

"All right."

"See Miss Ella?"

"She around."

"All right."

"Goat or fish?" Kenrai smart, him guess Horace business.

"Goat."

"Gimme soome, Horace mahn. Me need soome meat on me ribs."

Horace laugh and walk on.

"Fookah," call Kenrai. "Whore ass."

"Oh mahn, never hear dat one before," and Horace laugh some more, step lively onto roadside. Denise minding shop beside 'Tune, as Horace sometimes call Neptune. Horace want smile at her but him not want her see how him front teeth gone, so smile with eyes alone. Aw, she know it full well anyway.

"Denise, gimme piece of boola cake." Special cake Denise make real fine, ginger and honey mix so sweet.

"For fifty cents, no problem."

"No mahn, just gimme it. Me pay, me pay soon."

She not bother answering, only look away and pick at her nails. Horace laugh and step to dark cool inside of Neptune Café like him step into mouth of big fish, like man Preacher yell about from old Bible days. It real dark after daylight, so him wait near door til eyes get ready, stand with back against wall. Nothing to fear, truly, but still no reason to rush in until eyes are ready. Driver on tourist bus shoot pool drinking Red Stripe beer so cold it sweat down the bottle. Hmm, two of them go down smooth smooth smooth. Tourist sit at table near window, pink skin shining like light bulb. Them order mannish water, that a goat stew, and Horace laugh because that mannish water from Sheila-goat him bring last week.

Most likely Miss Ella sit inside her wood booth beside the bar. Them build that booth last tourist season. It got door in side but only little hole in front where money change hands like MoBay bank. Horace guess Miss Ella move so much money, she get to feel like bank. Handy spot to keep money safe from night thief too. It plenty big booth, and it sure need be plenty big because Miss Ella not getting smaller. Each week go by she seem wider wider wider, blacker blacker blacker, more more more gold chain round her neck. Horace feel a laugh coming, but him hold it because she would know why that laugh come up. Bad feeling before business not a good idea.

"Miss Ella," him say quiet at side of door.

"Coome, Horace," she call, over crack of pool balls.

Horace move easy to side door of booth, wait while she finish money count. Then Miss Ella turn on her stool. It take a while for her to turn all herself around. Horace make him belly tight so no laugh slip out.

"Now what you want, mahn?"

"Gotta goat."

"Me need ah goat," she say, red eyes more narrow, "but dis past goat him full of string and toof, mahn, real toof."

Now Horace just have to laugh. No way that goat tough, him know what that goat eat, what it act like, how it move, and that goat not tough. Miss Ella want price down, that all.

Miss Ella watch him laugh. If her just deal with Horace, price could get down to no money at all, just some cold Red Stripe and rice. But it not just Horace, it Horace and Horace father Manley and Horace brother Kozmo. Them bring more fish and goat than anyone. Without them, tourist come and go with nothing to buy at table. Men need her to buy from them, but she need them bring food to sell tourists. And maybe them need her less than them think. If them ever get together, make one trip to market with all the fish or goat, could fetch damn good price. Better keep them come to Neptune, think Miss Ella.

"All right, Horace," she say. "Even though dat last goat him toof, despite cuttin away plenty plenty string, me give same price—two-fifty ah pound."

"All right," say Horace.

"But dis time," Miss Ella push on quick, "we gonna weigh dat goat after him all butcher down, not wid all head and bone and throwaway piece."

When Horace hear this him laugh hardest yet. Papa tell him about this. Miss Ella use head and bone and every little thing for mannish water, just like she use fish head for soup. But she not want pay for everything, just for flesh. Papa warn him right about this trick.

"No, Miss Ella," say Horace.

"Well den, price coome down to two-twenty ah pound. I gots to make ah livin, mahn." She start bustling around inside her booth, pretend she got plenty to do.

"Miss Ella," say Horace, "dat one goat bring you how many tourist dinner? Ten? Ten more mannish water beside? At very very least. And what you charge tourist for dat? Twelve dollah for dinner? Six dollah for mannish water?"

"But me got cost you don't understand," she cry. "Overhead. Lectricity. Pool cue break. Employees needin pay." She think; Horace guess low. One big goat bring twice that much when mix in with plenty rice or potato and carrot.

"Miss Ella," say Horace, "two-fifty good price. Me tell you true now: Before me go two-twenty, me go two-seventy. Understand?"

Horace getting big, Miss Ella think. Him getting smart too. Time past when deal with him better than deal with Manley. Soon be better deal with Manley because Manley go back long way and Manley remember times before me get gold chains on me neck.

"All right, Horace," she sigh, "two-fifty—and one cold Red Stripe. One."

"Yah, mahn." Horace smile. "You get it tomorrow."

"You kill him?"

"Sure sure." But Horace not kill him. Horace try once, but him just not have the heart after raise him up and look in him eyes and see little babies cry bah bah when momma drag away. Him bring goat to friend of Papa who kill him, drain him, and take a slice for it.

All right, business taken care and go well. Horace step to road where plenty guys set up small shop for tourist traffic. One place sell shell and coral, plenty conch, coral just like man brain. Them sit under shade of bamboo sticks and sometime someone stop and buy. Another place just carving, all wood, them sit in back with chisel smokin spleef laughing and carving. But Clinton best, mahn, not just because him best friend. Everyone say it, Papa and Koz even say it. Horace see Clinton on way home from seaside.

"Hoi! Gapper! Whagwan?" call guy who get things from Falmouth like can of juice to sell roadside. Him call Horace "Gapper" because Horace teeth gone. Horace no like that nickname, and that guy know it. "Whagwan, Gapper?" him ask again, laugh laugh laugh.

"Nothing going on, Bigger," call Horace, think up name fast. That guy get bigger every day, lazybones.

Bigger scowl. Him not like new nickname. Good, think Horace, stepping lively past two places to new spot where brother of man with donkeys set up. Kettle of stew cook out back, and man feel Horace come, call for him to move around back. Two cars whiz by before Horace can come.

"Yesss, Horasss, yesss," say him, sweeping a few dread-locks under him hat. Stew smell good, all earth things, no meat. Ital cooking. True Rasta style. Horace wait. Stew bubble.

"Horace," him say after a while. "Me brother coome from bush soon. Yah got anything for him, mahn?"

Horace think on it. Plant not ready yet, but it be ready soon. Soon for plant mean different thing than soon for people, though. "What you mean by soon?" ask Horace.

"Four week time, mahn."

Him think like plant, think Horace. Him a Rasta. "All right, me know it now," and him prepare walk on.

"Wait, Horace," him say, and big wood spoon go into pot for some stew in hollow shell of coconut.

"Thanks, Rasta," say Horace.

"Give thanks all the time, Horasss mahn," and Rasta smile at him, full white white teeth shiny as clean shell in water.

Last shop before cutoff to old road to seaside, Horace know him friend Winston be there. "Hoi, Coomfy," Horace call. Coomfy be Winston nickname because when him born him one of twins, other twin die, but Winston small and easy to carry, so him be Coomfy. Now him big but name stick.

"Seaside?" ask Winston.

"Yes."

"Do me favor, mahn."

"Sure thing."

"Tell me old mahn me go MoBay, sell carving soon soon, if him need fish, line, or hook."

"Cool."

"All right."

Old road to seaside cut off from new road to seaside. Old road build too close to water and break up in storm waves, so them build new road farther away. Can still take car to where boats pull up on sand and where government water pipe come up, but no one drive cars except some Sunday when Church of Zion man come round or Miss Ella need something real bad real quick send bus man by.

When Horace reach beach spot him see that something going on. Pickneys scrape scales off bait fish, that normal, and men be gathered under shade of almond tree, that normal, but seem like everyone there, and instead of sleep on overturn boat wait for sun to cool or play dominoes or make patch, them all sit talking. Horace hurry up, but before it fly from him brain him lean over Winston papa, whisper message. Old man Winston hold up finger show him understand.

Otto talk, him nickname Rooster because him so feisty and strut around all the time. "Me not tief nothing," him yell. "Who can tief lobster from sea? No one, dat who. Me dive for it and me work hard for it. Soomeone think him can take dat from me got anudder think coomin." Rooster pick up spear gun and shake it like spear, look most at Horace papa Manley. Horace feel laugh come up inside.

Manley stay sit on dugout canoe make himself long ago, damn good one, maybe biggest on beach. Only thing show him mad at all is crossing arms at chest and muscles stick out more than usual. "Who say you tief, mahn?" him say quiet. "Dat word coome from only one mouth here"—and sudden Manley on him feet right front of Otto face—"YAHR mouth, mahn, YAHR MOUTH. No one callin you tief but You bring it out. Yahr insides coome out, mahn, yahr own thinkin 'bout yahrself step forth and you doan know it."

Rooster quick grab conch shell hold in him hand like to strike Manley. Horace brother Koz behind Manley on heart side. Horace quicker slip behind Rooster striking hand side. Just in case, just in case. Rooster not known for violence—by day.

"Clear yahr brain and listen to me now, Otto mahn," say Manley. "We got dis problem: Yahr spearfishin drive away all lobster. No trap catch no lobster no moore any-

30

where inside reef. Yahr fishing it out, mahn, and yahr driving price down down; bring in too many one time. Even worse, yahr takin lobster full of eggs ready to let go seed. Foolish, mahn, too foolish. Kill all dem babies, kill our future, for one lobster?"

Old man Winston stir in him seat. "Yes yes," him say, "and where you get money for air tank and spear gun, let you stay down under all day? Ganja money, not fish money do it."

"What wrong wid dat?" flare up Rooster, keepin hold conch, pawing sand like donkey. New nickname, think Horace: Donkey.

"Nothin," soothe Manley, "nothin at all. But dere be soomething else wrong, Otto mahn. Look dere by road, and think behind Neptune, whappenin dere."

Otto not have to look. Him know Manley mean waterline him sneak off government pipe at seaside back to him home. Line sprung two leaks, all day all night spray water until ground turn to mud and mosquito love it.

"Me not know yahr government mahn now, Manley Wynn," Rooster sneer. "Dem pay you good look after dem interests?"

Giggle slip out from Horace stomach, couldn't help it— but just at very very wrong time. Sound of it make something in Rooster snap. Him whip round quick as rat and swing conch hand at Horace head. Him strong but not so quick as Horace, so Horace slip to side get in shove at back of Rooster as him pass. Rooster slip to one knee. By then Horace hold stick over him head and Kozmo got bait knife at him neck. Rooster stop dead but him breathe heavy heavy heavy. Murmurs among men; Horace getting big but him still bwai, all know it, so Otto swinging at him not be a cool thing at all, not cool at all.

"Yahr sense, Rooster, coome to yahr sense, mahn," say

Dixon. Him Otto drinkin buddy, so that help calm it. Koz and Horace back off and let Rooster stand.

"Me tell you plain what me think 'bout yahr pipe," say Manley. "Me think yahr lettin cool clear water go to waste, mahn. Useless! But maybe worse, government coome, see it, and what dem do? Dem shut it down, mahn. Not just shut you down, shut down all us at pipe. Den what? No water clean fish. No water rinse salt off hand. No water at all when dry spell coome. It boolshit, mahn, boolshit."

Rooster look at him with eyes red, but say nothing.

"True speech," say Billy, nickname Shorty because him not so tall. "Dem two things make strain, Rooster mahn. Spearfish and water, two big things."

"Me bring water so Nellie can stay wid pickney bwai Neal," say Rooster, spit out words like sugarcane mesh. "Me spearfish get money use build home for bwai and Nellie. Could be soome you doan like seeing me push on, get ahead?"

"No mahn," say Manley strong, "not dat way. Listen me clear, here ah plan: You spearfish where reef meet point, morning sun side, but stop yahr fishin one rock throw from dere. Doan take lobster other side, leave dem for traps."

Rooster hop about. "Me see lobster, ten dollah in water, you say leave it?"

"Yah mahn, but doan look at it dat way, look at it like you already sell'em lobster by just leave'im dere. Because listen clear again now: You do dat, me family work with you, fix up dat pipe of yahrs so no moore leak. And den we bury dat pipe, get it? Bury dat damn pipe and hide it so so good that when government men show face, look all day if dem want, dem never never will find it. Seaside pipe stay cool, yahr pipe stay cool, give lobster time to coome back. Work from me family on pipe buy dem lobster you leave behind."

Men shift around when them hear this. Reason clear, offer good for both sides—even better for Rooster because him already fish out most lobster so what him really lose by getting Manley family help? Not much. But everybody get more lobster later on, and fixing and hiding bad pipe good protection against losing good pipe. Ideas like that part of reason Manley never have nickname that stick. First name good enough because it say the real thing about him, like best nickname do. Manley, him manly.

Rooster think him like what him hear. Drop conch. "All right, all right," him say. "Dat all right."

"When next strong wind blow, no boat. Start work on pipe," Manley promise.

Rooster turn to Horace. "Cool, Horace, cool, mahn," him mutter.

"Cool," say Horace, belly tight.

Knot tie up in everyone stomach unravel now. Some go see how pickney cleaning fish. Some tend line or see after orange and coconut for bait in lobster trap. Some just seek out shade or domino table. Horace walk to stand in water with Papa and Koz.

"Horace bwai," say Manley, "dat laugh of yahrs get you fooked soomeday truly." But Manley look at Horace full of laugh inside himself, knowing full well where Horace get that laugh from. "Now tell me, whagwan?"

"Goat to Miss Ella."

"Good price?"

"Yah mahn—include head and guts per pound."

Manley laugh soft. "She-devil, always probing for de edge. Dat just in her, like barracuda must snap him jaw. Always try cutting ah price."

"Gwan Rose Hill soon?" ask Koz. Him more quiet like Momma, real hard worker, on short side but strong. Horace more like Papa, meaning hard work too, but talk more. Koz find him girlfriend name Joanne, now them stay in place near seaside. Him not go up to district so much anymore.

"Going dere sometime," say Horace. "You too, Papa?"

"No. Night fishing. Tell Dorothy."

"And bring her dis," say Koz. Him give Horace some red snapper for Momma.

"Me take care goat, den coome fishin, maybe tomorrow at sunset."

Manley laugh again. "Horace and Koz both, seaside seaside seaside. For steady balance, need both seaside and bush, yah know."

"Yah mahn, yah mahn," say Horace, but it clear him not feel it. On board nailed to tree over where boats sit Horace see big marlin tail like two curve knives join together at handle. Manley get that tail, biggest in village ever. One day, Horace think, me get tail even bigger, ride marlin in to beach over reef, eat plenty sell plenty, nail tail to board.

Sun still high but past top. Horace want visit Clinton before seeking out that damn goat still in bush—that goat die tomorrow, him the one go in tourist belly him so hard to pen. So Horace wave off everyone, even that Otto-Rooster-Donkey, and step lively to road, cut through land between old seaside road and new seaside road, past hearing before Koz yell that him forget red snapper, and then him glad to see Clinton shop door open and hear sound of mallet on chisel on wood.

"Hoi."

"Dat you, Laugher?" call Clinton from around back.

Horace giggle at hearing him nickname. "Yah, Dreamer mahn, it me."

Clinton call Horace "Laugher" for same reason Horace call Clinton "Dreamer"; that what them both do all the time. But Clinton make him dream come true in a way, because him make carving to bring dreams to light. Clinton carving not like all the others, no no no. Sure, him make bowl or bird or dreadlock head, but him make many many other things more. Big mahogany bull, egret from light cedar, eagle and hawk from red birch, hummingbird from lignum vitae. Plenty statue too, stand to Horace waist and higher. Man and woman stand up, him dick inside her, or man alone big dick stick straight out, or woman alone nipple like mango pit. Horace giggle, but Clinton see them just like eagle or bird, just another part of him dreams show out. Clinton show them proud, same as show crane with long long neck standing so skinny and tall that Horace shoulder touch beak as he walk around back.

"All well?"

"All right. Rooster take swing at me head wid conch shell fist. Him too slow."

"Good thing, mahn. Otherwise you look like lobster after him mash it up."

Horace laugh and sit like Clinton sit with back on bamboo wall. Sometime them sit like that long long time. Horace love it when them do because Clinton light up him chalice, puff and work to free shape which him say trapped in wood waiting to come out, and them talk about dreams and secrets. Anytime all right to do that, not just night when most people talk dreams and secrets, because Dreamer think that way all the time and Horace him good friend.

Them sit. Thunk thunk thunk go Clinton mallet.

"What wood that be now?"

"National wood," say Clinton, because lignum vitae Jamaica national wood, like hummingbird Jamaica national bird. "Sometime me think lignum moore ah stone den wood, it hard hard hard, mahn. Specially heartwood, dark dark wood."

35

"Like skin," say Horace.

"Yah mahn, dat why lignum be national wood. Heart strong strong strong, and dark. Away from heart, lighter color but not so strong."

Horace giggle, keep up him Laugher nickname, then go quiet. Clinton just like that, see everything as part of everything else. Everything mean something deep too. Horace remember how Clinton know name of all manner of trees, where them come from and how long them take to grow. Him say that when slave boat pass by, strongest slaves escape, swim to shore, live in hills. More sneak away from plantation. Them all plant every kind of tree them can, keep different fruit coming all year round, keep something to eat. No need go near plantation, maybe get caught, lose freedom.

Clinton not born near seaside. Him born in mountains. Maybe that why him think that way, Horace think. Him have more deep deep mountain in him and Horace have more seaside in him. Clinton come to Rose Hill when him pickney with him momma. No papa. One day she leave for MoBay and not come home again. Clinton live like strong slave in old days, walk hills, see people, hear what them say, eat with them. One old man show him to work wood, share roof, and soon give him tools when old hands work no more. Clinton say it him path to carve.

Car pass on road whiz whiz. Donkey hee-haw. Bird come out now with sun lower. Day settle down slow. Sea calm too, men get ready to go out again.

"Thinkin, Horace?" ask Clinton.

"Yah mahn." Horace take deep breath. "America," him say, like name of beautiful woman.

"Thinkin America again, mahn?"

"Yah mahn."

"What dat dream like, Laugher?"

"Me go MoBay, catch plane go so high me eyes see clouds from top. Jamaica fall far far away in sea full of blue. Big marlin fish jumping on waves far far from fishin boat, middle dah sea, just jumpin for fun. Can see that from plane. Soon coome Florida, Mi-ah-mee. Get off dere, find sugarcane field needing workers. Work dere one season, just one, make plenty U.S. dollar. Den buy car, plenty gas cheap in States, and me drive about. Open road, yah know, no one stop you. Soon coome big seaside spot where men working big boat for fish. Me work dere one season, show dem how strong Jamaican can work. Dem see how me know where fish want to be, can sense it, mahn. Big fat fat mahn, him own one boat big enough for ten men, coome to me and say, 'Excooz me, Mister Horace sir, might I speak wid you for a moment, sir?' Me say, Yah mahn, it all right. Him say, 'Mister Horace sir, since you coome we catch plenty fish, mahn, plenty fish. What you say me have you skipper me boat, you stay wid me and you captain me boat?' Me sit back, tell him dat all right, long as every year me take him boat on trip somewhere along seashore of States, just for fun, see New York Chicago Boston L.A. Him say, 'Sure, Horace, sure, mahn. No problem.' After one moore year me send home for Belle. She stay wid me till we see cool spot for home. Den use fish money and build it."

"I think fat fat man have him cool-runnings daughter," Clinton tease.

"No no." Horace frown serious. "All me want from him be boat, dat all."

Them sit quiet again. Horace learn from Clinton to dream big long full dream, not just dream like walk down trail find piece of gold get rich live happy. Real-life dream. But still Horace not a dreamer like Dreamer.

"Thinkin, Clinton?"

"Yah mahn," and Clinton puff on him chalice until smoke make big hat round him head. Him open mouth to speak and more smoke come out. "Ah-free-kah," Dreamer say.

"What dat dream like, Dreamer?" whisper Horace.

"Nighttime. Tall tall green grass sway in cool night breeze. Me walking trail through grass wid walkin stick me carve from Ahfreekah wood, most black hard wood anywhere. All of a sudden, no warning, leopard leap on trail. Him black as night, two eyes shine like little moons. Me stop, but me not fearful. 'Brother cat,' me say, 'we both black as night. We can share dis Ahfreekah land we both know.' Leopard stand still, tail twitch, den him blink moon eyes to say all right, and him jump off. Me walk on home. Village where everything made from tall grass and black wood. Two tall carving, tall as tree, greet all peoples on trail near village. One mahn, one womahn. Me own carvings, mahn. Round village in circle more carvings from me own hand, one for each animal live near, show dem we know dem live dere, catch dem spirit so it all right. Always big fire made for sitting, talking, dreaming. Me take me seat, watch fire orange on black black night. Light me chalice and smoke. Good ganja, Ahfreekah ganja. Soon me womahn coome sit, her hair to waist shiny black and her skin smooth and her teeth ivory. She wear skirt of grass, nothing on her chest, just open to warm breeze. Touch her hand and she touch me shoulder. She take dat chalice and make soome smoke for us both to crawl inside, like blanket wrap round us."

Dreamer stop, smoke him chalice, thunk thunk him lignum vitae. Horace swept up in Dreamer dream, sit back. With each thunk of mallet, Clinton hum one little thing:

"Ah" thunk

"Free" thunk

"Kah" thunk

"Ah" thunk

"Free" thunk

"Kah" thunk

"Ai" thunk

"Free" thunk

"Ai and I" thunk

"Free" thunk

"Kah" thunk.

Horace know that Dreamer be into working rhythm now, like men be out from seaside and bird be finding food and goat be restless in pen. Time for Horace climb hill, find that damn goat before sundown.

"All right," Horace say to him friend.

"Al" thunk

"Right" thunk

"Laugher" thunk, and Clinton give big smile but keep him eye on wood.

And now come trail home. Today trail home longer than trail seaside. Not just uphill, longer all kind of ways. Horace wonder about that, because sometime him seaside one heartbeat then home next heartbeat, but another day him on trail long long time. Same trail, same feet, same heartbeat. What difference? Brain is different, and brain is a powerful thing. Sometime seem like everything else in body just set up to take care of brain. Thick thick skull protect. No wing, no claw, no fin, no fur, no big teeth, man is too small to be big and too big to be small, what him got is brain and brain take him to middle of sea, over clouds, make idea of pen for goat. Horace pass through Shire Hall, see man with donkeys clearing grass strip for ganja plane. Brain make business deal, brain cunning cunning cunning. Brain talk, remember like no animal. Brain can even think like animal to trick it, then think more than any animal. That the one big thing help man eat when him got no wings to fly or teeth to bite.

Horace use him brain get that damn goat. That goat can run through bush better, but Horace trick him to hollow with stone wall behind, and catch him good. Past red ant line six steps Horace find rope him hide for goat search. Take trail far past home, slip past barbed wire over old stone wall. Sure enough, that goat gone for orange tree, him love orange. Horace see where him jump up on tree to snatch orange, scrape bark with hoof. Quiet quiet, Horace slip down back side of Rose Hill where lagwood get big, then cedar, then mahogany. Horace know this goat, Horace know this goat go this way. And that brain in Horace do him right, because from mahogany trees Horace see clearing where that damn goat stand like him own all the grass on field for him own eating.

But see him and catch him two different things. Horace get plan, throw rocks behind both sides keep goat running toward pen, then trap him in hollow. Then, think Horace, leaning against old mahogany tree, then that damn goat get him insides cut out to fill up tourist bellies. Horace bring him to Miss Ella for, let's see, two-fifty ah pound, that mean—

BANG

Rifle shot bullet through tree near near him head. Horace crouch.

BANG

"Freeze if you know what's good for you," shouted a voice.

Freeze?

CHAPTER
THREE

MARTY Sanders strode full of purpose and power toward the mahogany forest where the trespasser he had just trapped waited, crouched and still, another human being obeying his command. Sure enough, all it took was a few days walking with his father and he had accomplished what the old man could not—get to the bottom of this wood thievery.

Shooting a rifle seemed less strange than he had expected, but by now a week had passed and many things seemed less strange. He was no longer stumbling and stung, no longer overwhelmed by the past. Every day he walked long distances, usually alone, sometimes with his father—although Father's slow pace and long rests proved maddening. At night there was not much to do except feel homesick, drink a little rum, and sit in the big room downstairs without so much as a TV. He would watch his father pretend to watch the wall while listening to the radio, and then when his father watched him he would pretend to be preoccupied cleaning his camera. When they did talk it was all so slow, so little said over such a long time. God, your mind could atrophy in this, sink like quicksand into silence. . . .

"What are you doing sneaking through our property?" Marty demanded, stepping close to Horace.

Him step too close, think Horace. Me want, can take that gun away from him.

"Goat," say Horace.

"What?"

"Goat, goat run 'way."

"Yeah, right, you were just innocently chasing your goat through our mahogany trees. I think you were trying to cut some of them down for carvings, that's what I think."

"No, mahn. Me got rope, no ax, just rope." Horace feel laugh come.

"That doesn't prove anything," said Marty angrily.

Horace giggle. "Me gwan take rope, throw in tree, pull tree down, carry it 'way, all alone at sunset. Sure, mahn, you catch me, mahn, you see it true."

Marty didn't know quite what to make of this and stumbled for an answer when he heard his father's "Hoi, hoi" not far behind. The old man was catching up.

"Father, I found us a trespasser," he announced, gesturing toward Horace.

Breathing heavily, Martin Sanders tugged at his brown cap, rested on his rifle, and looked at Horace. "Manley bwai?" he asked when he caught his breath.

"Yes, Marse Martin."

"Whagwan?" What's going on here, translated Marty to himself.

"Goat."

"What him like?"

"All black, brown stripe head to tail. Good size, ready tw'eat."

"Me see him, tie him up," Martin promised.

"Thanks, mahn," say Horace.

"What's going on here?" protested Marty. "I just catch this kid trespassing on our land, right where the mahogany has been getting chopped down, and all you do is tell him you'll help catch his imaginary goat."

"I know the boy's father, and I trust him," said Martin quietly.

"Well, at least make an example of him for the others. Maybe he wasn't trying to steal our wood, but he definitely was trespassing—he's standing right here right now. We should report him down at Long River."

"No, son," and the old man sighed. He was weary at the end of every day now and his son's insistence made him even more tired. "These are our neighbors. They mean no harm and they're welcome here."

"Then I see why you're having these problems," Marty muttered.

"Gwan hoome, Horace," said the old man. "All right."

"All right, cool," say Horace. Him turn away, thinking, not a good day. Two times, mayhem come close.

"Oh, Horace," called Martin. "See Manley, tell him me want talk soon soon. Tell him me visit Dagi day after tomorrow, if him not to seaside him can coome in mornin to Dagi."

"Him coome," Horace promise.

Horace vanished before Marty even had a chance to see where he went. Then, by the time he turned back, his father had already begun the slow walk to the house. From behind he seemed even older, more bloated about the middle, moving with the crooked legs of an old man, his shoulders rounded with age. His tan shirt was tattered at the collar and the middle buttons could barely reach to cover his stomach. It was the cancer that made him like that, Marty knew, and when he thought about how other men might have dealt with the slow eating away of their insides, the inevitable stalk of death, he knew that by all rights he should have great respect for this man walking before him. But somehow none of that could come forward. Yes, his father had strength, but strength wasn't everything.

"Why do you speak differently to that boy than you do around the house?" asked Marty. His tone accused.

"I do it because he understands me better that way, and you understand me better this way," said Martin.

"It reminds me of some stuff I hear back home. A black guy will be walking down the street, talking normally to a white friend, and then as soon as he sees another black friend he'll slip into this jive talk like he was born in the delta south of New Orleans. It always seems so stupid."

"I was born here," said Martin, "and so were you, Martinson."

He doesn't understand what I'm saying at all, thought Marty. It's useless to try to get through.

Why does he call over there "home," when this is his home? wondered Martin.

They walked on, slowly, keeping pace with the approaching night. A light went on in the kitchen; Cora was preparing dinner.

"I still think you handled that situation very poorly," said Marty finally.

A flash of anger pulled Martin Sanders erect. This had to be dealt with. "Now listen to me," he said, his voice deepening. "To have interfered with that boy would have been a stupid thing to do. What do you think this is, the back streets of Boston? This is the bush. People walk through here all the time. What's more, a few clues told me the boy was telling the truth, whether I knew his family or not."

"How could you possibly know that?" Marty demanded.

"First of all, if he had wanted to escape, in fact if he had wanted to kill you, it all would have happened before I ever got there."

"What are you talking about? I had the rifle."

"You walked up to him like you wanted to shake his hand. Do you have any idea how quick a man gets in the bush? Quickness means staying alive. He could have taken that rifle away from you before you even knew what happened."

"You underestimate me," said Marty angrily.

"No, you underestimate Jamaicans."

There was a pause. Then, sarcastically, Marty said, "All right, then, what was the other so-called clue?"

"He exactly described the strange goat we passed three times as we walked the land this afternoon. Didn't you see him?"

How am I supposed to know one goat from another? Marty thought. I haven't spent my life studying them. But he held his tongue. That seemed to be how he and his father were most of the time—holding their tongues, holding their distance. Silently they reached home and parted company.

That night the scene continued. Marty was cleaning the lens on his camera. Father was stroking one of the dogs quietly, staring off into space. It had been like that for a long time, maybe an hour, when finally Marty asked, "So what did the doctor say today?"

Martin shook himself out of a reverie. "He said that if I

45

wanted to, they could still try some kind of radiation and drugs, but it's too late to operate now. He wanted to know if he should try to check me into the hospital in Kingston."

Pause. He always stops halfway, thought Marty; it's such an irritating habit. "Well?"

Martin caught his breath and continued. "He said no one around here would have what might help, even in Kingston, so if I was serious about trying to stop this thing, we should make plans for me to go to a hospital in the States. As a matter of fact, he mentioned several Boston-area hospitals as being the best."

A chance to finish out this drama in Boston, thought Marty. A chance to fulfill family responsibility and still be home. "That sounds like good advice. What did you say?"

The old man leaned back. "I said it would be a waste of money and time. I said they sure as hell aren't going to bury me in Boston, they'd better bury me right here. I said once I leave this place I'm dead anyway, so why lose my last days?" He had told Doc Stephenson one more thing, which he didn't tell his son: This was his last chance to try to hold the family land together under family ownership, and that meant more to him than living inside some oxygen tent for a few more weeks. This was his only chance to convince his boy, somehow, that he belonged in Jamaica. But Doc knew all that; he was just presenting the medical options.

Marty's glimmer of hope for a quick return was stamped out. He wasn't surprised. "Did he talk time at all?" he asked, trying not to sound eager or impatient.

He really wants to get it over with, thought Martin. "One month, two months. Frankly, he said he's surprised I'm still walking around." Martin shifted in his seat, but the thing inside, a part of him that had nothing to do with him but everything to do with his time left, that thing didn't move. It pressed against his chest and hurt. It wanted him to be still—forever. For years he had sat in this chair and hunted that thing like he used to hunt boar. He searched his insides for it, tried to find it and corner it and kill it. Sometimes he thought he had, but it would always come back. Now he didn't have to hunt it; now it was hunting him. He was cornered. All he could do was bare his fangs and hold it at bay as long as possible. Life's trick was to turn him into the boar.

What's wrong with me? wondered Marty. My father is dying and what I really want to know is how quickly I can bury him. What's wrong with me? "I'm writing a letter to Mother tonight," he suddenly blurted. "Do you want me to tell her anything?"

Tell her anything? He saw her as she had been, seated in the kitchen feeding the boy a teaspoon of honey he had collected the day before. She looked up and smiled at him, then turned her attention back to Martinson. The two of them folded into each other and he watched them, so perfect.

"No, son," he said.

"Well, at least you could say something to *me* about it, then," Marty flared.

The old man pushed back the dagger in his lungs. "I guess I always thought your mother told you what you needed to know."

"Yeah, but I'd like to hear your side of it."

"My side?" She had let her hair grow out, like most black women do now but no one did then. It surrounded her face like a nest in the branch of a tree. When it was wet it looked like black seaweed stuck to a beautiful wooden carving that long ago had been thrown into the sea, features smoothed by the waves. He had never told her that.

"My side?" he repeated. "Well, you know we met at a

47

conference in MoBay, an international conference on hunger—some kind of title like that. She was part of a research team from the university and I had been invited, well, they said something about my 'firsthand experience with life in the bush,' but I'd gone to school with the foreign affairs secretary and that had something to do with it." He paused, gathering strength, forcing back the fire in his stomach. This was what he was living for, this was the first of his important moments before the end.

"She was ten years younger than me." He struggled, trying to say how he felt. It had been thirteen years since he'd even tried. "I found her quite beautiful. The second evening of the conference, I invited a group back to the homestead for dinner. The roads were better then, of course, and the place was more kept up. I figured I could give the impression of being a country gentleman."

"Which is what you are anyway."

"I suppose so. Anyway, I think your mother was intrigued by the idea of this kind of life. There was MoBay on one hand, the beauty of Rose Hill on the other, plus you know at the time it was very popular to talk about getting back to your roots. Jamaica isn't Africa, but it's black after all."

"You talk like you had nothing to do with her decision to marry you."

Martin Sanders smiled, trying not to show how much it hurt to breathe. He wasn't doing well enough, he wasn't getting through, he had to try harder. "I had something to do with it. At first there was a lot of love, a great deal of love. I know that must be hard for you to believe after all that's happened." He let a small cough escape. "The first ten years were good."

"Then what happened?"

Inside, he bared his fangs. The trap was closing. "It's

hard to say." He fought for breath, feeling his son's impatience and anger. "Well, your mother was brought up in America, and I was brought up in Jamaica. And I was older. Both things made me, well, slower than her. I seemed to be satisfied with less. She needed more, more stimulation, I guess. After the States, MoBay really is no city at all. We had no neighbors who could carry on a political or intellectual discussion. No movies, no fashions. She held on for a long time, but I suppose finally you convinced her to leave."

"Me?" I knew it, thought Marty, I always knew he blamed me for their breakup. Over the years the thought had recurred, barely allowed to surface, that he had beaten his father in some kind of competition for his mother's affections. The feeling always gave him a bitter thrill.

No mahn, thought Martin, no mahn, you're losing it. "Understand me clear, son: It wasn't your fault in any way. I like to think it was nobody's fault really, just the way things had to happen."

You don't want to admit it was your fault, thought Marty.

"Maybe your mother used your schooling as the excuse she needed. But I remember"—and the old man paused to breathe and savor the thought—"when you were a boy you were really at home in the bush. You did what every boy on Rose Hill could do. You flew down trails and you could climb and handle a machete. And you were smart smart smart. I saw you as an amazing mixture of us both, and both our cultures. You could go to school in Kingston like I did." He fought to continue. He had to hold on. "But your mother worried that you were shut out from the civilized world, as she called it. Tree climbing didn't make her laugh because it was backward and monkeyish. She wanted your education to be more formal and modern."

49

"But she never really belonged here," protested Marty, defending her with her own words.

Martin remembered how she was always scared of standing near the old well, how in the early years it was a joke but later it really seemed as if she thought she might somehow fall in.

"Yes, I suppose that's true."

"And I never did, either."

The old man mustered his energy. "Martinson, no. You may not remember now, but you belonged here as much as anyone on Rose Hill. I'm not telling you that you belong here now, but I know as sure as bees go to lagwood that you were a part of this place." Desperately he wanted to say that his son still fit in, still belonged, but with a father's instinct he knew that to suggest the idea would only make it more distasteful.

Yes, Marty admitted, he remembered. How could he not, coming back here? For years he had blotted it out, but here there was nothing to use to dam the memories. Maybe that was why he never came back. "So she took me and left."

"Yes. Do you remember that day?"

"I still dream about it."

So do I, thought Martin. "What do you remember?"

"I remember seeing you walking toward the house across the fields. I remember Mother hurrying, as though we had to be gone before you returned or all would be lost. I remember her crying at the bottom of the hill waiting for the bus. And I remember being on the plane looking out the window at the blue ocean while she slept."

"Yes, I think she was afraid that I wouldn't let her take you away and I suppose she was right. I guess that's why she left the way she did."

"You mean"—and Marty was astonished—"you mean you didn't know we were leaving?"

Martin shook his head slowly, his brown eyes blurred by sickness. "Let me put it this way: Your mother had already left in her heart. I knew that. But I thought there might be some reconciliation. I didn't know she was going to take you away with her."

"She never told me that," Marty murmured. "So the one time you came to visit, right after I'd enrolled in school, were you thinking about bringing me back?"

"Yes."

"But you didn't."

"You seemed happy. You had already started talking like an American. You seemed excited about starting school. You didn't seem in the least bit homesick. I began to think that maybe your mother was right. What do you remember from that trip?"

"I remember wishing that you would go away. You seemed so out of place that I was embarrassed by you. I didn't want my new friends to know you were my father."

That still hurt, even after thirteen years. The noise and the mad rush and the lack of real earth to stand on and the absence of good trees to admire had made him feel like a foolish country bumpkin. The air was bad to breathe and he was constantly lost, standing on street corners not knowing which way to go. Everything looked the same. He had come to take back his son and felt as though all of his strength had been drained away. He shifted in his seat, trying to force the pain farther down inside him. "Yes, well, I had to come home, it was obvious." Home to silence, night after night, year after year.

"But you drove her away," Marty cried, even though he was feeling some of his father's anguish. "She had to leave or just wither away out here in the bush. You had to be right all the time and you had to be in control."

"She said that?" and the old man slowly put a hand to his forehead. "Control is a funny thing, not exactly as it

51

appears sometimes." Control, yes. He had been arrogant, strong, with a beautiful American wife and a healthy son, tromping his land. At home, at the supper table, in bed, it was different. Control was a funny word. He wished he could explain all this, it was very important, but now, even if he could have found the words, his body wouldn't let him. Martin sank back, holding the ear of a dog as though it might help him catch his wind. "Son, I think I'll get some rest now," he said quietly. "Tomorrow I'll be around the house, because the following day I go to meet with Dagi and Manley."

"Yes, I know. What for?"

"Oh, I have a few things I want to talk about with them," he murmured, too tired to be specific.

He's so evasive about his dealings, Marty thought, the shell hardening again.

Martin Sanders prepared to get out of his chair. He desperately wanted to be able to do it alone, to walk the stairs and retire to bed as always. He paused, still seated, gathered his strength, and then launched himself onto his cane. He managed to reach his legs, but like a weight lifter who trembles halfway through a lift, he couldn't hold himself up. He crumbled with just enough presence to sink into the chair rather than sprawl to the floor.

Marty was at his father's side before he had time to think. "Oh God," the old man murmured, "I'm sorry to subject you to this."

"I'll help you up," whispered Marty, and for the first time he allowed his father to lean on him. Together, slowly, they climbed the stairs. By the time they had reached the top, each of them, for his own reasons, had tears streaking his face.

CHAPTER
FOUR

Dear Mother,

It's late in the evening and Father has gone to bed, so I
thought I'd drop you a line and let you know I'm all
right. Sorry it's taken me so long to write. Knowing the
mails down here, you probably won't receive this for a
few weeks. Who knows what will be happening then?

You really wouldn't believe how much everything has
deteriorated in these thirteen years. The roads? All dirt
and rock now. The house? Badly in need of painting and
maintenance. The fields? Clear only because anybody
who owns a goat within five miles knows they can come
here and let it roam as if they owned the place. The
goddamn bees seem to be the only things as good or
better than before—of course, my first day here I got
stung by one of them as a welcome-home present.

Father parallels the general situation with his own

health. When I first arrived I thought that I was premature. He was up and walking around, pacing through the woods with his rifle, of course. I was expecting to see a man at death's door. But then after a few days I realized that he really is terminally ill, but he's so stubborn that he won't let himself give in to it. He won't even let himself acknowledge the fact that he's dying. Isn't that typical? Stubborn and out of touch to the very end.

These days pass by fairly quickly. I take walks, lot of times with my camera, and there are plenty of interesting things to see. Believe it or not, I haven't made it down to the ocean yet, mainly because Father could never make the hike and he seems to like me to spend some part of every day with him. I don't know why, exactly; I mean we don't talk very much. He just seems to like having me around.

There is an unspoken pressure about things, though. It's as though he's trying to bend me, change me, without really coming out and saying what he wants to do. To tell you the truth, I think he wants me to stay here and take over the place after he dies, but he knows it's such a preposterous idea that he doesn't dare bring it up. God, that's my idea of masochism! To be here at this point, more isolated and backward than ever, would be torture. Seeing things from an adult viewpoint, I'm amazed you lasted as long as you did.

Speaking of such things, Father and I did have one fairly long conversation (for him) about the past—just this evening in fact. Is it true he didn't know you were taking me to the U.S. when we left? Is that why he came to see me, to try and take me back? I'd be interested in your opinion about one more thing: Is it true that when I was growing up here I fit into the whole scene? I had always assumed that I was sort of a misfit until I got to the States, but Father seems to think I did pretty well here. What do you remember?

I must say that I've chuckled to myself a little bit remembering what a stern and mysterious warning you gave me before I left. Frankly, I must have some kind of immunity to the "lure of Jamaica" that you kept alluding to, because I certainly don't feel the tug. And yes, the sense of the world and what's important are very different here, but I don't see any kind of hypnotic power about it all. It strikes me as a backward, uncultured, self-centered perspective, that's all. There is a charm to a more simple, agrarian life-style, just as there is a charm to going on a lazy vacation. That doesn't mean you'd ever be happy living that way all the time. Far from the siren's call, what I hear down here is the ticking of the clock of boredom, and what I see is wasted lives.

Despite it all, I think that my decision to come was right. Had I not, the memory of refusing my father's last request (only request, now that I think on it) would have weighed on me forever. And seeing him here, in this environment, goes a long way toward separating the myth from reality in my mind. Remember, I was only thirteen when we left. As much as I get restless, bored, even homesick, I think this is an important thing I've done—for my own growth if not for Father's well-being.

So there you have it. Say hello to the folks in the library for me, and tell them I'll be back in a month or so. Most of all, tell Trudy that I miss the hell out of her. The old post office is still here, so you can drop me a line.

Love, Marty

P.S. I asked Father if he wanted me to communicate anything to you. All he said was No.

CHAPTER
FIVE

DAGI and him cousin Bomba stand in bee suits, fill up the tin can of Bomba's handy gadget with twigs, green leaves, and a few strips of back issue of the *Gleaner*. Once paper and twigs get lit, leaves make plenty smoke and little bellows at back of the can puff puff smoke into bee boxes.

"Make dem bees so drunk dem forget stingin," chuckle Bomba, and him right. Drunk bees let the men steal away honeycomb in the bottom section. As them work slow from box to box, the first smoked bees sober up and buzz around with fierce fierce anger. Thieves! Robbers! They attack and attack and attack, try to get through the mesh and cloth. But both beekeeper suits perfect cover because if them get even the smallest split or tear them know about it in a stinging big hurry.

As Dagi work with great white hood over him brown head, moving slow and bulky because of padding to keep stingers away from skin, him remember a photograph seen one time in a magazine in MoBay. He look at it long time before taking himself to the clerk at cash register. "What dis from?" him ask in a shy but steady way.

"Astronut," clerk say.

"What?" Dagi pride himself on being more worldwise than anyone else on Rose Hill (except Martin, of course), but this a mystery to him.

"Astronut," say clerk, like Dagi stupid not to know. "Walk on moon, walk in black space outside blue sky."

"Him look like me." Dagi amazed at how much the space suit look like his bee suit. Him buy the magazine to show Bomba and him wife, Lilly, and when him tell the story Bomba laugh, say, "Good thing dat clerk not call police, coome take crazyman away."

Them working faster than usual, not so much because of meeting set for Dagi porch later in morning but because of rain. It coming, no doubt about it, and them not want to get caught in the bush. When bee suits get wet them take days to dry. When honey get wet it lose strength. And when Bomba get wet it one of few few times good humor leave him.

Last of the waxy comb, dripping gold honey, drop into trays and onto back of Dagi's old donkey. Bomba stand fanning Ephraim, as Dagi name donkey, make sure bees don't sting him and make him jump and run. It bees last chance for revenge on the thieves.

"Rain comin, get bees even more mad," say Bomba.

"Good thing God make dem small. Otherwise we be dead."

"Otherwise we be cuttin sugercane."

Off come the tents on their heads. Dagi, smaller and finer than Bomba, both with straight black hair and a sharp nose, thin mouth of India, yet both born on Rose Hill. Them parents come from elsewhere, brought here with others by British Empire to make money for Brits somehow or other. But they as Jamaican as anyone, as Jamaican as Chinese-looking shopkeepers or Spanish-talking car mechanics or bushy-headed pickneys in the bush. This home all their lives.

Them learn to read and write—bees give families a steady income and chance to go to school. Only at market did they hear talk among other honeymen, ones with families from India, about how their people had never been slaves, how their homeland won freedom from Britain while Jamaica waited for freedom to be handed to her. Perhaps a little bit of this talk take root inside Dagi, but it wither as soon as him get home. To Bomba, it stupid from the start. "Me no need boolshit history make me feel all right," him shrug after others gone.

Follow trail from bush back to road, pass near Manley's house. "Hoi," Manley call. "Me coome soon, before rain." Dagi not know Manley invite as well, though could guess so. It flatter him to keep such company, biggest most educated landowner (that Martin), and mayor of the fishermen, as Dagi think of Manley. Dagi hurry to set up chairs on porch and make sure there are some grapefruit within easy reach.

Meanwhile Manley sit, drink him cup of tea, watch Dorothy move heavy and easy. Before so so many baby, she move light and easy. Now heavy, still easy. One thing Manley wish as much as anything, him and Dorothy get some money, buy suit and dress, go to MoBay get real marry by justice of peace with gold ring. All this time them never can do it, still call her Miss Dorothy. But still now plenty other things need money first. House just one room, need more room for girls come to prime. Horace need boat soon. Plenty plenty things only money can get, more important than gold ring.

"How foot?" Dorothy ask.

"All right." Him step on spike on walk to seaside, stab him heel hard. Happen plenty time before. Just walk on front of foot till it close up. "What think Marse Martin want me for? Something about goat?" Manley ask Dorothy because Dorothy got a feeling him learn to trust, give him jump on thinking about meeting.

"No mahn," she say, lift big old kettle grandma give her to cooking shed. "Bigger den dat. Him bwai coome, him bloat up like sick fish. Him past ripe."

"Him sick," Manley agree.

From backyard Horace call down, "Him sick but him all right. Him bwai not sick but him fussy fussy."

"Too much in States in him brain," say Manley. "Too much momma. Not 'nuff papa."

"Dat woman not bad," Dorothy say from shed. "She get sour, but when she sweet she mighty sweet."

Manley stand up. Rain come, good day for meeting. "Later on," him call. Foot make him limp just a little.

As Manley come down the road toward Dagi's porch, Martin Sanders was a mirror opposite arriving from the other direction. He had started early that morning on foot, with his son as company for most of the way. They had taken their time, but unlike most of their walks this time it was the old man who was trying to hurry.

"They'll wait, you know," said Marty as he watched his father try to catch his breath yet keep moving on.

"Rain," said Martin.

Marty pushed back his glasses. "Doesn't look that bad; maybe a sprinkle." His father didn't bother to say more; it would only lead to an embarrassing argument. They separated at the Big Turn.

As Martin took the turn alone, moving as best he could with his cane tapping the rocks before him, he wondered if this would be his last trip on this part of the road. He wanted to seize everything about the place and hold it inside himself, he wanted his memories to be strong and golden like his honey. It had become an obsession, to stare at each and every tree and house and rock and try to brand them into his soul. He was not a religious man in any organized sense of the word, but he had some obscure idea that there was such a thing as an afterlife and whether you reached that new place had something to do with your state of mind when you died. None of this was logical or rational and there was no one on this earth he would have confided his thoughts to, but they made him concentrate on the world at hand. A sharp enough memory right at the moment of death—it could act like an anchor. It could keep something of himself here on Rose Hill, and he desperately wanted that.

The problem was that each day his lucid time seemed to get shorter. Mornings were sharp and clear, but afternoons were starting to lose their edge and by nightfall everything became gauze and haze. If he died in that murkiness he just knew he would be lost. If somehow he could summon up his clear vision at that crucial moment, maybe there would be something more, something else, something . . .

The old iron gate at Dagi's was open for him. Lilly was paying attention to the goats in the yard, bending over in her bright print dress and tattered shoes. Perhaps this is the moment, Martin thought, perhaps this is the one which will come when I'm on the verge. Remember how she looks.

Manley closed the gate and came up beside him, not walking in his usual free way. Martin thought Manley's manner was a kind of sympathy which he didn't want.

"Because I use a cane, you don't have walk like an old man, Manley."

Manley smiled. "No mahn, stab me foot."

Remember that smile, thought Martin, remember when Manley lost his teeth to sugercane and he came to me wondering about false teeth and I traded his fence-mending for a trip to MoBay to get impressions of his jaw and then the package showed up at the post office and suddenly Manley looked ten years younger. "No pineapple," the dentist had said, "pineapple ruin them." "Dat small price to pay," Manley had answered, smiling smiling smiling. Remember that smile.

Three empty chairs sat on the porch waiting for them. Dagi inside changing his clothes. Martin took the middle seat and gathered his thoughts together. Manley know Dagi like be near grapefruit tree overhanging the porch, so him take far side.

"Ever hear a thing called Riddle of the Sphinx?" asked Martin, buying time to catch his breath.

"No mahn," say Manley. "What ah Sphinx?"

"Make-believe creature. You hear it, Dagi?"

"No, mahn," and Dagi took his seat.

"Go like this: What walk on four legs in mornin, two legs at midday, and three legs at nightfall? Got any idea, Dagi?"

"Strange thing, whatever it is."

"You, Manley?"

Manley think on it. Why Martin have such riddle in him head? Him look quick at Marse Martin, then flash come to him brain. "Yah mahn," him say, but soon as him say it him regret saying it.

"Well?" say Martin.

"Naw, forget it. Me not know."

"Come, mahn, yah got idea. Say it."

Manley not want make Martin feel more bad than him feel already, but now him got no choice. "You," say Manley.

Dagi sit up. "Whagwan?"

An amazing man, thought Martin. Can't really read, barely can write. One of the most amazing men I've ever met, including the man he was named after, Norman Manley.

Dagi sit back. "Me see it," him say. "Baby crawl, full man walk, old man use cane." Dagi reach for Bomba's latest gadget to show off. It a metal stick with pincers at end, control by piece of wire running down the stick. With pincers Dagi can reach out, pluck grapefruit off tree, and not even lean forward. Him do it three times, sitting back like a king, offer each a grapefruit. Give men something to do with them hands. Him start peeling his.

"First thing," said Martin after a while. "Thanks to you both for coming today. More than that, thanks to you both for being the neighbors and friends you have been."

The first raindrops hit the awning above their heads. Within seconds the light patter became a hard drumming. The downpour they all expected had arrived. Martin knew it gave each of them a good feeling; they were where they wanted to be, they had done what they needed to do, and now they could talk while the barrels and cisterns around their homes once again filled up. It was the best time for talking because there was no sun tugging at them to do something else.

Manley raise him hand, let it fall back on knee again. Martin Sanders have no need give thanks. If anything, other way around. Now come time to show that.

"My time come soon soon soon," said Martin. "That all right, truly dat all right. But I got a gnawing feeling inside and you two can help clean it out. When I leave, whagwan happen everything I work on all these years? House, land, bees?"

"Your bwai coome, him take it up," say Dagi.

Manley watch Marse Martin when Dagi say that. Him just sink in chest like him hit real hard. Bwai lose Jamaica sense, think Manley. Him heart in States.

"Martinson does not want to live here, dat plain," said Martin. "What I wish and what can happen are two different thing. Now I see dat de family of Sanders on Rose Hill reach the end of the road."

The sound of rain had become a steady drone overhead.

"Good thing him coome even if him not stay," say Manley. Him want Martin to know no hard feeling about Horace and goat and rifle shooting.

"Long as him not kill your bwai." Martin smiled.

Dagi hear about that. Him smile too.

"So I need to tell you two what I want to have happen when I die. This way there is no question, because you both know and you can remind each other. No one doubt your two words together.

"First thing: Cora can stay in house as long as she want. If she want bring family, she can. But get me clearly now: No one sells the house to anyone outside Rose Hill. I'll tell me bwai so him know too. No one sells the house, not Cora or Martinson or anyone. All right?" He had to stop, the knife in his chest stabbing.

"Now for bees. Dagi, can you take over me boxes, mahn?"

"Me and Bomba can do it. Bomba bwai coome up big now, soon him ready."

"Well then, work'em good, have plenty sweetness from dem. I just want to know they won't rot away and queen bee just leave for new hive in bush."

"Guarantee," say Dagi.

"You can use the bottles and honey-sorting house too, if you need them."

"Many many thanks, Martin," say Dagi. Simple words mean big things, think Dagi. Trail clear to become a wealthy man.

"Manley mahn, here what me thinkin 'bout: Plenty goat, some cow, couple donkey, sure to be left behind. I want you to make use of them all. Work them, eat them, breed them. But more, I want you to look after the land. Mend fence when them bust up; keep fields clear; don't let carvers take all dat good mahogany. If window bust in house, patch it if you can. Use goat money pay for things. If Cora not gwan live there, keep place nice till someone come. You can stay there yourself, mahn, if no one come. Use it, dat the big thing. A place must breathe to stay alive. Otherwise, it soon soon die, like people. You give it breath, mahn."

"Shall be done," say Manley.

"Can you do this even though it take you so far from seaside?" wondered Martin, already tiring from lack of breath.

"Yah, mahn. Me tell you plain: Me bwais gwan seaside now. Dat trail up and down, down and up get long long, time soon coome for me stay here in bush more den go to sea. So dis fit right in, mahn, right in."

"Good, good, you make me rest easy." I could write a will, thought Martin, and I could do a lot of legal things, but here goodwill means more than any paper. I've got a better chance of saving it this way than anything any barrister could do.

"Still not clear how your bwai fit," say Manley.

"Less him has to do with Jamaica, more him seem happy. Before it over, I'll tell him this plan."

The rain droned on, sometimes softer, sometimes

harder. Martin finished peeling his grapefruit and put a section to his mouth. It was sweet and juicy, full of life and yellow sunshine. Remember this taste, he thought, the pulp and seeds and skin and membranes. This might be the crucial moment.

Marty had decided to be adventurous, taking his camera along a trail he'd never traveled before, and he was tromping along at a good clip when he heard the first tentative patter on the leaves overhead. Just a sprinkle, he thought. In about as much time as it took him to wonder why his father was so panicked at a little rain, the tropical downpour had begun. He turned in his tracks, stuffed his camera under his T-shirt as best he could, and sprinted back to the road. Within minutes he was soaked and his only thought was to get under a roof as fast as humanly possible. There was the store on the road toward home—by the time he reached it he could barely see through his speckled glasses, and his camera certainly was drenched.

"Shit on a stick," he muttered, standing under a corrugated tin awning beside the tiny old grocery, listening to the rhythm of the rain overhead like impatient fingers drumming a tabletop. There were no walls, just wooden supports for the roof. At his feet the earth was dusty, and chickens pecked at nothing.

"Hee hee hee," cackled a voice. "Rain bring Martinson visit Miss Ethel, just like when him pickney bwai."

Miss Ethel was leaning out of the semicircle hole in the dirty wall through which she handed over bottled drinks and crackers to the men when they played dominoes on the earthen porch. She looked Marty up and down, sizing him up. She was even fatter than ever, but it was a droopy kind of fat. Her hair was motley gray and not combed, the lower part of her face had wrinkled up like an old prune because she had no more teeth—she is the ultimate hag, thought Marty.

"Hee hee hee, coome big man Martinson, coome show yahr learnin. Say hello Miss Ettel." She was used to playing the fool when she needed to, but no fool could have kept her small market open year after year after year.

"Hello, Miss Ethel," said Marty, meaning it to be sarcastic and condescending, but suddenly feeling like a bashful schoolboy before an old nanny.

"Yah talk foony, hee hee, can yah talk plain and straight?" She broke off a small piece of cracker and sucked it into her mouth.

"I talk straight, you talk funny."

"No mahn. Dis Jamaica, yah talk foony." She dropped her head just the littlest bit and looked at him coyly. "Think yahr better, talking dis way? Think it make yah different? Outah Many Peoples, One. Dat Jamaica. You Jamaican, mahn."

She seemed obscure, but he knew she was trying to lecture him. The rain beat down; he was captive.

"Hee hee hee, rain rain rain. Rain good for us, true?"

"Yes, yes, rain is good."

"Trees dem love it."

"Yes, yes." Not exactly your intellectual conversation over a cup of espresso.

Miss Ethel shrugged. "Dem teach you new speech, dem don't teach you manners, bwai."

Finally he turned and looked at her. She was still gumming the same piece of cracker, her elbows leaning on the wall, her old tits flabby in a faded dress, But her eyes watched him with a new hardness.

"I'm sorry, Miss Ethel, I didn't mean to be rude."

"Cha!" she cried, banging her hand on the wall. "Just when me think me get ah good fight to pass rain time, him say him sorry. Cha!" But her eyes softened and she smiled again, showing bits of cracker all over her gums. She handed him his own cracker as a peace offering.

Just then Horace flash through last open spot between trees and jump into Miss Ethel's, laughing and shaking off rain. "Hoi, Miss Ettel, cool runnings. Gimmesoometing-mahn."

Marty looked at Horace in total amazement. "You're not even wet! How'd you stay dry in this downpour?"

"Me wet, mahn, me wet."

"But look at me. I'm wet. You just have a few sprinkles on you."

"Me wet, mahn, me wet. Some rain yah can hide from, some rain just hit you. Me wet. Hoi, Ettel, gimme something."

"Yahr lucky lucky, bwai. Me just give him cracker and you know it. Here."

"All right, thanks." Lucky day, Horace think. Not so often Miss Ettel give something for nothing, not so often get good rain help things grow, not so often find pin. Him look proud at pin stick on him shirt.

"Whaddat?" ask Marty, not even noticing his pronunciation had slipped.

Horace stick out him chest, show it off.

"What does it mean?"

What it mean? Horace fold him arms. "It ah pin, dat all."

"PNP," read Marty.

"What about PNP?"

"That's what your pin says: PNP." Suddenly Marty realized what was going on; Horace couldn't read. Horace flash in him brain: That pin got writing on it. Now fookah from States show off him can read.

"Hee hee hee. Good thing not JLP, Horace, or you be fighting everyone in district."

"What she mean?" Marty demanded.

Horace think, him can read but him not know much. "PNP mean People Nashnahl Party, Michael Manley. JLP mean Jamaica Labour Party, Edward Seaga."

"Everyone like Michael Manley?"

"No, mahn, not everyone. But no one like Seaga. Him try smash ganja trade for bush peoples, the one thing bring some money to district, but den him let big guy from MoBay, Kingston, Negril, do whatever him like. Seaga for rich rich rich, not for poor. School shut down, no more lunch for pickney. Them say electricity too dear. But no, mahn, dat not real reason, him for rich."

"Well, of course the IMF cut the legs out from under Manley, but really it was a bit imprudent of him to ally himself so closely to Castro when he needed Western loans to keep the economy afloat."

Horace shake him head. "Me not know such thing, me know from heart. Manley all right. Seaga, no."

Simplistic, thought Marty, simplistic, and he doesn't even want to know more. But when you get right down to it, how much different is that from most American voters?

"Neither one care 'bout me, hee hee hee," chuckled Miss Ethel.

If not for rain, Horace not even speak such waste-of-time foolishness. Talking to Marse Martin son like talking to pickney—him know nothing, every little thing must say one two three four time, make brain feel dry and old. No more foolish talk.

"Hoi, Miss Ettel, gimme some rice," say Horace in new loud voice. Him know Momma need rice.

"Me no got rice," she say. "Rice all gone." But not looking at him straight.

"Yah got rice, me know yah got rice. Gimme it, mahn."

"Already give ah cracker, now yah want rice too?"

"Me pay for it."

"Show it."

Horace reach in him pocket, get dollar, and wave it in air. Marty, distracted from the beat of the rain, couldn't help but smile at the way Horace did it. Like offering something sweet to a kid as a bribe.

"Hee hee hee, not enoof, mahn, need dollar twenty." Clearly Miss Ethel was enjoying this.

"For rice? No way, mahn, me know rice at sixty cent ah pound, me want pound and half. Ten cent left, so me take hard candy too."

"No no no, hee hee. Can of tomato; rice seller make me buy one can tomato each pound rice or him not gimme rice. Rice sixty per pound, can sixty. Dollar twenty. Take it or leave it."

"No mahn. Cannot take it, cannot leave it. Need pound and half rice, Ettel, dat all. Momma grow tomato, no need can tomato."

Miss Ethel slam the wall. "Takeit or leaveit. You buy just rice, me got can tomato sit here. No one buy it from me, but me must buy it from seller. Me pay for it, yah know. Me sell yah just rice, me lose out, mahn."

Horace know now she serious, not just pass time until rain stop. Cha! Got some rice at home, but not much.

"I'll buy the can of tomato," Marty announced. He pulled a fifty-cent piece, a ten-sided coin with the image of Marcus Garvey for heads and the Jamaican national seal with a big lizard perched on it for tails, and slapped it down on Miss Ethel's counter.

"You need it true?" ask Horace.

"No, mahn, I don't need it. You take it."

Horace cross him arms. "No." Him shoot me one day, give me money next?

"No mahn, no mahn, me need it," Marty scrambled. "I forgot, Cora said she needed tomato. You take the rice, I'll take tomato."

Horace keep him arm cross. "Den you pay me ten cent."

"What?" Christ, just trying to help out and it's impossible. But what do you expect from a damn illiterate?

"Can tomato, sixty cent. Me give one dollar, you give fifty. You must give me ten cent for it, or me pay for your can."

It took a second, but Marty realized Horace was right. He would be getting the can for only fifty cents. He laughed. Damn illiterate? Maybe so, but he can add all right. "Yah, mahn, true," and the feeling of the moment swept Marty along. "Tell you what: I will do it if Miss Ethel give us each one rock candy."

Horace feel laugh come up, but Ethel slam hand on wall and shake her head, talking fast. "No, mahn, me-already-give-ah-cracker and now yah-wanna-candy."

Marty shrugged. "All right, then, you lose dollar fifty." He watched the rain, trying to keep from laughing.

Miss Ethel work her gums on her cracker, finally let herself break into a smile. "Martinson, me tell you you're Jamaican, now yah prove it." She pull herself out of her half-moon hole in the wall and lumber to her secret place where the rice hide—look back every second make sure neither Horace or Martinson see just right spot where she keep it. Horace look straight forward at rain—but Marty didn't appreciate the protocol and her privacy, so Miss Ethel had to fidget about the store until finally he turned away. And then, no rush no problem, Horace get him bag of rice, Marty had his can of tomatoes, two hard candies stuck to their plastic wrappings banged on top of the can, and Miss Ethel have dollar twenty. Once more they all turned to watch the rain, the two visitors standing side by side, Marty sucking the sweet, Horace have it under him tongue so it stay long long time.

To Marty it seemed they stood that way for an age, nothing happening. The spark of their bartering died away, and once again he was filled with the boredom of this life, the emptiness of time with nothing to do but wait. Finally he broke the silence just for the sake of breaking it, to change something.

"Tell me, Horace, how old are you?"

Horace have candy on heart side of mouth, but standing most on other side foot to keep good balance, just getting in nice with dirt at feet and rain in eyes when Marty speak.

"Eighteen, nineteen," Horace say, keep balance while talking.

"Which one?"

"Between dem."

"There's no such thing as between them."

Horace shrug, move sweet candy to other side. "What difference it make, mahn?"

Marty started turning over all the little ways that nineteen was different from eighteen, but he stopped. When you got right down to it, didn't matter here too much. No drinking ages, no driver's licenses, no sophomores and juniors. "No difference for you, I guess."

Hmm, think Horace, him take long way around, but him say me right. All right. "Me got a question den, mahn: Why you see me in bush, yell 'Freeze'?"

"I wanted you to stop."

"Yah, mahn. How come yah not yell 'Stop'?"

"Oh, I see. Well, back home, when it gets real cold, water will freeze into ice."

71

"Me know ice," say Horace. "Me loove ice."

"And when water freezes like that it just stops moving."

"But happen slow slow, not quick."

"When it's cold enough, it happens quick quick quick. Just like dat," and Marty snapped fingers.

"Just like dat?" ask Horace, full up with doubt.

"Truly, fast as that."

Horace smile for first time, show him open space. "So me run," and him pretend while him stand under Miss Ettel roof, "and you call 'Freeze,' den me just become like stone," and Horace stop right in middle of step, "or like lizard when him think bird near." Horace stand there, one leg up one leg down like him stop run in middle of step.

Marty laughed, thinking that there are mimes who would give their eyeteeth to be able to make that move right there. "Yah mahn, dat what it mean."

"Hee hee hee," laugh Miss Ethel. "'Freeze' mean do a thing fast fast? Sound like ah joke."

The rain filled their silence again, and Marty liked that because it made him more comfortable standing around. Behind them a few roosters were still pecking around the earthen floor, investigating for crumbs. Miss Ethel broke up half a cracker and threw it their way, watching them jump about. Horace fix him eye on one spot across road where leaf drip drip into puddle. Drip getting slower.

"You fish, Horace?"

"Yah mahn, me fish plenty."

"What you catch?"

"Snapper, barra, longjaw, some lobster, all kind of fish. Soomeday me catch marlin but no marlin as yet."

"What's a 'barra'?"

"Big fish, mahn. Real name barracoodah but me call him barra."

"Sort of like a shark, right?"

"Smaller, but him fight like shark, true. Dem got barra in States?"

"Where it's warm, but not where I live."

"What kind fish yah got dere?"

"Cod, haddock, flounder, tuna, swordfish."

"Me want swordfish, mahn, me want catch'im but him too too strong."

"Yah mahn, you need a big boat to get a swordfish."

"Papa, me, and Koz can catch'im, but reef cut him up when we drag him seaside. Too big to get on boat."

"Where's your boat, Horace?"

"Seaside, mahn, seaside."

"Hee hee hee," laugh Miss Ethel, "him think boat in bush?"

"Yes, yes, but where at seaside? How do I get there?"

"Start at road, do one thing: Follow brightest trail, always brightest trail. Come to seaside."

"Brightest trail? What's that mean, brightest trail?"

"You'll see it, mahn. Brightest trail."

"Sunday good day go seaside," Ethel call from shop.

"Everyone coome Sunday, whether it good or bad," Horace say.

"Sunday me coome," announced Marty. "I mean, I'll stop down on Sunday." It would make a good sociological study, interesting to see how everyone spends their weekend day of rest down at the beach. It gave him something new to look forward to after so many similar days.

Again the rain filled up their quiet. But now, instead of chafing at the delay, Marty began to enjoy the halt that nature put on everything. You really had no choice, so hell, might as well kick back and cool out. It was like a national holiday. Funny how having a little structure, even a small thing like a plan for Sunday, made time seem less heavy. He smiled and snuck a glance at Horace, who keep look at drip drip puddle. But Horace can tell Martinson look at him with different feeling than before, so him smile with him eyes.

It's like one of those psychology tests, Marty thought. Is the glass half-empty or half-full? Is the conversation the important part or is the silence the important part? Back home there's no doubt that the silence is little more than empty space between words. But here—and the realization was so fresh that he had to grope for words—here it seems like it's the silence that matters, the way of the silence, much more than the words. People seem to communicate on a more physical level here. He thought of the many nights he had already passed with his father, sitting in silence, fidgeting, railing inside about how little was going on. Maybe he was missing the important part of it. Maybe his father thought a lot was happening. He pictured his physical self and contrasted it with the young Jamaican beside him; he was paunchy in comparison, not very muscular, he couldn't even see without manmade lenses in front of his eyes. Horace was strong and lean even if his teeth were bad.

"I've lost touch with my physical self so much that I didn't even know I'd lost touch," Marty muttered, the words slipping out.

Horace let giggle sneak up. "True, mahn," him agree.

"You know what I mean?"

"Sure mahn."

"How do you know that?" Marty demanded, trying not to sound too defensive.

Him not really want to hear, but him ask just same, think Horace. "Smell," Horace say anyway.

"Smell?"

"Yah, mahn. Stand here, can tell from yahr smell dat soomething wrong."

"Hee hee hee," Miss Ethel cackled.

Marty laughed too. That was one he'd have to remember for party talk back home. "My smell gives me away? Shit."

"Yah mahn. Dat what it smell like."

A week ago Marty Sanders would have been offended beyond words at such a conversation—but a week ago he wouldn't have allowed such a conversation to get started. Now he laughed some more, cloaking his emotions in the role of sociologist, the next logical persona to keep himself removed once he had opened the taxi door and stepped into the movie screen.

Horace feel bad for saying that smell thing to Martinson. "Yahr just in yahr brain and mouth, mahn, dat where yah live," him say, try to make Martinson feel all right. "Me not live so much in brain and mouth, more in arm and leg."

He thinks he hurt my feelings, Marty realized. Well, holy shit, maybe he did. "It's all right, Horace, no harm. No need to apologize. But you know, I think maybe you can't be right in your brain if you're wrong everywhere else. Everything's connected." There's a concept for him to chew on, thought Marty.

"Everything work for brain, true," Horace agree.

If I was sitting around at home talking like this it would seem so ridiculous and dumb, thought Marty, but here it seems all right. He picked up his camera. "Say, can I take your picture?" he asked Horace.

"Sure mahn."

Marty looked through the viewfinder and he saw Horace, arms folded across his chest, leaning against the post of Miss Ethel's rude porch, PNP button bright on his shirt. The light was diffuse from the clouds and awning but there was plenty of it. Behind Horace some rain dripped and the road was covered with puddles, but within the frame there were plenty of green plants soaking in the water. Horace was smiling but he was trying to keep his mouth closed. Finally the laugh had to escape—just as Marty got the right shutter speed and focus. He snapped it as Horace broke into his big open grin, and Marty realized that this was the first time since his arrival that he had taken a picture of a person rather than a piece of scenery.

"Thanks," say Marty.

"No problem."

Miss Ethel stand in her window, pushing her hair away from her face. "Ready," she say.

Marty look at Horace like to say, What she mean? Horace move him hands like him got camera to say, She want you take her picture, mahn. Marty smiled, turned, and focused. In the viewfinder she looked old and sagging and wrinkled, but somehow she didn't look so much like the hag he expected to see. No, she looked sharper than that, and at the same time sweeter. Click went the camera.

There was a rumble on the road. Without looking, Horace know what it is. "Dagi car," him say.

"Dagi car? It's still running?"

"Only special time, mahn, not all time."

"I wonder what's so special right now?" Marty wondered. He looked at Horace, who looked away. "What you think, Horace?" Horace say nothing. Marty knew; his father couldn't make the walk home.

The car slowly drew up to them, Bomba driving with Dagi up front and Martin in back. Horace let air out him belly when him see Marse Martin sit up. Not so bad yet, Horace think, but bad enough him have to ride. If Marse Martin could walk, even if it take all day, Marse Martin would walk.

"Think I'll jump on board," said Marty as they got close. "See you Sunday, Horace."

"All right, mahn, maybe so."

"Hoi, hoi," Marty called to Bomba. In the back seat Martin turned quickly. His son calling Hoi?

Marty stuffed his camera under his shirt again and ran for the car. He had almost reached it when Horace, still with Miss Ethel (who had already slipped the forgotten tomato can under the counter), yelled above the rumble of the engine, *"Freeze."*

Involuntarily Marty stopped for just a second and heard Horace's crazy giggle. As he jumped into the little truck he laughed and held his third finger up high. The truck bounced on.

One finger up, think Horace, must be States way to say All right, cool. Must remember that. Him take off see papa now that meeting over, bring rice to cooking shed, practice raise longest finger up say good-bye. Take bush trail, stay off road, and stay more dry. Horace soon find Manley moving slow and quiet near home, little limp still on stab foot, little limp in brain as well. Horace fall in with papa for last bit of walking.

"Know dem cedar trees near garden?" say Manley.

"Yah mahn."

"We gwan cut dem down, get a ripsaw for makin boards."

"All right," say Horace. "Whagwan use for?"

"Coffin."

CHAPTER SIX

Dearest Marty,

Your letter finds me very well and now relieved of more than a little worry about you. When I hadn't heard from you for those first few weeks I had the sinking feeling that the Jamaican bush had swallowed you whole like one of those horror movie monsters, and you were gone for good. Your letter was most reassuring.

You'll just have to forgive my irrational fears about your trip, a journey which I agree was the proper thing to undertake. No doubt a psychiatrist would have a field day with our situation—my obsessive fear that you will reenact my past, your father's sickness drawing you to him, a twisted Oedipal triangle big enough to stretch across the Caribbean. I know all this yet still I let my emotions get the better of me, and find myself staring out the window of the office wondering what you're doing, how you're managing, how you're making the time pass day by day with so little to do. Believe me, I know that feeling. Then I try to shake it off and get back to reality.

There's plenty to get back to, that's for sure, and news from the real world is varied and complex as usual. Every few days on my way to the office I stop by the library to see how old Charles is doing without you—and to keep his memory of you intact for your return. He is his usual scatterbrained self, mumbling and shuffling about. How that place functions without you is incomprehensible to me, and the mountain of work you'll be facing on your return is no doubt staggering. He sends his regards, mumbled something about Errol Flynn's widow overseeing a ranch near Port Antonio. Strange as ever.

My own work presents the usual daily problems but remains palatable. The Government Department is presently in a protracted fight with the administration about funding a new professorial chair. To be honest about it, even though I never got my Ph.D. I think there's a chance they'll offer it to me if it comes open. I've been lecturing for five years now (five years? Dear Lord!), and of course I have the twin advantages of being a black and a woman. As with everything around here, it's largely a matter of politics and playing your cards properly. So far I'm simply biding my time.

Things around the Square are typically crazed, the usual melting pot of characters hustling about. Trudy stopped by my office yesterday, wondering when you might be back. She really is sweet; she simply looked in my eyes and said, 'I miss him,' just like that. Of course I said I felt the same way.

The students are pushing hard for the university to make some kind of stand on divestment of South African—related stocks. Bok holds that divestment means the loss of all leverage, a position which makes a certain amount of intellectual sense but has absolutely no moral underpinning. The university has accepted investments in South Africa for generations, and what has all that leverage produced in the way of a more humane society? Precious little that I can see.

Even so, I played the devil's advocate in lecture the other day, arguing the administration's side in front of two hundred rabid sophomores. It was quite extraordinary, because after all they couldn't resort to the emotional charges of racism against a black woman, now could they? I never let on where I truly stood, hard as that was, because I thought that revealing my real position would undercut my point: Argue cogently, argue the facts, and respect another intellectual position even if you don't agree with it.

I wish I could give you some more cultural news, which I'd imagine you're starving for, but without you around I feel somewhat out of it. I noticed a big line in front of Swift's the other night, waiting to hear some band or other. And then, oh yes, I read that the Insquare Bar has closed—is that the right name? Didn't you like to go there sometimes? Oh dear, I'm afraid you'll just have to come back and find out for yourself. Trudy mentioned that she had gone to see a movie featuring a band you liked—the Speaking Heads, is that right?—and it was one of those times when she missed your company. I assured her it wouldn't be long now before you're back from your mission and resettled.

Well, you asked me several questions in your letter, and I suppose I've been beating around the bush (so to speak) about answering them. First of all, yes, it is true that your father didn't know we were leaving for the States before we left. I never discussed the details of that time with you, frankly, because I suppose they were too painful and complicated for me to talk about. And I wasn't proud of my actions. But in my defense let me offer a few thoughts:

First, things had been deteriorating between me and your father for a long time. The exact timing of our break might have been unexpected, but anyone with a modicum of awareness would have known it was coming. I think he did.

Second, there was a real doubt in my mind whether

your father would let us go. Let me take that back; the doubt was whether he would let *you* go. I suppose I was a little bit scared, about how he would respond when I told him what I was going to do. Your father is not a violent man, but he is a physical man, and he has always been a little bit, well, unpredictable. It's a Jamaican trait and something I was never able to grasp in nearly fifteen years of living there, how people could explode in violence or physical confrontation one minute and then be passive and reasonable the next. Don't misunderstand me. He never so much as raised a finger toward me during our marriage. But this was really the last straw. Even though he and I had become nearly strangers to each other, the family still meant everything to him. To take away his only son, his namesake, even if it was for that son's own good—I didn't know what he would do.

So I ran away. Yes, he came to try to take you back, but once you were here it was obvious you should stay. Besides, once we were here we were on my turf, not his anymore, and I felt much more confident about how to deal with the situation. And he, of course, was like a fish out of water. He loses all his authority when he leaves that place. I pity him for that; a man with such potential trapped in his crumbling, backward little world where the major topic of discussion is how much honey the bees made. And now it's coming to an end for him, the potential never realized.

When you wonder whether you ever fit into that place or not, I say to you that you never really fit in. Yes, you could climb the damn coconut trees (every time you did my heart was in my mouth), but intellectually you were far different from the average Jamaican boy. Your interests didn't stop at their level, your curiosity was wide-ranging, and it was your potential which made me take you away. I didn't want to see you squander your life by following your father's footsteps. I didn't want to see a big personality made small by the limits of his environment. In that climate, and I mean climate defined physically and intellectually, a person atrophies. To see that happen to you was something I simply could not bear.

So there you have your mother's perspective. I hope this doesn't sound too "ethnocentric," to use the sociologist's phrase. I hope it doesn't sound too judgmental. I wish I could see you face to face to know how you receive all this. I'm so scared that you'll be lured back there by this romantic myth about the simple beauty of rural life. There is an attraction there, granted, an idealistic, anachronistic magnetism. Believe me, I know what that attraction can do because it drew me to a life for a decade and a half in which you were the only good, lasting thing I produced. When I finally broke away it was as though I'd broken a magician's spell, or overcome a debilitating addiction. Please, I beg of you, don't get caught up in that. I wouldn't wish that withdrawal, that inevitable, painful withdrawal, on anyone—least of all you. You're doing a good thing, a noble thing, by being there now. When your father's time is done your time there will be done too.

I hope what I write next doesn't sound terribly callous, but to tell you the truth when I left there thirteen years ago it was as though your father died for me. I mourned him then and my life with him came to as complete a halt as if he were already dead. I never expected to see him again—when he came here it was like seeing a ghost. Your going to him now is like your going to the Underworld as far as I'm concerned—it scares me that much, like watching Orpheus return to save Eurydice. By all means, learn from his catastrophe and Don't Look Back.

So I understand when your father said he didn't have anything to tell me, and I feel much the same way. We had our chance together, we did as much as we could, and it didn't work out. I had hoped that you would never be put in the position of being caught in the middle between us, but now, at the end, that seems unavoidable. I hope it's not too much of a burden, and I hope you're bearing up under the responsibilities you have there. You're a good son to do what you're doing.

82

Well, there you have it. Somehow I feel that my words have to pierce a dark veil, like they have to be as sharp as I can make them, as sharp as a machete, to cut through the distance between us. If they sound strange and foreign, don't recoil, *please*. Instead, realize what that means as a change in your perspective—a month ago they wouldn't have seemed strange at all.

I know you're fully capable of making your own decisions, and I know the textbooks say that I should avoid interfering in what are now your adult affairs. But I cannot stop my strong feelings about this. Call it mother's intuition, if you will: Thirteen years ago I felt as strongly, and I think time has proven me right. Keep your sensibilities intact, Marty, keep your world view in order. It's crucial to your well-being.

Oh Lord, I suppose I'm really blowing this entire situation way out of proportion. I've extrapolated far beyond what your letter implied, and I know what people say—that phobias have a way of making themselves come true. It's just that when I look out the window, day after day, my fantasy fears take on a life of their own, and grow bigger by the hour. A little reality cuts them down to size again. And I'm so anxious to hear from you, but most important, I'm anxious to see you. That would be the most reassuring thing of all. Until then, keep me posted.

Much love,
Mother

CHAPTER
SEVEN

SUNDAY come.

Manley sit on him stoop in door to house, watch family get ready go seaside. Most Sunday him go seaside, but not this Sunday. Feeling tired, slow. Not so tired just lay about, but so tired just want stay close to yard. Koz say him come up, two them finish rip cedar Horace help cut down.

Maybe it seeing a life slip away make Manley feel tired. Watch a man, Martin, know him gwan die soon soon soon now, see the spirit slip away day by day, that enough make any man feel tired. What is it make that happen? Little bug sneak in him when him not ready, little bug feed on him grow too strong drive out. Sometime Manley catch big fish, say barra or even marlin, cut him open see spots inside where something else grow, or even all through fish little bit of it everywhere, like bubbles in meat. Some men say forget it, just eat it up, but Manley say *No* mahn, disease, make everyone sick. Such a little thing can take over a big man or a big fish, strange but true. Sometimes body seem so strong nothing could stop it, not machete or even bullet. Other times body seem so weak, littlest little thing could just kill spirit no time at all.

Time come for Martin. Him time come sooner than for some, later than for some. Him try to get everything set up, put all in place so it be smooth when him go. That all right, that a form of righteousness. If you kill fish at seaside, don't leave him blood and guts just sit there for someone else clean up before him can cut own fish. Clean it up yourself. Take care your own. Fish cleaning a small way, Martin now doing it big way. How you live, how you die, somehow it all as one. Not like Preacher put it, but close like that.

So Manley sit, thinking, watch him family move about. Him not want think it, but one reason him not go seaside is foot. Still bother by stab. Skin close up now all right, but inside healing not done. If it still open him go seaside get seawater in it, but now it close so just stay off one day see how it go.

Dorothy tie red cloth round her head, little ones stick close. Them want get going soon as soon can be. But Dorothy take it slow. She worry about Manley. Not like him to stay here on Sunday. More like him to go to seaside Sunday, talk with peoples, play with children, keep everything smooth. "Foot all right?" she ask.

"It all right, it all right," him say.

"Say it so so quick, me think not."

Manley just shake him head, smile. No hiding from her. She can see in in in. "True, Dorothy, it getting better. Koz coome, me work here." Him stand and move close to her. So so many kids now just can't have no more, but sometime it very hard not to make them.

"Well, all right, we meet Horace down dere."

"If him can break from Belle one second, den you see him." Manley laugh. Horace go early on him own, get boat ready take Belle to reef.

Dorothy laugh too. Horace do plenty help around and it be sad not see him every day laugh and talk, but it be more more sad see him not have girlfriend with own house and family and full life. She proud that boy come from her and Manley, she walk anywhere straight up look anyone in eye because she know Manley is right and she is right and the children show the two of them together is right. No need for gold ring prove it.

"All right den, Mister Manley mahn, me gwan down dere."

"Don't let Preacher scare your brain wid devil talk," Manley say, eye shiny. Him know Dorothy more like to hear such thing than him.

"Cha. Me got enough worry, no need devil worry too."

Him put arm around her, walk down yard to road. She feel like she little bit him cane, foot still not right. Make her worry again. "Boil soome water and stick yahr foot in it, mahn. Do it good."

"All right, Dorothy love, don't bust your brain 'bout it."

Manley give each little one special rub, one behind ear and one top of head and one on nose and one in belly and one between eyes, and them run on with their momma just like baby goat. Him sit in yard, drink tea, wait for Koz, and think about what it feel like when the spirit begin to leave. If the time is right, Manley want to ask Martin about that—but him time might be over before it ever be right.

Right then would have been a good time to ask Martin Sanders such a question, because in the mornings he was his strongest and clearest. Marty knew this, so even though his father seemed almost eager to have Marty walk down to seaside, he felt a twinge. Later in the day things might not be so good and he would be gone.

"Son, it would make me feel much better if you went down. What can you do for me here that Cora can't? Anyway, I'd be interested in the news and today's Sunday. In fact, you could do me a favor while you're down there."

"What's that?" Marty was loading his camera.

"You could stop in at the Neptune Café where Miss Ella should be. She sometimes brings messages for me into MoBay. Tell her to tell Doc Stephenson that his patient is hanging in there. No need for him to come up."

"You sure?"

"Absolutely." Doc had offered to bring some powerful pain-killers—he had even hinted that he could bring enough to allow Martin to end it quickly if he chose that option. But no, thought Martin, if I take the drugs what would happen at the crucial moment? I might be so out of touch that what I will need to anchor myself, the grasp I will need, will slip away in a haze. All of my preparation and care and concentration would be lost. Especially now that Marty seems to be thawing out a little bit.

The old man would not say it for fear of driving his son away, but to see Marty eager to go to seaside gave him more reason to live on than any attention he could get at bedside. If he could just hang on long enough to let this little growth in the boy take root, to give this world a fair chance to show its beauty—that was worth the pain, that and being right there at the crucial moment.

"All right, then, I'll see you at the end of the day."

"Truly, Marty, don't rush."

"Cool mahn," and they smiled at each other.

Marty slung his camera over his shoulder, stuck a pen and some paper in his pocket, and took off. The bees hummed as he passed, Miss Ethel's was closed for the day—the road was quiet. He had barely begun to get his walking rhythm down when he reached Big Turn. God, on his first day that walk had seemed like an eternity. Now—strictly a stroll. The sun seemed to be pouring down and it felt warm and gold on his skin. Good thing, too, because how could he find the brightest trail without the sun?

He saw a path that looked promising and turned into the bush. So long as things generally went downhill, he figured he couldn't go too far wrong. And Marty remembered something about an old road, part of the Shire Hall plantation system. He used to take his slingshot back there to see if he could pick off a bird (never did), or a mango (sometimes). The trail was steep and Marty thumped along until he found himself a nice walking stick made out of a straight stalk of red birch that must have snapped free during the rainstorm. Sure enough, before long his trail opened into the rocky remains of an old road. So far, brightest trail easy to follow.

Even in a completely decrepit state, the old road was a marvel. It was built through what must have been dense forest along the side of a steep ridge, the stonework underneath still intact. Looking at the crumbling remains of old retaining walls, seeing what an engineering feat it must have been to carve such a road out of the land, gave Marty a sense of history about the place. But wait a minute; what does it really mean? Was it such an engineering feat or was it the abuse of many cheap, powerful slaves that could get such a thing done? And what was the road for anyway? Probably to move sugarcane, which meant even more slaves. He tried to imagine what this forgotten pathway looked like, say, one hundred years ago. Donkeys pulling carts laden down with green stalks led by slaves sweating in the sun, overseers with wide straw hats, whips flicking at their sides, on very special occasions the lady of the house sauntering up the hill to see her domain—no, she'd be riding sidesaddle on her beautiful mare with a white veil over her head, marveling at how strong the black shiny slaves were and how cheerfully they greeted her as she passed, how happily they toiled. Where were my ancestors in all this? Strange, but Marty had never figured that out. Were they the Uncle Toms for the white owners? Were they the rum makers or the planters? Were they the laborers? As he walked along he couldn't believe he didn't know, that he'd never asked or never been told whether he asked or not. Why hadn't he been told? A spark of resentment fired his thoughts, but unlike the bitterness of the past, it was a feeling directed at mother as well as father. He must speak to his father about this before it was too late, to find out where he came from—everyone had the right to know that. Father would know.

A twitter overhead made him pause. He looked up, saw nothing. But when he started walking along again he heard another sound that was very familiar. What was it? It sounded just like—no, not exactly but almost—like Horace when he giggled. Marty turned around quick and there was a little pickney who had climbed into an overhanging tree and was playing a trick on him. "See you, mahn," called Marty, laughing. The little boy scampered down and walked up to him with his knuckles in his mouth, eyes big.

"Where are you going?" asked Marty, rubbing the kinky black wool of his hair. The boy just looked at him.

"Where gwan?" repeated Marty.

"Seaside," whispered the boy.

"All alone?"

The boy pointed down the trail. "Momma," him say, and he skipped away. Marty watched him bouncing along the rocks and roots, moving much faster than Marty ever could—him on bare feet, me in the best running shoes money can buy. Incredible. Seeing a chance at having a guide, Marty picked up the pace, hoping to catch up with the family.

Sure enough, Dorothy waiting where trail split one way to seaside, the other way through Shire Hall to the Neptune, then seaside. She hear someone stamping along the trail, not sound like anyone she know, stick tap tap tap as him walk, make so much noise step on every loose stone. She wait see who that; when Martinson come in view everything make sense.

"Hoi," him say, breathe heavy.

"Hoi."

"Going to seaside?"

"Yah mahn." Pickneys spread out along trail all come run see new man. Stand round her dress.

"You have nice children," Marty said to this quiet woman.

Dorothy smile big. "Thanks." Them all keep stand there; him want something else?

"Me gwan see a Miss Ella at Neptune Café. Is this the right way?"

"Yah, mahn."

"You gwan there? Can I walk with you?"

"Me not gwan dere. Me gwan straight seaside. You walk Neptune side, then seaside. Walk dere till see Shire Hall, pass hall on heart, den turn. Keep on brightest trail, brightest trail whenever it split. Den you reach 'Tune."

Marty laughed. "You're not the first one to tell me to use brightest trail."

"Who else?"

"Guy name Horace."

Dorothy smile. "Him say dat to you after me teach him dat when him first learn walk seaside." When Martinson look at her like him not know what she mean, she say, "Me Horace momma, Miss Dorothy. Dese Horace brother and sister."

"Well, all right," cried out Marty. "I'm Marty, I mean Martinson Sanders."

"Yah mahn, me know."

"Horace at seaside?"

"Already dere."

"I'll see him there, then. First me walk to Miss Ella with a message. If you see Horace, tell him me come along visit him."

"Sure thing. How papa?"

Marty hesitated. "Well, in morning him fine. At night, him get weak."

"Dat the way of sickness." Dorothy nod her head. "If yah need soomething, can coome and ask me."

"Thanks. See you at seaside?"

"Maybe so. Pickneys not stay so long." Dorothy not say she want come home early be with Manley and him foot.

They smiled and turned to pick up their different paths when Dorothy paused. "Mister Martinson," she say soft.

"Yah, mahn," Marty answered, stopping.

"You not know den whagwan so it all right, and no harm done. But now yah got idea for doings in bush." Dorothy raise her hand up, something she almost never do. "Me not care where you see him, anywhere in dis world: You shoot at Wynne family again and any good thing between us it over, mahn, over. And bad thing grow when no good thing dere. Get me clear?"

Marty felt blood rush to his face. "Miss Dorothy, it clear clear clear. In States, when two people understand each other, they do a thing together. They shake hands to say everything all right. Want to shake hands?" Marty put out his hand.

She smile. "Yah, mahn." They stood at the split of the trails, the children around her legs, Dorothy barely reaching to Marty's shoulder, and pumped their handshake up and down. Then they moved apart.

I wonder if I'll ever live that down, wondered Marty, banging his walking stick on a few of the rocks along the trail. I'll probably be remembered as the guy who showed up when his father died, took a shot at Horace Wynne, and disappeared back to the States before anyone got to know him. If I'm remembered at all.

He came to the wide-open fields at the end of the upper trail, passing a man with several donkeys hauling empty burlap sacks on their backs. He was clearing rocks out of the field. Marty was going to stop and find out what possible reason he had for doing such a thing—but the man looked at him with obvious hostility, so he moved along. Besides, Shire Hall loomed ahead, and this was a place that stuck in Marty's memory. He remembered his parents talking about how people had taken over the house after the last of the Brookshire family died, and how it was slowly crumbling because no one really took care of it anymore. Yet here it was, at least thirteen years later. He was wondering what might be going on in there when he looked up and saw a large woman bending over a steaming kettle in the yard behind the great hall. She was beckoning to him, waving for him to come visit her. He turned off the footpath through the field, stepping up a crumbled concrete stairway. As he got closer he saw that the woman was standing over a large hearth that had been built up from what once must have been the stone patio.

"Soome tea?" she ask, stirring her black kettle with a big wooden spoon. "Pamela famous for her tea."

"I take it you're Pamela."

"Yessss, me Pamela."

"Me try soome tea, den," said Marty.

Pamela smile, look at him with deep brown eyes seem to flash every once in while with lightning streak through them. She a big woman, bigger than Miss Ethel even, but a different kind of big. Mostly muscle, real true big instead of just fatty sit-around big. "Tea nice for Sunday. Nice relax day." She pour dark dark tea in cup, add little bit honey, stir up with back end of spoon, hand over cup as her eyes light flash, then go quiet again.

Marty tasted the brew. It was woody and musky, covered over with honey. "Where honey coome from?" he asked.

"Marse Martin box."

"Like dat honey better than Dagi honey?"

"Depend. Both dem got good honey, best honey. Depend on queen in box." Pamela stir up kettle. "Tell you another thing: Me say just dat whether you Marse Martin bwai or not," and she laugh and flash her eyes into tea.

"How'd you know who I was?"

"Me know, mahn, me know."

"But how?"

"Word travel, dat all."

The more of the tea he drank, the more he liked the taste. "You live in Shire Hall, Miss Pamela?"

"Yah mahn. Plenty peoples live Shire Hall, plenty peoples coome and go. Me live here long time. Could almost say dat Shire Hall like bee box, me like queen." She laugh, face wide-open. "But me not boss everyone around like queen bee."

Marty laughed too. He liked her style. "That why you make so much tea, for everyone to have some?"

"No mahn, me sell it."

"Sell tea?"

"Yessss, sell it."

"Where?"

"Couple of tourist place MoBay, but me bwai take it Negril and sell dere. Younger tourist like it moore, and younger tourist in Negril."

Marty was confused. "I don't understand. Why is this for tourists? Why sell them tea when they can get it in any store?"

Pamela eyes flash and she throw back head laugh to heaven. "No store can get dis tea, mahn. Special, special tea. Only get it after rain like few days ago, get up early early in morning before sun burn up field where cow graze."

Marty drained his cup. "Well, I like it. What it made from?"

"Mushroom, mahn. Mushroom tea."

Finally Marty realized what she was saying. "You mean I just drank some psychedelic tea?"

"What you call it? Me call it mushroom tea."

His first impulse was to stick his finger down his throat to make himself vomit, but he imagined what that would mean to Pamela, who had invited him over for her special homemade tea. Shit. "This tea make you see strange things, Miss Pamela?"

She look at him sideways. "Soometime, depend on you. Soome peoples see thing, soome peoples feel thing, soome peoples just relax." She see him all of a sudden be strange, like him worry about tea. "What you gwan do today, mahn?"

"Seaside."

"Well, all right, den doan worry for tea, mahn. Tea just inside you like orange. Forget you even drink it, just walk-on talk-on do whatever your heart say do. It just *you*, mahn, not something strange to you. Just *you*. Even more"—and she look him straight in eye—"tea coome from Pamela, so you know it all right. Ask your papa and him say it too."

"Him drink tea?" ask Marty, not believing her.

"Soometime, soometime most everyone drink Pamela tea, just like soometime most everyone drink Marse Martin honey."

Just when I begin to think I've got an idea what's happening, thought Marty, just when I get a fix in my head, something like this jumps me. Jamaica.

"Thanks, Miss Pamela. Me walk on to Neptune Café."

"Yessss, Martinson, yessss. Just enjoy your Sunday, mahn, no worry."

"All right."

"And tell papa one thing: Him want strong strong cup of tea, help ease him, him can have it."

"Me tell him."

He picked up the trail again, supersensitive to every little thing he was feeling as if he was a time bomb ticking. No, maybe like a flower about to bud. Or maybe more like fruit about to fall from a tree. Or maybe . . . like Marty Sanders walking down a trail in Jamaica. Him laugh, throw him arms up and around in the air. Camera get in way.

The path from Shire Hall to the coast road had several branches to it, some turning back into the bush, but Marty simply followed the brightest trail. Of course it's brightest, he reasoned; most people walk it, so the rocks get worn and white, the brush cleared by swinging arms and legs. Once he realized that, the way was as obvious as a highway back home. Soon Marty was passing small clusters of homes, and then a muddy field (not a swamp ever since, unknown to Marty, Rooster's water pipe had been fixed and buried), and finally the Neptune Café beside the coast road.

The door to the Neptune was blocked by a large tourist bus that had pulled right up to it. Marty had to walk around, noticing faces staring down at him from behind tinted green glass. Suddenly he realized that he hadn't seen a white face in weeks, let alone a tourist bus full of them. He stopped and stared back at the people sitting in their seats high above the road. They seemed pudgy and sickly—the green-tinted windows didn't help show off their white skin. Quickly they looked away.

He stuck his head into the bar cautiously. After all, this was the infamous Neptune, the 'Tune, the place his mother forbid him to set foot in ever, under any conditions; the place where there were drunks and fights and smashed bottles and loud music late into the night. Now he remembered how his father had laughed, saying that visiting Miss Ella would be safer than walking through the bush. Momma had said, Well if that's the case, he shouldn't be walking through the bush alone. Then Father stopped laughing, stopped smiling even, stood up, and walked away.

It was dark in there, even in morning light, so Marty stood for a moment to catch his bearings, leaving his walking stick propped up outside the door. The bus must have disgorged a load of tourists because there were lines at the bathroom doors, several people were gathered around the bar, and the pool table was in use. Some sleepy Jamaicans were grouped at the far end, talking quietly with a woman loading beer bottles into the cooler.

"Ah, EXCUSE ME," said one tourist with dark glasses and a floppy hat covering his face.

The woman tending bar looked at her friends, shrugged, and slowly walked to where the man was standing. She stared at him.

"Got any lite beer?"

"No mahn. Red Stripe, Watney, Heineken."

"Aw, give me a Heineken. What the hell, Joey, right? On vacation, right?" He slapped a buddy on the back.

"Ow, my sunburn." His friend winced. "Make it two."

"Two Heineken." Slowly she sauntered along the bar, dug out two lukewarm beers, and returned. "Want glasses?"

"Sure," said Mr. Sunburn.

"No, no," argued sunglass floppy-hat. He turned to his friend. "I read in my travel book that if you're not sure what kind of hygiene is practiced where you're eating, it's best to drink directly from the bottle. Cuts down on the chance of getting a bug, you know?"

She looked at him. "Glasses are clean, mahn."

"Oh yes yes, I'm sure they are. How much do we owe you?"

She looked at him again. "Ten dollar."

"Remember," said sunglass floppy-hat, "that's only two U.S. First one on me." They left their glasses on the bar and walked over to the pool table.

Marty skirted around them, hugging the wall as if they had a communicable disease he would catch if he got too close. He joined the small group of Jamaicans, who stiffened as he came near but otherwise ignored him. Marty waited quietly until he saw that they had relaxed. Then he leaned in. "Me look for Miss Ella."

Them not look at him, but one them nod him head. "Denise, Miss Ella?"

Denise walk to other side where wood booth set up with hole in front pass money in and out, poke her head into door at side, talk to someone. As she do it same tourist guy come back again.

"SAY," he yelled, pounding the bar for service. "We'll take another round."

"Hey, man, why don't you show a little manners," blurted Marty. "You wouldn't act like that at home."

The tourist looked up. He saw not one black American but a group of Jamaicans slouched over the bar. They looked sullen and dangerous. "C'mon, Joey, let's get back on the bus," he said. "I heard about racial hostility down here, but I really didn't believe it until now."

Marty feel laugh come race up out of him belly, make him break out with a chuckle. Few them other guys sitting around kind of smile too, few don't smile at all. Then big fat black woman, gold chains hanging around her neck, come slow rolling toward Marty with Denise behind.

"Miss Ella?"

"Yah mahn." She look him up and down, red eyes small.

"Me name Martinson Sanders. Coome with message from me father."

"Coome round here, den," and she bring him to her private place at wood booth. "Now, what him say?"

"Him say tell Doc Stephenson no need for him to come up. Everything all right."

"Dat true?"

"True enough." He thought of Pamela, brewing her tea at Shire Hall, and he looked at Ella, so fat fat fat. A tingle, almost a cold shiver, passed through him. Pamela fat from her heart; Ella fat from her pocketbook.

"All right, den, me pass it on." She lean back far as she can in booth, which not too far. "So yah coome home, mahn." If him take over honey trade, keep breeding goat and cow, Ella sure want to know him good and have him know her good.

"Coome back help me father. Not stay too long."

Hmm, that different. "Well, listen, den, Martinson; yah just drive away some biz, mahn. Me not say dem tourist cool or nice, but dem tourist got money, mahn, and dat what me here for. Yah can hold yahr tongue better."

"Not all Americans are like that, you know," answered Marty. "Here or in States, when one talk like that, treat another person like that, then people can say it's wrong."

"Denise can speak for herself. She not need you take care of her." Behind Miss Ella stand Denise, smile kind of shy.

"All right, Miss Ella. I see what you're saying."

"Cool. Now have ah Red Stripe. No charge." Him still Martin son, whether him stay or go, think Ella.

"No mahn. Me lose you customer, me pay for beer."

"All right." Miss Ella not one to fight if man want to pay instead of get it free.

Marty left her in the wood booth, where she was counting the take from another Saturday night, and returned to the bar with Denise. He pulled out five dollars as she place an ice-cold Red Stripe and frosted glass in front of him. "Two dollar," she say, push back three.

"But . . ."

Denise smile. "Five loud-mouth tourist price. Three dollar pretty nice tourist price. Two dollar real nice tourist and Jamaican price."

The same laugh and shiver came up inside. Marty smile big at her like it best secret in the world she just tell him. She see him laugh inside and smile back. Denise. Marty would know her name the next time.

It was the first beer he had tasted in weeks and even on Sunday morning it went down real smooth. He left a dollar hiding under his glass for Denise and went to the door. His camera banged against him as he walked and with a sudden inspiration he returned to Ella's hideaway booth. "Miss Ella, know someone soon go back up Rose Hill?"

"Sure, mahn," she say, not looking up from money count. "Plenty gwan home Sunday afternoon."

"Well, if you can, could you hold on to this camera for me? And if someone go to Rose Hill, them can bring it to my house? If not, some other day me get it from you."

She look up. "Not want it today?"

"No. Me gwan swim, walk on beach. Just get in way."

Him use it say him trust me, Ella think. Not a thing someone do if him leave district soon soon. "Sure thing, mahn, me take care."

"Thanks."

He felt much freer and not so much like a tourist now that the camera was gone. At the front door he found his wooden stick still propped against the wall—it looked good to him, like an old friend, and he grabbed it with pleasure. The stick banged against the tires of the tour bus a few times and then Marty was walking the road, headed toward the beach.

But take it easy, seem like there so much to see between Neptune and seaside. The road was quiet, he could hear the slap and murmur of the sea. The sea turquoise wash over the land and the sunlight yellow wash over the sea. At the horizon the two meet and no one can tell exactly where that happens, or maybe it never happens, it only looks like it happens. Whoosh, calm wave break on shore. *Honk honk*, car keep him at side of road. "Say, brother, whagwan?" say a voice from little shack. "Coome here."

Marty let the man's voice tug him over like the moon tugs a wave. Placed on wooden tables were many many things from the sea—coral fans like open hands of white lace and coral globes that looked just like brains pulled out of skulls and spiny fingers and shells with open pink mouths like babies or toothless old men. They were beautiful but they were all dead. It was like skeleton bones heaped on a table for sale.

100

"Where you stay?" ask the man selling everything.

"Rose Hill."

"Rose Hill? Whaddat? New hotel at MoBay?"

"No, mahn, Rose Hill."

"Rose Hill Resort, Rose Hill Holidays, like dat. True?"

"No mahn, Rose Hill, period." And Marty pointed up at the ridge.

"All right, all right, cool," and the man backed off. "Take it easy. Anything seen, it for sale."

Marty picked up a big brain coral. "Alas, poor Yorick, I knew him well." He laughed.

"Whagwan?"

"You know Shakespeare?" ask Marty.

"Robbie Shakespeare, sure, mahn. Everyone know him. Best studio musician in Jamaica."

"No mahn, not same one. Shakespeare me think about was a writer. I said a line from him."

"Cool, mahn. Seen." No hustling someone from Rose Hill on Sunday, so him sit back, scrub some coral, let Marty walk on.

Another guy, a big man selling canned juice and fruit, call to Marty to come see, but Marty not stop. Him just wave and walk on. The crunch of his foot on seashells, heat from the road shimmering up, sand bleached white at the edge of the aging asphalt. He wanted to feel the sand, so he took off his sneakers and walked barefoot. Once upon a time he did that often, except he would have to wait until after he left the house and then hide the sneakers in a good spot so his mother wouldn't know. The hard part was remembering to put those silly sneakers on again at the end of the day.

Near where the old road forked off to the public beach a man sat on a stump in front of his shack sipping from a coconut shell. His hair was long like tough rope. Dreadlocks. Everyone in the States talks about the Rastafarians, but on Rose Hill they don't seem to be much around. He looked up from over the rim of his coconut, eyes white and clear. "I and Ai give greetings," him say.

"What that mean, I and Eye?"

Man look at Marty without saying a word but seem like him face ask a question, answer the question, then smile. "I and Ai mean Oneness wid many thing, Oneness wid Jah. Me give you greeting, it ah greeting from all manner of thing, not just from dis shell of a body before you."

Sun beat down, heat building toward midday, no cars passing, sea sound mix with bird calls. The high ridge he had just come down looked green and gray and blue, but it didn't look scary anymore, it look more like backbone of old cow stick up under skin. Rastaman see Marty look into high bush. "Coome from dere?"

"Born dere, not sure if me coome from dere or not."

Rastaman nod him head. "True Rasta say it no matter where you coome from, where you live, so long as spirit clear and Jah spirit shine through." Him throw back him head and laugh, dreadlocks swing like coils of rope. "But for me, on de path but not yet true Rasta, living in city make me lose balance. Maybe because me got to wear shoes."

"Yah, mahn," and Marty laugh too. Suddenly everything seemed very very calm, like in the eye of a big storm. He knew he was going to swirl out again, that was the way of things, but right then it was calm. The tea.

Rastaman watch him close. "Moore den meet de eye wid you, mahn. Moore den you tink gwan around you, too. Moore den moore den mooreden everywhere. Good thing to remember."

"Yes, Mister Rastamahn. So me walk to beach, see some moore of dis mooreden."

"Sure thing. But get ready"—and Rasta jump up sud-

den—"get ready for FIRE AND BRIMSTONE, ETER-
NAL DAMNATION!" Just as sudden him sit down again.
"Preacher mahn." Him smile.

Marty got the giggles and let them come out like soda
bubbles overflowing a glass. "All right," him say, walk on.

"Mooreden mooreden mooreden," call Rasta.

"Yes, Rastamahn, cool cool." Man, thought Marty, he's
a preacher in his own right.

The road hot on his feet, but the old road that branch
off cooler because it a lighter color. Some wild bees buzz in
and out of big red flowers. He stopped to watch them,
wide red petals like swollen pouting lips covered with the
brightest red lipstick, but a long stem in the middle not
like a tongue at all. Male and female combined into one
living thing. The bees were busy busy busy as always.
They come to the color but they don't seem to love it, just
something they've got to do. They hum but not a nice hum
to pass the time while they work, more an angry voice.
Then again maybe all this is total bullshit, what's the word
they put to it in school? Humansomething? Attaching human attributes to animate or inanimate objects. Person-
ification. What would the Rastaman call it? Oneness.
Because we can think such a thing, does that make it so?
Because the bees can't think such a thing, does that make
it not so? Which birds eat bees anyway? Do they get
stung? Do bees eat anything except pollen? It must be
their wings that make the humming sound. How often do
they make honey? Come to think of it, it's entirely possible
that bees put me through college. Mother would never talk
much about money except to say that there was enough.
Could bees make enough honey to pay tuition? Ha, there's
a question to ask Father. He looked outside himself and
realized he had walked to seaside.

It was the colors more than anything that overwhelmed

him at first. The pink of the sand and the light blue of the water, the green of the seaweed and the different green of the almond tree's broad leaves. And then on top of these fields of color, like dabs of paint, were the colors of everyone who had come to seaside for a day of rest. A red scarf and an orange dress pulled up to go wading and a green T-shirt and a pair of purple striped pants and a blue hat and white shorts on a pickney bwai and yellow sunglasses and pink knee socks and always the dark dark skin from brown to black shining in the water. Far out he could see where waves broke white on the reef that protected this long stretch of beach—half-moon reef, half-moon bay, that is the name that came back to him after so long, how could he forget something for years, forget he ever knew it even, and then remember in a moment? He saw some canoes in the water but more of them lined the beach overturned. Even their bottoms were colorful, painted pink or green or blue. A small boy wading in the water cried out as if he was hurt, and heads turned, but it was nothing serious, so everyone settled down again, slowly finding their comfortable spots like black cats.

He found a quiet place near the canoes, pulled out paper and pen, and began the letter he had planned on writing:

Dear Mother,
As I was walking along this morning I stopped to look at some shells a man had for sale in his little shack at the side of the road. They looked like bones to me. Some looked like skulls and brains, so as I held one up I said, "Alas, poor Yorick, I knew him well." Of course, that totally mystified the Jamaican, who when I asked him if he'd heard of Shakespeare said, "Sure, he's a good musician here in Jamaica." Can you believe it?

*   *   *

He stopped, reread what he had written, ripped out the page, tore it into small pieces, and buried the pieces in the pink sand. *That's not how I really feel. That wasn't a stupid thing for him to say—any more than it was stupid of me not to know who he was talking about. She always made me feel in a subtle way that Jamaicans are all stupid. Why? Why? She's scared of me liking it too much here. If everybody here is so backward and stupid, what's there to be scared of? Why did she stay so long?* He dug his forearm into the sand, and when he pulled it out it was covered by fine pink sand. Not really sand, more like millions and millions of shells pulverized small as grains of sand. They clung to his skin, making it look almost like a white man's. *Am I racist, like the subtle racism of an educated white man? Was I brought up racist?*

Dear Mother,
   I'm sitting on the beach. It's Sunday. Lots of people (by Jamaican standards) are playing around the water, although of course by Boston standards this beautiful beach is nearly deserted. Despite the poverty, every person I see is wearing something different, a different color or style. That says something to me about Jamaican culture. Everyone expresses himself in his own way and that is very important. This is a culture of individuals. If anyone tried to make it drab and uniform like some Communist country, even like Cuba, they would have a fight on their hands, mahn.

A small girl with nothing on at all come running out of the water to him. Heads turn; when Martin smile and rub her woolly hair glistening with rainbow drops everyone settle down again.

"Me want write," say pickney girl.

Marty took a clean sheet of paper, gave the girl the pen, and let her scribble away. "What's your name?"

105

"Carla," murmur girl, very serious about her writing.

"Here, me show you something." He took back the pen and wrote her name at the bottom of the paper. "Dat how to spell your name. Carla."

She take it from him and stare at it long long time. Finally, look up at him, she ask, "Me take it home?"

"Yes."

She run away, find momma sit in sand just where little waves hit legs, talk talk talk about her name and give momma paper hold keep safe. The woman look over and smile Martin way. Him smile back, returning to his letter. The first thing he did was cross out the word "mahn," and then:

I realize now that I've given this place little or no credit. That attitude is just wrong, plain and simple. I think about the reggae music from this island that has swept the world, and all the interest in Rastafarianism, and a history of fierce independence. I'll tell you the truth, I even find the language appealing, not simply lazy British. It's much more than that. I don't always understand what's being said, and two people can carry on a conversation in front of my face while I don't have the vaguest idea of what information is passing along. But the rhythm of it is always clear. That's the amazing thing. The rhythm of this place vibrates and transmits through music, language, and daily living.

What's more, I think something else. I was born here. My ancestors lived here. Why do I know so little about my birthplace, really my birthright? I feel as though I've been shut off from a piece of myself, and being back here now I feel like I'm beginning to find that piece of myself again. How ironic to find that only as I'm losing my father—almost like one had to happen before the other could.

I hesitate writing to you like this because I sense your disapproval. Well, frankly, I'm beginning to wonder about more than a few things. "More than" seems to be the phrase of the day, so here goes:

Did you keep me away from Jamaica all these years because you were afraid I'd want to stay here? You talked about Jamaica's mysterious attraction and all that, but it's not like some kind of black magic. Things might have turned out badly for you here with Father, but that doesn't mean I shouldn't know where I was born and raised or be proud of my heritage. The longer I'm here, the more I feel like I've been denying some really wonderful things about me and my homeland.

Homeland? He paused to catch his breath and reread. He almost tore it out and ripped it up again, this time because it hurt so much to write those things—it was the same as admitting them to himself—and what was more he knew that such a letter would cause his mother great anguish. She would freak out, she would think it was proof of her fears coming true—when actually it was the honesty necessary to reconcile the situation in a healthy way. He stared at the page for a long time, the words turning into foreign squiggles, inchworms, dirty scratches, then words again. This time he wanted to send it:

Father is holding on remarkably well, deceptively well. I get the idea that he's fighting this disease every step of the way, keeping himself intact, but when he finally breaks down it will be quick and complete. The foolish stubbornness which held him back in life is now holding back his death—now, finally, he has something worth being obstinate about.

So it's hard to say when the end will come. A day, a week, a month? I really don't know. Although he's losing strength, we seem to be getting along better. I guess I've gotten used to his silence. It's like words aren't as important to him as they are to me and you. So I've had to learn how to interpret silence and gestures, like absorbing a new language. I can imagine how frustrating this must have been to you over the years. But it also adds a dimension to relating with people that I've never really understood before.

Marty looked up, his attention caught by some noise. A crowd seemed to be gathering down the beach a bit, and Marty caught a quick glimpse of a man dressed in a dark suit and white collar.

Well, I hope this letter hasn't upset you, and I'd be interested in your reaction to my thoughts. Please take them in the spirit they're intended, as positive questioning. At any event, it being Sunday, I think I'll get myself a little religion. Preacher coome, as they say around here. Preacher coome to seaside.

Love, Marty

By the time Marty fetched his trusty walking stick (to leave it behind would be like leaving an old friend behind) the preacher had already taken off his dark coat, hung it on the limb of a nearby tree, rolled up his sleeves, and begun exhorting the flock to gather round. He was a big man, a bull of a man, white shirt already darkened with sweat, possessing a voice that needed no amplification to be heard. He lived in the district in a house built from high-class cinder block, wide windows nice roof all brought from MoBay. His church was small and broken down but it had electricity for a guitar to help the singing. The big MoBay church would pay for missionary Preacher's house, but if Rose Hill expect to get nice church all its own then people have to put in enough collection money to buy materials plus find time to do the work. Powerful as Preacher be, it a measure of feeling that Rose Hill church stay small and run-down—after early morning service if Preacher really want to reach some people him come to seaside.

"*Praise* de *Lawd, praise* Him," say Preacher, warming up.

"Amen," say a few women, warming up too. Preacher particular favorite of certain single women because him single too, big powerful man like that bound to be a good catch with nice house and all. Rumors even say Preacher seen sometimes at night hanging around Miss Stacia—strange because Miss Stacia not one to be singing the Lord's praises inside any kind of church, walls or no. No one hold it against him; Preacher might be a man of God but him a man just the same.

"'HALleLOOyah,' I say."

"HALleLOOyah," say one woman.

"I'm talking about de LAWD . . ."

"Yah, mahn."

". . . de Lawd who give him ONLY Son so we might be SAVE, Jesus Christ the FISHerman, the SAVior, our in-spiRAYtion."

"Praise Him."

"We doan need no roof to sing His praises, we doan need no four walls to give thanks to de Lawd, all we need is in our hearts and souls. We come to God on this Sunday on this beach because Him EVerywheere. Praise God."

"Amen."

"LET Him into your life and gain ETERNAL SalVAYtion. And what must you give back in reTURN? Just TURN from evil. TURN from sin. TURN from coveting your neighbor's possessions. TURN to de LAWD, dat all yah must do."

"Yah, mahn, say it, Preacher."

"We all KNOW dat Jesus could walk on WAter. We all KNOW dat Jesus could fee the HUNgry. We all KNOW dat Jesus could raise up the DEAD. LET His strength be yours in RIGHteousness."

Marty stood at the edge of the crowd, swept up in the energy and rhythm of the Preacher, but one image filled his brain. He saw Christ hanging on the cross, wrists and side dripping blood, head bowed under a crown of thorns, long straight blond hair blue eyes pink skin shining under an angel's halo. White God, always a white god. Same god left over from the plantations and slave ships. Jamaica has its own gods, not need white god. But the Preacher certainly didn't see it that way.

"There is a HEAthenism at loose in our land, a HEAthenism dat threatens our salVAYtion. I'm going to SPEAK to dat HEAthenism today, I'm going to ROOT OUT dat sickness."

"Do it, Preacher, do it."

"Dey let their hair grown LONG, not like God-fearing Samson of old, no, like HEAthen spirits out of our DARK DARK past before the light of JEsus come into our hearts. Dey disDAIN civiliZAYtion and live like ANimals, reFUSing the good order of soCIety and hiding instead in smoky back rooms wid the evil WEED they cannot live without. They PREY on weak young people when they should be PRAYing to the Lord Jesus Christ for forGIVEness. They are the SNAKE and ganja is dere APple, they WOO away the faint of heart from the path of eTERnal BLESSedness. Dere red and bleary eyes reveal MUCH, for as the poet says, eyes are the gateways to the SOUL. Them SOULS are red and bleary, full of SIN and Evil."

A few people Amen to that, but more just wait patient for Preacher to move on to next subject. They know him got to speak against Rastas and they know Rastas not have faith in Jesus Christ the Savior, so them damned forever, but still Rastas—true Rastas, not just trendy boys with dreadlocks—true Rastas hurt no one, live simple, and don't speak out against Jesus Christ unless Him take people away from natural things. Some people even compare Rastas to John the Baptist wandering around with holy ways. Maybe that why Preacher against them so much; maybe also because one Rastaman live way up in hills seem to come down around new moon just when Miss Stacia seem disappear for night or two. Wicked thought like that come out between giggles of women at water collect spot.

"But even for DEM, even for those of you who have been seDUCED by dere ways, dere is STILL time, dere is STILL hope, because de LAWD, with his unQUENCHable comPASsion, give us His ONly SON that we might be save. While LIFE still breathes in your SOUL there is STILL time for you to reTURN to the flock. JESUS Christ is our shepherd, in HIS hand is the STAFF of everlasting life. ACCEPT Him and JOIN us with the clear CONscience that makes life on this earth easy and the life thereAFter a PARAdise."

Marty felt the strong wood of his own staff, Jamaican hardwood, and he trusted it more than he trusted the staff of Jesus. Back in the States, he was cynical about religion because everyone around the university was cynical about religion, but here there was more to it than that. Which branch of history should carry on in the Jamaican soul? The Rastas might be simple and foolish but at least they were never a part of oppression. You could be sure that the man back on the coast road with the dreadlocks would either have been a slave or have escaped into the bush. But how about the Preacher? Maybe, in another time, he would have become the black overseer for the plantation owner with just as much righteous zeal as he is the

Preacher now. Marty turned his back on the meeting, dug his stick into the pink sand, and started to walk farther down the beach.

Little did he realize that doing this was like walking out of church down the center aisle in the middle of the sermon. Preacher pause, regard him, then raise his voice again. "Some among us cannot hear the RIGHTeous word of God without TURNing their backs. The words HURT too MUCH, they spark our GUILT and unHAPpiness with such strong diVINE LIGHT that we cannot face the FLAME. Our SOULS are like dry sticks just WAITING for a flint to be conSUMed in inFERnal heat. I PITY SUCH SOULS. . . ."

"Amen, amen."

"I PITY THEIR EMPTY SADNESS. . . ."

"Say it."

"THEIR SHALLOW SEARCH FOR MEANING WILL NEVER END . . ."

"Preacher righteous."

"UNTIL THEY FIND THE SAVIOR, JESUS OUR LORD. . . ."

Marty walk on, keeping him head turn away because a laugh come racing up him belly onto his face. A sneaking-out-of-church laugh; a mushroom-tea laugh.

At a safe distance he waded into the water, not caring one bit if his pants got wet, splashing cool liquid light all over himself. His skin looked as if it was glowing and beads of water dripped off his fingers like jewels from the deepest diamond mines of undivested South Africa. His glasses were covered with salt water, making him blind to everything except light, wet light everywhere, and he wished he could have ditched them as he had ditched his camera. He pulled them off and set them on the sand beside his shoes and staff and notebook. Up close things seemed hazy but far away everything clear. Him laugh, wondering what Horace might think about eyeglasses—eyes prove you too much in brain, in book reading, and not enough looking out to keep the balance of sight. Where is Horace anyway?

He looked among the men stretched out on their canoes, hoping to catch a glimpse of him, but no. Instead he heard a sound that seemed to thunk through his chest, a deep sound repeating rhythmically over and over. It seemed to be coming from behind the almond tree near the boats. Slowly, blissfully, he waded along, leaving sneakers, glasses, and walking stick behind, to search for the source. He found a man seated with his back against the trunk of a tree on top of a wooden box, knees spread wide, both hands dangling between his legs. In a lazy slow way he seemed to be plucking something on the front of the box, and when Marty looked closer, squinting, he saw what looked like five tongues of metal, all of them bolted to the front of this box, which also had a hole cut out of the face. Of course! It was a bass, and the man was plucking on the metal to make a low vibration that hummed through the box. The sound was clear and deep, it seemed to roll right through him and call other people too. A guitar appeared, and a gourd with seeds inside that made a nice rattling sound. The beat was calypso, not so hard as reggae, but it swung and carried people along.

"Mahn, dat box got nice sound," said Marty to no one.

"Roombah box," say guy stand next to him.

"What are those metal pieces made from?"

"Take ah saw, cut blade into five tongue, set each tongue in different place, make different sound. Roombah box."

The makeshift band seemed to slip into a rhythm, gliding through a series of chords over and over again, until

113

the roombah box player began to hum for a while and finally break into a song, slow and steady, quiet but full—like Sunday, mahn, like Sunday:

> *Never let ah womahn know*
> *How much yah loove her*
> *Never let a womahn know*
> *How mooch yah care*
>
> *Ah womahn is like a shadow*
> *Ah mahn he like a arrow*
>
> *Ah womahn she like a shadow*
> *Ah mahn he like a arrow*

The verses came and went but the chorus always returned: "Ah womahn is like a shadow, ah mahn he like a arrow." Marty sat in the cool shade of the almond tree, watching dark and light play on the sand. Shadow place to rest, shelter, always hug the earth, but shadow can't make itself, must be made from something else. A woman like a shadow? What would Mother say? Or Trudy? Him smile and chuckle. They wouldn't like it, they would think it was sexist—but to see it only that way is to miss the other side of the feeling. It a simple little line from a folk song, but it run deeper the more you think on it. The cool protection of shadows, the best place to be in the heat of the day, the welcoming, beckoning relief from a harsh sun. No, it's not all one way. A little ditty is more than just a little ditty. Mooreden. Jamaica still water.

He was ready to sit there all day, sink into the sand and let the music wash over everything, hear some men behind him sit down to a domino game on the beach, touch the bark of a tree trunk rising out of sand, stare into the eyes of a curious child, regard a huge fishtail on a hut or nets dangling in the sun, but this Sunday that feeling was not meant to last. This Sunday the calm was broken by the sound of a car coming down the old seaside road.

The music lost its beat and then died away as everyone see a small dark blue car with lights on the roof pull up to the beach, and two men in full police uniforms climb out. Marty jump up and move to get his glasses and shoes and walking stick and writing paper—it just feel like he should have everything right there close at hand with him. As he gathered them, he saw two canoes coming hard for shore. In the first one a woman sat in front while in back, paddling strong, head down, back glistening, sat Horace. In the second canoe a woman and child sat in front while a strong man behind paddled even harder than Horace, like his life depended on it. Something happening, think Marty, but him have no idea what that something might be.

CHAPTER
EIGHT

For Horace and Belle, it a beautiful Sunday morning. Them start early while sea like glass, sun rising over reef not beat down hard yet, Horace paddle make ripple stretch in every direction catch the sunlight like streak lining the water.

"Know ah zebra, Horace?" ask Belle.

Horace frown, shake him head no, keep paddling like serious man.

"Me see it in photo book 'bout Africa. Zebra look like horse but him got stripe all over, black and white."

Horace smile, get it. "Sun and paddle make zebra water today?"

Belle eyes say yes. That how them talk, look at things and say about them, or remember something and laugh about it. Most times them have no need really finish their talking, because halfway both know what the other mean. It make things easy between them. Belle not gossip gossip all the time like some, she learn read and write real quick, and all her teeth white in the sun. She near as tall as Horace and wider some places but skinnier other places. Him like that part of her just like him like most every part of her—except sometime him feel like she too smart for him, know too much. But then Horace remember what him know, plenty things, and then think him not feel good about that part Belle only because him wish to know more himself. Maybe a little jealous. Cha, good man got no need be jealous.

This Sunday extra special more than calm sun because Belle borrow two mask and snorkel from brother of cousin work at Lyman Hall Holiday Inn. Horace just love to snorkel at the reef. Right in the middle of the reef, farthest place from where points of reef touch land like big hook, right in middle best spot for snorkeling. Reef big there, plenty fish love hiding in little holes, then bottom drop off quick all sand no black spiny urchin stab up feet. On calm day can stand behind reef, look far back to seaside where everyone look like little dots on the sand, then take few steps be in deep water. Good for Belle too because she not as good a swimmer as Horace, not done it as much, so she feel safe where it shallow but still see plenty pretty color fish.

Them start at reef point sunrise side, side where Rooster do him lobster fishing now, and slow and easy paddle along inside of reef toward middle. Horace run out a line with little baitfish on it, just in case some snapper might want breakfast Sunday morning and instead turn into Horace supper Sunday night. Belle bring mango out of her dress pocket, peel skin back like petals of a flower to show

117

bright orange inside around pit. She suck on it little while, then give to Horace while boat skim the quiet water full of light. It a nice one, not stringy.

"How sewing?" him ask.

Five day a week Belle get up early early, climb on King Alphanso bus, go to Falmouth and sew. She work real good with needle and thread, mend most anything anyone want mend. Some night she stay too late to get King Alphanso coming home, so she have to walk. It a long long way, even through bush. Horace wish him know what days that be so he could run there, meet her, walk back. But never can tell.

"All right," she say. "Owner think me doin fine, but him say me got to own me own machine. If me can get it, him pay much much better."

"How much for machine?"

"Machine hundred dollar or moore."

Horace throw mango pit in sea. "Him should pay for it. Him make plenty money from your work."

Belle shrug; that not the way it go in Falmouth. "Me not get machine, stop gwan dere soon. Moore pay if me just get fruit, sell at market."

Make Horace mad to hear such talk. Belle can sew like no one else him know, but everyone can sell at market. For her not to sew be wrong, wasteful, like him not fishing. It just the thing she should do. But it take money to make more money—money feed upon itself, money it own bait, money it own seed. Unless you got some to start up, then growing it like planting ganja with no seeds. No matter how hard you try, ganja not gwan grow there.

"Anyone got it?"

"No mahn, hundred dollar too much. But me hold on long as me can, something may just coome along change it."

Them reach nice spot in middle of reef, so Horace set down big stone him use for anchor, keep line short so boat stay away from reef smashup—tide coming in no wind, so it hold right. Them all alone, so Belle take off her dress, swim in water with just little white underpants. When she stand in shallows water reach right to her nipples and them get hard from coolness and Horace. Horace swim underwater to her legs, wriggle between them like big eel, come up other side with laugh bubbles blowing out him nose. Belle turn around laughing too and Horace feel her warm belly against him and smooth arms round him neck and sharp bite of her teeth on him shoulder. She know that make him mad because him can't bite back. But it a good mad. Him give her a kiss but as kiss happen he wrap one leg round her and push her into water to where it over her head. She get scared and him laugh and laugh while she splash back to shallows, shaking fist at him and laughing too.

Horace spit on inside of both masks, give one to Belle. She want stay in shallow, walk about watch fish slip in and out of reef wall. Him want to stay with her but him want to swim about too, so at first they walk together with masks and snorkels in the water, holding hands sometimes or pointing to things other times. Many many many tiny blue fish all move together, all change direction at once. How them know to move as one? Out of Many, One. Wavy black fish with yellow streak make kissing move with mouth. Skinny yellow fish dart into hole in brain coral, stick nose out see if them give chase. When bottom drop off, the water stay clear clear, and below Jim point to where small barracuda gliding and twisting along the sand like barra do. Belle get scared and back up. Horace shake him head in water: No fear, barra just like dog, not hurt you unless you attack, him even more afraid of you than you afraid of him.

Belle feeling a bit cold, so she go back to sun in boat, but Horace swim along. Seaweed like waving ocean hair, covering sandy skin below, hiding all manner of things. Never put a foot in there, never. Along the way the grass meet with the rock, them mix together so sometimes can put a foot there if you can see a rock clear and go right to it. But it get deep so quick it not worth it.

Horace swim that way plenty strokes, follow reef in half-moon hook it make, when he see something make him pull up quick. Up ahead plenty bubbles floating to top from deep down. Could be bubbles from rock settling or big fish just dive, but no, bubbles keep coming. Those breathing bubbles, no doubt. Those diving bubbles.

Move easy, think Horace, move easy see whagwan. He keep him shadow behind, stay on surface but feet and arms under so no splash. Not much farther him find where the bubbles come from: Man down there with tank, diving deep at base of reef, silver shine of spear gun in him hand. Horace know that man. Horace know it Rooster, and Horace know Rooster far far far from side of reef where him agree to hunt lobster in return for Wynne family fix and bury pipe. Now Rooster here on Sunday morning, no one out and around, and him lobster fishing on trap side of reef.

Rooster thinking so hard about spearing lobster him not see Horace above and a little ways away. Slow slow Horace turn around and swim back to where Belle and boat wait. Him look up and see Rooster boat farther down the reef. "Belle," him say, pulling up stone, "we gwan over see dat boat."

She get look at him face. "Trouble?"

"Yah mahn."

Horace paddle hard for Rooster boat, so when him reach it Rooster still diving. Up top Rooster wife, Nellie, sit with boy Neal at her nipple. When she see Horace coming her eyes go wide because she know damn well whagwan. She bring Neal close to her with one hand while other hand reach for diving knife.

"Hoi, Nellie," say Belle in her quiet way like nothing in world wrong. Nellie say nothing. Horace look inside boat and see plenty lobster, six or seven good-size, already stab. Him also see what Nellie other hand doing.

"Belle," say Horace, bringing both boat together, "reach and pick up dem lobster dere while me steady boat. Hurry." Horace steady it with paddle stretch across: paddle just so happen stretch across Nellie knife arm too. Him want Belle to hurry because him not want meet Rooster here alone, him want meet Rooster on beach where rest of village gather.

Belle see what happening. She grab lobster bucket while Horace push off, paddle hard as him can for shore while looking for bubbles same time. Rooster must have seen second boat shadow because already bubbles come toward boat with Nellie. Horace know Rooster one strong strong man, can paddle faster than Horace. More than anything else, Horace want to reach seaside before Rooster catch up with them. Then Horace feel much much easier.

Horace put him head down, look at nothing but arm and paddle, wishing for a second paddle in boat for Belle. She know to crouch down, keep low in boat and low against wind. She become Horace eyes.

"Otto in him boat, tear off tank, just start paddle. Air tank slow him down, heavy in boat, we got good start, still halfway seaside but me think him faster. Gwan be close."

"Knife," gasp Horace. Belle find it and lay it near at hand. But Rooster begin to tire just a little from extra weight. Him get nearer and nearer to Horace but him can't catch up all the way. Horace keep him head down pushing right through to the sand, running boat into seaside harder than him ever do it before, Belle and him both jump out with lobster bucket soon as them hit. Even so, Rooster so close him almost catch them before them both look to shore—and everything change. There, full uniform car guns everything, stand two police.

"Now I know," one of them say in real British English, "that not all of you are deaf and dumb. So I will ask again: Where is all the excess water use coming from in this district? Hurry up, we don't have all day, and if we can't get to the bottom of this now, then someone might just have to keep us company down at the station until we get some answers. Hey, you two," him call to Horace and Otto, pay no attention to the women, "you get over here too."

Horace breathe hard walk over with lobster bucket and Rooster walk over with spear gun and to every man on that beach it clear as fresh water what happen. Sunday morning, Rooster sneak out, break deal on lobster spearing—and Horace catch him. Of course police have no idea whagwan and every man look away from every other man because just a look might be enough to make police single out one of them and take him away. But running through all of them like rope through a herd of goat is the feeling that what happen next is Horace decision. After all, Horace family strike pipe deal with Rooster. Now Rooster go back on it, cheat. Horace oldest Wynne here, so if Horace want to pay that Roostermahn back right now, him have that right.

Horace stand there just like everyone else, head down, hands flat at sides, but him thinking like crazy: What would Papa do? Bring police in to protect village, punish Rooster-Donkey-Otto dat Fookah? We do plenty work

122

help him out and him sneak to thieve lobster at reef. Now like stroke from heaven police show up at very same moment that thieving discover. Turn him over? Not turn him over, risk police just take someone from village who got nothing to do with it. To protect Fookah-Donkey? What would Papa do?

Thoughts keep run run run through him brain, Horace wishing they would slow down. But each moment passing by make him more sure of what right: Problem between him family and Otto. It a district problem and answer come from district. Police know how to shoot and kill and take away, them not know how to help truly make things right. Them hurt and hurt and nothing more. Live by sword, die by sword. Police? No. Horace move him feet apart, put weight on both equal, face straight on like him ready for anything. That little motion tell everyone from Rose Hill standing about that Horace reach decision: Keep it here. No police.

Tension that fill up the moment gone now that Horace sure what him want. No one change how them standing, but air between them relax like now them ready stand there all day need be. Police not know what happen, but know that something happen and their chance gone now. Their turn to make a move: Take someone away? Give up? Keep searching?

One take nightstick in him hand—Horace remember Clinton say what terrible use that is for hardest heartwood of lignum vitae—and smack it on heel of hand. But other policeman seem like the leader. Him look around, see dozen or more strong men standing against just him and partner, one man even have spearfish gun which on land is deadly as bullet, and him think him not really give a fuck about water use out here. Save face, save pride, and get out—that what him shoulders seem to be saying to Horace.

"Well then," the officer announce, "we'll just have to return with a full contingent of men and scour this area until we find the culprit."

Everyone know that bullshit. Pipe could be cut anywhere from MoBay to Falmouth, all same pipe. Him just bluffing.

"And in the meantime, as a gesture of goodwill, we will accept a few of these lobsters as your payment for wasting our time today." He turn to Horace, point him stick in bucket.

Horace feel laugh in him belly but him make damn sure to hold it there. Otto begin to paw ground just the littlest bit. There go Donkey again, think Horace. Keep belly tight. Turning to police, he take two lobster out, two smallest, hand them over. Small price for keeping things cool.

Leader give them both to second policeman, who hold them up. "These are the smallest in the bucket," him say. "Either give us two more, or give us the biggest two."

For first time since police come everyone look straight at them. Some hands come off sides and get crossed on chest. Horace look at them two, uniform cover the brass gleaming in sun all clean and iron and starch with tall round hats. Them try to act bigger and better than everyone but them greedy, greedy for power. That what lobster mean to them. Power.

"Two yah got dere good enough," say Horace quiet.

"Is that right?" say second police, reaching for stick again.

"Yah, mahn," say old man Winston, stand other side. Police turn him head.

"Yah mahn," say Dixon, drinking buddy of Otto, stand side by almond tree. Police turn again.

"Yah mahn," say Belle, stand beside Horace. Her eye look like it stick a knife in that police heart.

Air get tense again. Then lead policeman nod him head up and down, look in each eye like him taking photograph of every one of them. "You haven't heard the last of this," him say, like to scare everyone. Them both turn away, black boots spray sand, walk to car, and drive off.

Amazing, thought Marty, leaning on his staff, totally amazing. He expected the group to pass congratulations around, break up, and return to regular Sunday activities. He didn't know enough to know that there was still one more confrontation before this drama could end.

As police car drive away Horace reach in lobster bucket, take out lobster one at a time. First lobster him give to old man Winston. "Thanks," Horace say.

Rooster explode. "What you think you're doing? Me catch dem lobster!"

Horace go to Coomfy, give second lobster. "Thanks," Horace say.

Rooster move like to come at Horace. Horace whirl around yell right in him face: "Yahr divin other side. Me family pay for dese lobster wid hard hard work and you tief dem Sunday morning. *Fookah*. Without Manley Wynne you be in prison right now—and you *still* tief lobster. Me talk to Papa and Koz, decide what next. But meantime, dese lobster for *me* give *me* friend." Horace turn to Dixon, give third lobster. "Thanks, mahn," him say, but him heart still burning up at Otto. *"Fookin tief,"* Horace yell. "Dat be last time Wynne family stand up for you, fookin *tief*."

Horace turn to Belle to give her last lobster, start to say thanks to her. At that instant Marty realized that Rooster (or Otto, he seemed to be called both) had slipped to the fringe of the group as fast as a rat and was reaching for his spear gun. He had to cross near Marty, whom he ignored as though Marty didn't really exist in this Jamaican world. Belle screamed as the silver sheen of the spear gun rose up, pointed at Horace. There was no time for thought but there was enough time for Marty to bring his hardwood walking staff down on the spear gun just as Rooster pulled the trigger. The spear drove into the sand at Horace's feet and the force of Marty's blow wrenched the spear gun out of Rooster's hand to the ground, where it lay bent and broken like a dead snake.

Rooster look at Marty and Horace, Horace and Marty, eyes wild and red. Horace reach down, take spear, and bend it in his hands until it useless. "You try it twice now," say Horace, quiet but straight clear into Otto face, "yah try it twice but now yah know: Yah can never touch me. Yah doan have dah power of hurt over me, Fookah. From now on yah got new nickname always: Fookah."

Horace and Belle turn and walk to take care of boat. Group split up slow, but everyone, even Dixon, stay away from Otto now. Marty, his body tingling and weak from the rush of the moment, walked to where Horace had stowed the boat while Belle cleaned the lobster. He stood there quietly while Horace rinsed off the wooden hull of his canoe with clear water. Finally Horace stood up, and when he did his face was smiling his biggest laughing smile his front teeth all gone. With both of his hands he was giving Marty the finger—just like he had been practicing since the day of the big rain.

"Coome over me friend Clinton shop, eat some lobster," say Horace.

"Sure thing," say Marty, and looking at each other, them both start giggling from the belly out.

CHAPTER NINE

W HEN the three of them reach Clinton shop, sun just beginning to get low. Two big pieces of wood on hinges swung shut across front, show that Clinton closed, but out back thin line of blue smoke show him there.

"Hoi," call Horace, stand out front.

"Coome, Laugher," call Clinton.

Them come around and see where Clinton and Vernica, Clinton best friend beside Horace, have kettle cooking over fire made from Clinton wood shavings. Belle hide lobster behind her back until she can't hide it no more. "Got ah present," she say, hold it up.

Vernica laugh. "Good thing we not ital cooking. Throw it right in."

"What him call you?" Marty asked Horace.

Horace giggle. "Me nickname: Laugher."

Clinton look little bit worry. Saying someone's true nickname in front of stranger not a cool thing—it give him power over you. But him not know stranger with Horace.

Horace see that look. "It all right," Horace say. "Martinson can hear it. Him already got me life in him hand."

Clinton look him over. "Welcoome, mahn. Me name Clinton, but yah can call me Dreamer."

Marty knew this would be the time to tell them his secret name, to complete the circle of trust, but he didn't have one. If he did, what would it be? He spoke before he knew what he was saying: "Mooreden."

Clinton look at him with question in his eyes.

"Real name Martinson Sanders, nickname Mooreden."

Horace laugh. "Moore den meet de eye wid him."

Clinton smile. "Seen," him say, and turn attention to kettle cooking.

"Hope dat lobster real real tasty," sigh Belle, sitting down on mahogany stump against bamboo wall. "After all we do gettin it, better be good."

"Whappen?" wonder Vernica.

"Wait, lemme guess it," say Clinton. "Dis lobster spear—dat mean Otto. Hmmm. Me see it clear: Otto tief lobster from trap side, you catch him. True?"

"True, mahn," say Marty. "Horace give Otto new nickname: Fookah."

They all laugh at that one. "Otto take spear gun, try kill me, mahn, kill me dead," say Horace, "but him can never do it. Mooreden knock dat gun out him hand, bust it up. Spear drive into sand instead of into me belly."

Vernica look at Marty with new feeling. Her eyes deep brown and she wearing white white T-shirt cling to her body real close. Marty looked at her for a second but then he turned away because she and Clinton were together and if he looked any longer then she would know he wished that wasn't so. But when she stood and moved across the little yard to gather up some wooden bowls he couldn't take his eyes off her, so graceful, long, and slender.

They sat quiet together, wait for stew be ready while shadows get longer and longer all the time. Marty could see many of Clinton's larger statues, the ones him do for him own heart sake and not for tourist, and they were magnificent works of art. He knew that if they were displayed in the posh galleries or museums of Boston or New York they would be a sensation, commanding exorbitant prices. Yet here they sat, barely covered by the rain, of no interest to the tourists because they were too big to carry home and too unusual to be accepted as more of that nice work those natives do with wood.

"Your work is truly beautiful," said Marty.

"Many thanks, mahn."

"What kind of woods do you use?"

"All kind grow round here, depend on what me want make."

"Well, what that dark wood there? Seem like you use it a lot."

"Dat mahogany, mahn. Real good carvin wood."

Horace shift on him seat just as Marty ask next question: "And where dat mahogany coome from?"

Clinton see shift, not answer direct. "Soome me buy, other me find 'round district."

Marty sat back, leaned over to Horace, and whispered in his ear, "What think, Laugher? Me shoot rifle over Clinton head?" Horace say nothing, just giggle giggle giggle.

Stew steaming hot and ready, lobster give nice extra taste to it. Vernica and Clinton make sure plenty pepper all through, bring out taste of yellow potato and green bean.

Pepper make stew hotter than Marty usually eat, but after first taste him like it. It reminded him of . . . of Sundays, of course, the one day of the week when his father would cook. Father never made stews exactly like this, but always there was the heavy hand with pepper, his mother protesting (good-naturedly or not, depending on the day) that he was drowning out the taste, Father ignoring her and dumping it on.

By the time the stew was done, day near its end too and blue shadows take over the land. Clinton keep fire going while reaching for special chalice. Him carve it from extra sweet cedar to give the ganja nice scent as him draw it through stem. Head of pipe got face and mane of a lion carve into the wood—reminding Marty of the face on the front of the King Alphanso bus. Best chalice for best time of best day of week. Dreamer fill it up, make cloud of smoke round him own head, pass it on to Vernica, who do same. Even Horace smoke some, one of few times him feel like it. Belle, like Horace, smoke less, and when it come to Marty him puff away too. It feel like a peace pipe, all must share or the purpose lost. Chalice go around one more time and air fill with scent of high mountain ganj, kind Clinton get in him travels, stronger than ganj Horace grow near seaside, more sap darker leaf taste bluer smoke but still not harsh, no no. Smoke not bite your insides because it grow in thin air free from bad fumes, nothing bad in dirt, just grow as it please and man who grow it not worry all the time about police or thief or nothing, so him brain clear too. At least, that what Clinton say to Horace when Horace ask him why that ganja different.

Sun finally disappear altogether—seemed to Marty that it hovered on the horizon forever—and Clinton build up fire so everyone can see everyone and get some warm keep the cool edge of night away. As Clinton tend to wood sticks for burning him see Horace with head back, eyes shining. Horace not smoke much, so when him do then ganj really go inside him deep.

"Thinkin, Laugher?" ask Clinton.

"Yah, Dreamer mahn," Horace sigh and smile. "Thinkin 'Merica."

"Whah thinkin?"

"Me sneak on cargo plane from MoBay, gwan Atlanta, no problem. When get dere sneak off, run run to big city. Plenty light flash all over, day and night, and first day or two me just walk about, hungry, tired and nowhere to sleep. But den, mahn, me meet up wid mahn who makin ah movie. . . ."

Marty laughed. "Not too many moviemakers in Atlanta."

Clinton give Marty quick look but Marty not see it.

"Dat all right," say Horace. "Only need one. Him big big mahn, fat belly. When him see me him say, 'Scooz me, sir, but me needin mahn who know 'bout fishin Jamaica style to star in brand-new movie.'

"Me say, 'Well, yah coome right place, mahn, me know it.'

"Him say, 'Only thing, dere got be ah scene in dis movie where hero get in fight, get him teeth knock out. Cannot fake it, mahn, must be real. Yah willin?'

"Den me just open me mouth, show him how me teeth not dere. 'Willin,' me say.

"'Cool cool,' say fat mahn. 'First part movie shoot here in States, den move everything Jamaica seaside near MoBay. Know dat place?'

"Me just smile, say, 'Yah mahn, me know it.'"

Marty laughed again. "Yeah, but first you got to join a union."

"What ah union?" ask Horace.

"Everyone in movies must belong to the union or else you can't work. They make you pay a lot of money to join."

Horace hesitate in him dream, stop smiling, and slump over. When Marty looked up from inside his ganja laugh to see why Horace was waiting, he saw Clinton's eyes glittering like black diamonds staring at him with such energy that they pinned him against the bamboo wall. Not a word was said, but suddenly Marty understood and felt ashamed: This is dream time, say Clinton eyes, this the time when everyone free and no one can try to stop that free flight. Anyone who does is not welcome.

"But guess what I just remember," blurted Marty. "Only U.S. citizens have to do that thing with the union, so no problem, Horace, no problem."

Horace face brighten up, lean back again. "Cool, cool. So we shoot first part of movie in States, den coome Rose Hill, where dem bring big boat seaside, camera take picture of me in boat. Finish movie and dem pay plenty plenty money for me as well as leaving boat behind as thanks. Fat fat mahn coome, say, 'Next year, Sir Horace, next year we coome back, make new movie.'

"Me say, 'Cool mahn, me be here.'

"Him say, 'Next year, first part movie in Africa, den coome Jamaica. Yah want go dere?'

"Me say, 'Sure mahn, can do it. See you den.'"

Horace smile and sit back, dream done. No one say a thing, but everyone feel that now it Belle turn tell her dream. She not done it as much with Clinton as Horace, but she done it some and she feeling free in her brain. It take a little while, but everyone got plenty time. Soon enough she start in:

"One day me sittin in Falmouth at de shop sewin ah seam. Door open, little bell ring just like every time door open, in step older gentlemahn dress in real nice suit made from wool wid little gray lines runnin through dat fabric. It lunchtime and everyone but me gone. Walk up and say, 'Yes, sir, what can I do for you, sir?'

"Held in him hand is a vest, vest fit wid suit him wearin. 'Madame, me vest got tear under one sleeve. See it?' Sure enough, tear dere. 'Madame, I need dis vest to wear for big speech I will make dis very day. Can you fix it right away?'

"Me got plenty other thing gwan, but him need it quick and him speak so nice me say, 'Yah, mahn, me can fix it.' Me take needle and thread, find just right color thread, make each stitch just clean and small and right. Soon dat vest good as new, better den new.

"When dat mahn see what me can do, without even machine, him open him eyes wide wide wide. 'Madame,' him say, 'dat cleanest stitching my eyes ever seen, and I coome from Kingston where dere are plenty seamstress. Tell me, do yah own dis store?'

"'No, sir,' me say. 'Just work here.'

"Him rub him chin. 'Well, lemme ask you dis, den: After me give ah speech, one thing I gwan do is go MoBay and look for something invest me money in. Suppose me find ah dress shop me want buy? You want to run dat shop for me, becoome manager or even part owner dat shop?'

"Me say, 'Yah mahn,' and me tell him me know two, three other girls good as me—almost good as me—and can bring dem to work too. Well, sure enough dat mahn show up next day, park him big black car right front dah shop, coome in, and take me MoBay where him find true true place, five or six machine dere, all Singer machine. Him hand me key to dat store, him say, 'Dis shop for you, madame. Me coome once every week see whappenin and if yah needin anything like more thread or needles. But if

133

yah work hard here, surely you shall make plenty money. Before I return Kingston, I gwan stop visit all me friend in MoBay, plenty rich friend, tell dem all bring dere clothes here.'

"Sure enough, plenty peoples coome, shop get plenty biz, me and me sister and me cousin all get real good wage for work. And when dat old mahn die, him leave store in me name in him will."

Murmurs pass through them all and the fire crackle hot like it enjoy that dream too. No better or worse than Horace dream or any other dream, just Belle close-to-home dreaming. And because it close to real life it have a sweetness blending into it, like lagwood honey in dark tea. Sometime Horace wish that Belle dream bigger dream, faraway dream, but Clinton tell him that such thinking is foolishness and Horace soon agree. Marty found himself wishing that he could find that old man, or he could be that old man himself.

When everyone heartbeat settle down to slow steady thump again, Vernica, sitting next to Belle, make little sound clear her throat and then start to talk:

"One day me takin walk through dah bush, deep deep in heart of high mountain country. Just walkin, yah know, walkin and thinkin 'bout dis and dat, not payin heed where trail gwan. When me coome to me senses, looking around, me not know where me at. Strange strange place, trail along side of mountain above valley me never seen before. So so steep me slip, slide, and fall down to dis valley, and look up see me never can get back up dere again.

"At first it seem real bad, but after short time, looking round, seem not so bad. Every kind of tree grow in dis valley, and dem all seem ripe all times. Mango not one string in it, orange juicy juicy juicy, lime sweet, bees buzzing round plenty honey. 'Where dis place?' me wonder, saying it to de air because no one else around.

"Deep deep voice behind me head answer; 'Dis country *my* country.' Voice scare me straight to me bones, but me turn and see who saying it. Big big lion saying it. Him licking him paw not like little kitten but like him thinkin 'bout eatin me.

"I and I be tryin to think what kind of answer a lion might like hearing, when another voice say, 'Not just him country, it all us country.' Me turn and see big big bull, big horn close to me arm, could stab right through me. And coome up behind bull lot of different animal—bird and goat and rooster and donkey and tiger and horse and squirrel. Even snake and rat all coome see me. Seem like dem all can talk because everyone chatter away sayin dis and dat, dem sayin Coome here, Coome dere, Doan fear lion, See me, Climb on me back, No no, fly on me wing— all dat kind of talk till valley seem full of noise. Seem so funny dat me start laughing, but soon as dat happen all dem animal get quiet quiet quiet.

"Lion speak: 'What dat sound?'

"Me say, 'Laughing, mahn.'

"Lion eyes get narrow. 'Never hear dat sound. No other animal make dat sound—laughing, yah call it?'

"I and I laugh again. 'Yah mahn, it a happy sound. When peoples get feelin good, dem make laughing sound.'

"All dem animal try make laughing noise, but it coome out crazy like loud hee-haw coocoo waaa—soo soo much noise me start laughing all over again. Dem stop, listen to Hahahahahaha, but dem cannot do it.

"Soon lion roar, make dem all stop. Him say, 'All right, every animal got something no other animal can do. Yours be laughing. Now doan be scared, coome down on all four leg and coome to river where we live.'

"Cannot help it, me just got to laugh again. 'Me walk on two leg all times, not just when me scared. Shall walk to river on two leg.'

"'Suit yourself, mahn,' cackle rooster nearby. 'You're trying to be like me and dat a good choice.'

"We walk to river, sparkling clean water flow through dat valley, and animal got homes set up dere near each other along riverbanks. Even though some animal seem like them want to eat another animal, like lion want eat goat, dem get along all right. Me not know why or how, but dem do it. Peaceful, yah know. Animal help bring me wood for buildin tree house. Me find nice tree wid big limb over river, sun coome shine into tree in morning, and dere me build nice house for sleepin and restin. Crow and starling, even hawk coome bring grass make roof over house, make house like big big nest. Animal think all peoples like living in tree, but tell dem me not like all peoples.

"It a beautiful valley, everything sweet and cool, 'cept one thing: All animal coome wid one other, but me coome single. Gettin kindah lonely even though it so so nice. But den, one day, me walkin near where me fall into animal valley, just walkin and singin and talkin, when me look up and see—"

Vernica stop, look shy at Clinton. Him look at her and laugh. That the end of her story, at least the words part.

The circle come around to Clinton now, Dreamer himself. For a moment it felt to Marty like Clinton might pick up where Vernica had left off, take that dream one step further into Eden. But no, Dreamer not dreaming that way. Taking a puff on him chalice, back straight against the bamboo wall him build with him own hands, surrounded by friends close at hand and all this surrounded by carvings that glow in the fire with life of their own, Dreamer peer into the dark night above the fire. Small

136

whiffs of smoke rise from him nostrils like dragon breath, eyes go far away and seem to take the black night all the way inside him heart and soul. That where inspiration come from, him body seem to say to Marty. And then Dreamer begin:

"Dust fill sky late in day, dust from many many camel moovin through desert wid men on dere back, thumpety thumpety thumpety on sand. Camel spread out in big V like when bird flock fly long way, 'cept inside V fill also wid even moore camel, many many many men ride through desert. Men wear long white robe round dem, white cloth round dere head too. White for coolness, yes, but white for righteousness as well. Ridin ridin ridin, up and down camel moove moove moove, thump of camel hoof soon fill air like thunder.

"Lead mahn at point of V holdin long pole wid flag wrap round it, flag tie up so yah cannot see it. Every mahn riding at outside of V holdin ram's horn in him hand, must be hundred or moore ram horn dere. Sun gettin low in sky, gold-red color.

"Just when first tip of sun touch land at horizon, just right dat moment, every one dem mahn holding ram horn raise dat horn to him lips. Lead mahn untie flag him carry on pole. Men blow into dem horn and sound like trumpet coome from each one. Together dem fill de sky wid sound of trumpet blowin, sound of dah shofar in time of old, sound bring down wall of Jericho. Lead mahn let him flag fly, gold and red of sunset shine onto white white flag wid golden lion in middle of flag. Lost tribes of Israel return! Lost tribe coome again to Ethiopia homeland. JAH! JAH RASTAFARI! JAH! Them call him name as them coome to Ethiopia.

"Rider wid white white horse, only one not on camel, coome chargin through dem all, break past V into lead.

Him stand tall in him saddle. One and all know him to be Haile Selassie, descendant of David and Solomon, ruler prophesied coome from Ethiopia and unite lost tribes of Israel to JAH. Him ride to sunset, gleamin gold and red just like lion flag dat bear him likeness. JAH RASTAFARI. Ridin hoome on de shoulder of JAH, de wing and wind of JAH, de mighty fist of JAH. Every step them coome, V get longer and longer, moore and moore join in celebration of JAH, he rule dem all wid him messenger Haile Selassie.

"And when yah look into dat great army, into dat big V gettin longer all de time, not at one wid ram horn near edge, not way up front or way in back, just one of many many many coomin to JAH, white robe flying behind and camel hoof makin thunder on sand, when yah look close at dat one mahn in middle of so so many many—well, den yah shall see me."

Clinton white teeth gleam in firelight, then him puff on chalice and grow quiet.

A gentle quiet settle down among them, and Marty knew his time had come. He knew it would, yet he had been so lost in the fantasies of others, in the swirl of marijuana and the long suspense of mushroom tea, in the fire and the night, that he had given no thought to the dream he should offer. What could he say? This would be his dream, the others would see into him by the images he conjured up, and all he felt was empty and observant. A sociologist is not supposed to participate, he is supposed to watch, but he kept getting pushed and pulled into action, not by choice but by necessity. He saw himself sitting in the middle of nowhere, in the middle of everywhere, carvings watching and protecting them all, fire defining a place, these people patient, relaxed into the night, trusting and worthy of trust. Then see his own self awkward and shifty beside them, not so complete and centered feeling, and him wish him body not be that way. So Marty took a deep breath, let it all out, took another, let it all out again, and suddenly found himself speaking without any certainty of what was coming out, or what it meant:

"I'm thinking about a child—me think 'bout ah bwai, not little pickney, but good-size, maybe twelve or thirteen. Jamaican boy. He loves to walk around in the bush, try to sneak up on birds with his slingshot or climb tall trees for coconut or soursap. Happy boy, father got land and animals and honey, so him have plenty to eat. Mother gentle and like taking him into MoBay to see the sights, or sit him on her lap to read a story and show him what letters mean what sounds. Him grow up strong, him know that other people live other ways, but the way he lives is the best way for him.

"Everything seem fine, like nothing could go wrong and everything go right, but soon trouble start coomin. Bwai's momma and papa start to fight at night, or if they don't fight they don't talk at all. At night this bwai would lie in bed and hear them argue in loud voices, yell at each other back and forth. But him not understand it, because during the day them both treat him real good, no yelling at him, no yelling at each other, they just go about doing what each one want to do. So bwai think it gonna be all right. And him feel so good to run around see everything and everyone that him think they must share that feeling. It never crossed this child's mind that him parents could ever split up—how could they? His parents him parents, dat all dere is to it. Sun could stop in sky, moon could never rise, sure, and him parents could not be together in them home, sure.

"But just like a stone rolling down hill, nothing could stop it getting worse. Quiet times get bad quiet, not good quiet, and loud times get angry loud, not happy loud. It get so bad that even for the bwai the days seem cloudy most of the time, gray and sad. Him stop seeing how pretty the flower look and how quick the bird fly. Him feel like him sick all the time, like the whole world turn blue.

"Finally that bwai just can't stand it any longer. He kept thinking that maybe it him own fault for what was happening, that if he wasn't dere maybe mother and father would see clear and be happy again. So the more he think on it, the more one idea keep coming to him: Go away, sneak away for a little bit, give momma and papa chance to get everything straight, then come back and everything be cool.

"So dat what the bwai do. One night after parents finish fighting and go to slepp, him sneak away into the bush with slingshot and machete. Him use them to get all manner of food as well as build a little house for himself out in bush. Him get strong and know the way of all animals so they don't mind him and him know where the honeybees at if him need a sweet thing, or where wild pig run, so he should stay away. Him live dat way for month after month after month, growing bigger and stronger all the time. And then, one day for no reason that the bwai can really explain, it just coome into him brain that it time to go home, that mother and father fix everything up and now it time to see them again and get back home.

"Sure enough, him take the long walk out of the bush to home, and there him find parents waiting. Them both cry out when he coome walking through the fields, swinging machete high over him head in greeting. Them coome running together to greet him, tears streaming down their faces but good tears, welcome-home tears. Everyone seem to understand why he went away, they don't punish him for it or anything like that, and even better them like each other again and tell him that the bad time over, never have that kind of fighting every day ever. The bwai live on in Jamaica, and now him even stronger and know more about everything than before. His momma teach him more reading and writing and him papa teach him all secrets about the land and sea so when him older him move easy in town or in bush, in Jamaica or even across the sea in America. Him happy and strong because his roots go deep and spread wide."

Marty stop, eyes bright with tears under his glasses. Horace realize the most but everyone see that this dream closer to truth than others, closer but just as faraway as any dream. A sweet dream, yes, but bite inside the sweetness and find bitter bitter bitter.

"Gettin late," say Clinton soft. "Anyone want sleep here at seaside can coome me home."

Marty sit up. "No no, mahn, got to get back to me father." And then came a rush of panic: He hadn't a prayer of making it back up to the top of Rose Hill in the dead of night—not without someone who knew the mountain trail much much better than he did. It would be literal suicide to try. Marty looked at Horace, but before he could . . .

"No mahn, thanks," say Horace. "Me and Belle gwan back up. Feel like coomin wid us, Martinson?"

Marty just nod him head yes, and the three of them stand. Before leaving the firelight, however, Marty leaned over. "Clinton mahn," him say, "you're welcoome to cut mahogany from me family land for your carvings."

Clinton look him in the eye. "When me cut, me cut with care," him promise. "Me keep forest strong, and me watch make sure other carvers know dis forest must be save."

"All right," say Marty, and him gone.

CHAPTER
TEN

THE hike home became a dream. With Horace leading the way and Belle behind, Marty slowly climbed through the night. The moon was low but it cast enough light to make the rocks glow on the path—even in the night they could follow the brightest trail. At first Horace would slip ahead without realizing it and Belle would be right on his heels, but soon Marty's eyes became more accustomed to the night and he picked up the pace. Pitch blackness would come in pockets, but open stretches in the canopy allowed the eerie, heatless light of the moon to show the way. Sometimes it seemed like the less attention he gave to his feet, the easier he could climb, as though the awareness of all the rocks and sticks he could stumble over attracted those very things to his feet. So Marty tried to listen to the wind breathe in the trees, to hear rocks scrabbling together as a goat jumped out of their way, to sense the rush of a bat wheeling near their heads—all without fear because Horace led the way, and anyway what animal would dare confront the three of them? Crickets screeched their tune and a donkey brayed his answer into the night, full of stubborn anger. A red birch dropped a long finger of leaves into their faces, mimicking a thorny bush that scraped his ankles. Without eyes, the trail took on a fabric and weave like patches of a huge quilt, a quilt stitched from sound and touch and smell.

At only one time during the long walk home did they see signs of other people. Near Shire Hall, before the upper end of the old plantation road began, Marty could see some yellow lights gleaming along the open pastureland, like contained balls of fire set up in two careful rows side by side. They were obviously set, not some kind of raging brush fire. When Marty asked what they were, Horace didn't even look up.

"Ganja strip," Horace say. "No plane come around tonight, them wait till moon gone. But dem make sure fire ready, strip clear—soometime pilot fly over check it out before real trip."

"When will they make the real trip?"

"Two week or so. When moon gone, mahn."

The hill seemed to keep moving under their feet, seaside far behind and below, on and on and on. The trail became steep and narrow, then flat and broad, then dark, then mottled with light. Footsteps became a part of a ritual, a mindless repetition that must continue, that could not stop any more than the moon could stop rising. The closer Marty came to exhaustion, the less attention he paid to the hill, to a large animal close at hand bounding away in fright, to the profile of a branch like a serpent crawling on

143

a stone wall, to anything except each step and each breath, step no more a matter of will than breath, breath no more important than step.

"Careful, Martinson," whisper Horace, push branch from trail, not want foolish branch whip back in Martinson face.

Keerful, Martinson, keerful, little bwai. The taunt of childhood returned, rousing him from his trance. There was Horace's back before him, a black outline moving easily, soundlessly. He could vanish in an instant and I would never know where he went, or he could turn and end my life before I could so much as blink. That first meeting, he could have taken that gun away from me before I had the vaguest idea what had happened—Father said that, and he was right. Behind came Belle, protecting his back. Would any Jamaican man let a woman protect his back? No, he would protect her back, no Jamaican would dream of going in this order. I'm not Jamaican, thought Marty, they treat me different because I am different.

Belle voice lift up in the night. "Feeling the hill, Martinson?"

"No," he answered with sudden hostility. "Why do you ask?"

"All dah sudden yah walk different, dat all," she say mild, thinking that him tired, so him get angry up inside.

"Me feeling it plenty," say Horace up front. "Good for us dat moon shining so bright, make it easy."

It's in my own head, thought Marty, it not that they think all these things about me. It's me thinking them about myself, put it into them brains, their consciousness. If I could just stop doing that I'd be much better off. That kind of self-consciousness is so stupid, so limiting, like a stone wall across the trail. Makes a man have to stop and climb over; better thing to do would be knock it down, get it out of everybody else's way, get it out of your own way for the next trip on the trail. Yes, that self-consciousness makes you break stride, lose feeling of hill, lose present tense. Left with—just tense, no present. Marty chuckled into the night, forgetting how he was moving and so moving easy again.

Him all right, think Belle. Him get tired and sad but then come back again, put out laugh and feeling that everything all right.

Cool runnings now, think Horace. Long-part past, short-part come. Martinson give a lift, no more dragging, so him soon be home safe and sound.

And when Marty had forgotten why they were walking, or that they even had a destination that would end the footsteps, they tumbled into the main road of Rose Hill. Now he knew the way, and without hesitating he took the lead as Horace and Belle stepped aside. They crossed over the clearing and began the short descent down the backside trail to his homestead. No big thing—it him family trail, him should take lead. Yah mahn, no big thing, but in an unspoken instant it belied his insecure feelings on the trail. A light twinkled through the trees; Marty knew that Cora had left the blue porch bulb burning. As they came close to the house, Horace stopped, cocking his head. A bleating goat cry rose up nearby. He reached out and like a magician produced a rope from out of the darkness. It was tied to a tree. The other end tethered the goat.

"Remember him, mahn?" ask Horace.

"The goat from the first time?"

"Same fookin goat. Someone catch him at long last."

They arrived at the porch and now, after so much that had happened and so many changes in such a short time, Marty felt strange about their splitting up. The three of them stood in the blue electric light until Marty said, "If you would like, you can spend the night here. We got plenty of room."

Idea of sleepin in big Marse Martin house appeal to Horace—him never been in there before. Him look at Belle, ask with him eyes what she think. She shake her head no, then she turn to Marty. "Thanks mahn, but house full of sickness, family worries. Not right for us sleep dere right now. Another time, truly."

Marty nodded. "Cool, Belle, you're right."

"All right," say Horace. The understanding between them getting strong so them not need to say thanks or good-bye, just look and smile and be on their ways.

Marty watched them melt into the night, listened to the sound of their bare feet on earth, stood on the porch for what seemed like a long time, and then turned to go inside. As he did he recoiled quickly—something was swinging past his face near the door, small and black like a bat. There it came again, but this time he saw it clear: his camera, hung from its strap on a hook near the door. Miss Ella had sent someone up to return the camera he had forgotten completely about. He smiled, opened the door, reached for the kerosene lantern he knew would be on the table directly inside, lit the wick, and slowly walked upstairs.

"Marty?" His father's voice, once so deep and full, barely made itself heard down the hall even though the bedroom door was open.

"Yes." The lamp threw flickering shadows into the dark room.

"Marty?"

"Yes, Father, it's me." Marty set the lamp on the table near the bed and sat down. His father was covered only by a white sheet. He lay on his back, belly bloated, cheekbones protruding above the deep hollow where his face had once been full.

"Marty?"

He was asleep but it was fitful, and as he shifted, Marty could see a line appear on his forehead, a line that seemed to split his face in two and then slowly melt away. A line of pain.

"When lagwood blooms the honey becoome clear," he murmured. "Just before lagwood blooms the honey is darkest. Soome like the dark but most like the light. Do you understand?"

Marty leaned forward to see if his father truly was talking to him or not. No, he was sleeping.

"Baby goat must stay with their mother. When they're first born the vultures will try to grab them and eat them. Their mother will protect, but sometimes to shoot a vulture is not a bad thing. The others stay away for many days after one is shot. But don't shoot too many. No no, not too many. Mothers protect." A spasm of pain wracked the old man's face. His eyes opened, catching the light of the kerosene lamp. He turned and saw Marty sitting nearby. "Well well well"—and he tried to smile—"I understand you had a little meeting with a spear gun today."

Marty could see that his eyeglasses were reflecting the lantern glare into his father's face, so he set them down. "Yes." He smiled. "Now me and Horace are even. How'd you hear?"

It only took that moment for Martin Sanders to drift away again. He talked in a quiet monotone, each word clear yet attached to the next: "The minute something is built it begins to decay. Heat and water and the bush. Everything grows so fast it wants to cover any sign of anything human as soon as it can." He lay in bed, eyes open, staring at the cracked ceiling. Spasms would pass over his face, making him tense and relax as though he was moving in and out of focus. "It takes so much energy just to hold it

back, just to keep from getting overrun by vines and ter-
mites, that you need all your strength to stand up, let alone
make any headway. It seems easy here, but it was never
easy, always pushing against something, somewhere,
somehow." He fell into murmuring, head lolled to Marty's
side, and there was his son again. "I'm sorry, Marty. How
did I hear? The boy who brought your camera saw it happen. Did you see where he hung it by the door?"

"Yes."

"He seemed to think you were a hero. Dat true, mahn?"

"No mahn. It just happen, dat all. The only reason I
could do anything was because the guy—they call him
Rooster or Otto—the guy didn't think I'd interfere. Kind
of like I was invisible, the way tourists are invisible, you
know?"

"Never again," the old man sighed, "never again. I'm
the invisible one now. But I don't want to be that way. I
need something to hold on to, that's all, something to give
me a root. Can you keep a root and go that high, pulled
way up that way, pulled right off the earth? Something
stays behind buried in that hole, so why can't it be more
than food for worms? If I can just get to that one thing,
grab it with all my might, shake it up and down and yell in
its face and make it tell me about the secret wire that connects here and there so I can string up that wire while
there's still time—then wherever that place is will be all
right because it will be part of here even though it's not
here anymore. It's got nothing to do with a purpose or a
reason or any of that, it's just a connection, that's all, a
connection. A telephone number, the right address, an appointment, a schedule, a birthday to celebrate, a calendar
attached to electric poles, getting the post office put in,
clearing deadwood off the road, knowing the trail between
here and there . . . Do you understand any of this?"

"I think so; I'm not sure, but I think so."

"Do *you* see any way out? Do you see any way to stay in even though it's time to get out?"

How do you answer a question like that? "I don't know, Father, you're asking about something people have been wondering about forever. Isn't that what God's about?"

Martin Sanders sank down. "I can't believe in God. Sometimes I've tried, lately I've tried, but I just can't believe in God. It just doesn't ring true to me, even now when—well, when it would answer all these questions at least until I stop breathing. But it would be like fooling myself with a little child's trick to pass the time. I don't want any little trick to pass the time. You live all your life like you have forever to get done what you want to get done and then the end looms up like a roadblock and the last thing you want is some trick to pass the time. God? Jesus Christ died for my sins? Ridiculous."

"But you feel like something remains after—after your body stops?"

He shifted on his back, covered in a white sheet, like a bloated seal on ice. "Maybe it's a different name for God, but there does seem to be some kind of force—something behind everything—sometimes I feel like I get a glimpse of it when the bees buzz around their boxes or the sun hits the pasture in a certain way. But it's not God, it's not something you can appeal to or act a certain way so it will like you, it's just There, that's all, it's There, and if I could just know how to connect to it and see it clearly, then I think it would be There just as much for whatever is left of me. There could be Here, I wish There could be Here." He stopped, wincing. "The deathbed ramblings of an unhappy old man who tries to make his own end into something bigger than it is. It's just me dying, that's all. Old things have to die to make room for new." He didn't look at Marty, just at the ceiling with the crack that got a little longer year after year after year.

Marty searched for some way to distract him. "I walked through Shire Hall today and met Miss Pamela."

A smile passed over the old man's face and Marty was glad he'd thought of it. "Pamela is something, isn't she? She holds the place together with her spirit. How is she?"

"Well, she gave me some tea, for one thing."

The old man struggled to pull himself to a sitting position, but fell back. "You drank some of Pamela's tea?"

"Yah mahn, early dis mornin. To tell you the truth, I didn't know what I was drinking until after I drank it."

"She is something else, but she wouldn't try to trick you on purpose. I bet she just assumed you knew because everyone knows Pamela makes mushroom tea."

"Now I know too. She told me to tell you that if the pain got too bad, or for whatever reason, she would bring you a real strong cup of tea. That's what she said—I didn't know you drank that stuff."

The old smile returned. "Got to soometime, mahn, better den rum for getting a new idea of things." Yes, Pamela's tea—maybe I should drink a strong cup of it, maybe that would be a way to hold on to something, see something of Here and There at the same time. But to drink it and just lie here, not walk the hills, not watch the shadows, not visit neighbors, that would be torture. . . .

"Did Mother ever try that tea?"

The smile faded. "No, no. She had an American idea of drugs, you know, that it was very dangerous, not to mention illegal—no idea what might happen if you did something like that. I tried to explain that it wasn't like bush rum that could make you blind, it was a natural sort of thing, but she never was convinced. And with that feeling inside, I didn't think she should drink it either. Such a thing is not meant to be forced on someone else, because then fear and paranoia would be the feelings the tea feeds on. It got so I wouldn't drink Pamela's tea around the house because Louise didn't like it."

To talk to his father like this was so new, so strange. To hear another side of a past he thought he understood, but truly did not, made a feeling like panic rise up in Marty's throat. It was weird and sad and ironic that such talk could happen only now, as the debilitated old man lay there so close to death, no longer a threat, no longer immortal or invulnerable. The beginning and the end come together.

But Marty didn't want such feelings to paralyze them, he just wanted to talk if he could, to share the intensity of his day with the one person in this world who could understand the schizophrenia of it all, of America and Jamaica colliding. "The experience was, well, mooreden and lessden I thought it would be, all at the same time. After I drank it I expected some kind of scary thing to happen, some apocalyptic event. But then the rhythm of the day established itself and all I felt was real good—real aware of everything and just, well, high. I forgot it was even in me most of the time."

The old man forgot his fatigue, which was the best gift Marty could offer. "It's not always like that, you know. Pamela makes her tea fresh, she picks the mushrooms herself and they come from right around the district. The combination of all those things makes the tea right for us— at least, that's what some people say. They say that when she sends her tea to Negril it tastes different and does different things to people. I don't know how much of this to believe, how much is voodoo about mushrooms, but I think there's some kind of truth to it. I remember once, oh, must have been twelve or thirteen years ago, I drank some tea that a guy made on Orange Hill, that's near Negril, and it was nothing like Pamela's."

"What was it like?"

"It was dark, not the color of it, but the feeling. Kind of evil, I guess. It made me think that everything was sinister instead of when I drink Pamela's and everything seems right."

Marty couldn't believe that this man, talking this way, was his father. It was so contrary to the image he had built up over the years, an image that really had little to do with the man himself. Marty realized that more and more. "Let's see," he mused, speculating as he would with an equal, "that was twelve or thirteen years ago. Maybe it wasn't the tea so much as your own state of mind and the tea sort of magnified it. What was going on at that time?"

Martin turned and looked at his boy as his answer. Of course; son and wife had just left.

The kerosene lamp flickered, strange shadows jumped on the far wall. The old man's profile became larger and smaller, stronger and dimmer, as the light sputtered. "I wonder if this old place is going to become like Shire Hall when I'm gone, taken over by a bunch of strangers."

"It could be worse, Father. It does give a lot of people a decent place to live."

"No no no," and Martin struggled up again. "People should make their own place to live. You don't have as much respect for a place if you just squat there for a while, move in, and take over. Pamela is the exception, but the rest are like those birds that steal another bird's nest, what are they called?"

"I don't know," said Marty.

"Oh hell, once I knew their name like my own—it doesn't matter. Listen clear, Marty: This shouldn't be a communal house. So I've passed the word that Cora and

152

her family can stay here if she wants after I'm gone. Lord knows she deserves it."

"But what about me?" Marty blurted before giving it any thought.

Martin looked at his son. "What about you?"

"Well, I mean—shouldn't I be a part of deciding what's going to happen?"

Martin sank back into his pillow. He felt like he was playing a fish who needed all the patience in the world and a delicate touch to know when to let the line go and when to tug hard. But he didn't have the will and sensitivity left to know how to reel his boy in. "If you want to be a part of it, it's here for you. If you don't, it's gone with me." He resigned himself to that unvarnished fact of life and death, allowing only a small hope that maybe Marty would want to stay on.

Marty said nothing. He knew his uncertainty was depriving his father of the one thing he wanted most from his time left in this world, but he couldn't bring himself to lie and he surely couldn't say he was going to stay here and carry on in his father's footsteps. That would go against everything he had been taught and everything he had believed during all his years in the States. Father talked about There and Here and a connection and all kinds of things like that, but Marty knew damn well what the true connection could be, what would bring peace to the old man. The connection was blood, not anything outside. Marty knew that and he guessed his father knew that too, only the old man was afraid to say as much. And why should that be expected? Why should Marty give up his own goals? Marty had his own life—his purpose couldn't be perpetuating his father's existence from the grave and beyond. The question he had to answer was more selfish:

Where did he belong? Here or in the States? Father or mother? No no, not father or mother, what's right for *me.*

"Tell me about my ancestors, Father."

"Hmmm?" He had dozed away.

"Tell me about your parents. I don't know a thing about them."

"My parents?" He struggled back to the surface. "My parents—they're both buried at the very top of Rose Hill, beyond the end of the road. That's where they'll take me too."

"But what were they like? How did they live?"

"Oh, they were different than me, different than you, different from each other." Martin knew he was losing strength, so he fought back yet again, trying to conjure up something specific to say to his only son, his boy who had come back to watch him die. "My father, your grandfather, he was no slave but he was the son of slaves. He could work harder than any man on Rose Hill. They wanted to make him foreman of the sugarcane operation, but he wouldn't do it. He wanted to be his own man. He wore a red scarf around his neck—people said it attracted bees to him and that's how he first got started with bees. But that's not true—it was Mother who first got him going on bees. She was no slave's daughter, oh no, she was from the hills. Real wild. She taught him how to grow and plant and set up the bees. He showed her how much work one man could do. When the cow got sick she knew what to use to cure her, but when the fence busted open he could fix it with his bare hands. And between them were six children."

"Six children? You have brothers and sisters?"

"Two died young. One died in the war. One left Jamaica. One lives in the outskirts of Kingston. I was first son, the one they sent to school. They wanted me to become a teacher, let one of the others work the land, but I came back when . . ."

"When?"

". . . when my father was dying and no one else was left who could do it. On his deathbed he moaned about what a waste it was to make an educated man work here."

The wheel keeps turning, thought Marty, turning and returning. "But what about the house?"

"They took it over before I was born. There had been a fire, a death—this is the slave quarters of the original house, you know."

"Really? I didn't know that."

"Yes, my mother got a big kick out of that, she liked the idea of it. Dad didn't care so much—it was in such bad shape that he needed to rip it apart and rebuild most of it, so by then he considered it his own. It had been vacant for a long time and plenty of people thought there were bad spirits here. But he just laughed at them and cleaned it up. Even after the earthquake he laughed at the superstitions."

"Earthquake? I remember an earthquake."

"That one was only the latest in a series. The first one cracked the foundation and dried up the well. Dad just plastered over the foundation and dug the well deeper. That's what he was like. Everyone else was sure it was a sign to get out—even Mother began to wonder—but when he laughed the spirits ran away. That's what she said. So long as he could keep on laughing she could keep living here."

"What were their names?"

"Her birth name was Valerie, but her given name was Pulse. Papa heard a doctor call a heartbeat that one time, and he liked it, so he gave her that name. Your grandfather's name was Wilson, but his real name was Willin, because that's what he was."

"What's your real name, Papa?" Marty whispered.

He sighed. "Not many know it, not many use it, but I'll tell you: Keeper. Keeper me real name."

"I got a real name now too, yah know."

The old man smiled; he looked at his son with a smile that seemed to spread across the parched landscape of his face like a sunrise, the warmest smile Marty had ever seen him make. "So I've lived to see the day when Martinson got a real name. I'll be damned. Do you want to tell me what it is?"

"Yah mahn," and Marty leaned forward. "Mooreden. Dem call me Mooreden."

The bed began to shake, and Marty could see that his father was laughing but it hurt too much to laugh, so he was crying too, laughing and crying both so hard that his body was making the bed shake. It was scary. Marty put a hand on the old man's shoulder to settle him down. Finally Martin could talk again. "Mooreden," he wheezed. "Dat true right name. You are Mooreden." He lay watching the earthquake crack in the ceiling. "Mooreden, do dis for me: Turn off the lantern and listen to me now. I got some things that need to be said tonight. Will you do this?"

Marty turned off the light and pulled his chair closer as an answer. A glow from the full moon through the window was the only light.

"Hear me now, because there is still some time left for me but I doan know how much longer and how I will be for talking: Fence posts made of cedar, walk them and you will know the boundary of our homeland. Inside fence posts, for animal pen or any other reason, never made from cedar post. Cedar post fence never made from barb wire, just regular wire. Barb wire for inside fence, outside fence just meant to show the land, not keep anyone out or hurt dem if dem want jump it. Pay no attention to stone

156

walls, except where dem follow cedar fence. Stone walls made by slaves in olden days, got nothing to do with free Jamaica today.

"All right, cows can graze wherever them want, but goat need to be moved from time to time here and dere. Them rip up grass roots. Think about gettin some pigs, them smart and get big and sell for good price. Make pen where yah can throw things for them to eat and it not matter if place get all muddy. Doan be afraid to ask someone for help, mahn, but remember that help means something and yah should return help for help, not with money so much as time and thought. Dagi, him know everything about bees. Trust him, mahn. When he tells you something it right. Share with him. The house always always needing help here and there, but doan let it bother you too much. As Manley say, Don't bust your brain about it. If you let it bother you, you're always working on it instead of enjoying it. You'll know when something really needs work. Bush always coome, always coome, always got to push it back, but you can do it. State of mind, doan let it become obsession. Now, keep listen me clear: When lagwood blooms honey gets clear. Just before dat bloom the honey get dark dark, talk to Dagi. When baby goat born some vulture like to try to eat him. Momma protect, momma always protect, but if two baby and them spread apart in open field den vulture got a chance. That nature's way, but every once in while shoot vulture if them get too close and strong. Shoot one, them all fly away, many days. Suppose window break in house? Go MoBay, them cut you new one if you bring frame with you. If not, get big enough piece to cut yourself, but dat mean painful glass splinter in fingers. Speak to them, ask them, they will do it. Roof shingles easy, do it in two days if leakin start. Mahogany trees need protecting, dem rare and special. If yah need wood for any reason, say fence posts, or burning, or yah want build something for animal, den yah can follow trail from backside of house. . . ."

His talking continued in a low monotone long after his eyes had closed, on and on and on until Marty was dozing in his chair, hypnotized and asleep, the words still pouring over him and into him. In fleeting dreams he would picture the situation his father was speaking about and see himself doing as he was advised, wearing a tan cap and a tan shirt and tan pants with black boots and a black rifle under one arm. Then he would see himself in Cambridge, walking through Harvard Square wearing a down vest, kicking at an old gray patch of snow, with a Christmas package under one arm and Trudy walking beside. Then he saw Denise, the woman from the Neptune, serving him a cold Red Stripe while he hammered cedar posts into the warm red earth. When Marty started awake as false dawn lit up the windows, his father was finally quiet, so quiet that for an instant Marty thought it was over. But no, he was only sleeping peacefully, his face calm and his chest moving deeply up and down—as though he had been holding his breath underwater for a long time and now he had come to the surface and could finally let go.

CHAPTER
ELEVEN

MANLEY hear talk one time about strange doings in island them call Haitee. Easy to remember what it called because name same as plentee only hate instead of plent. That place sound wicked, mahn, like it got the true name. Government there real bad, so bad peoples just take into the sea and swim for their lives. Government got to be real bad for peoples to do that. And them got peoples in the hills who make little dolls look like someone them hate and stick pins in the dolls make that person hurt in the same place. Plentee hatee in Haitee. Jamaica hills breed Rastas, preach love even if them not always act love. Haitee hills breed people stick needles in dolls. Jamaica way better.

But Manley think on this Haitee business because him

159

feel like someone stick pins to put a curse on him. Nothing special wrong—stab in foot heal up fine—but him tired and dragged down all over, like a fish after fighting a line long time just run out of fight. This how it feel to get old? Cha, not old enough yet to limp around with pants falling down like useless drunk. Got things to do, got plentee to deal with and not letting no hatee stand in way. Him clack the fake teeth a few times in mouth as him walk the road. Manley always do that to get mind right and spirits up.

Sound of chatter tell him plenty women at water collect taking care of wash. Manley pull himself straight getting near there, not want to look bent. As him get close the chatter keep up—that mean them not talking about Wynne or sneaky gossip not meant for men ears. "Hoi, Manley mahn," call voice, sound like Miss Stacia. "Whagwan?"

"Kindah slow, kindah tired," him admit.

"Too much Miss Dorothy?" Chatter become giggle.

"No mahn." Him smile, teeth shining.

"Too much tomcatting in dah bush?"

"No mahn, why gwan bush when best is at home?"

"Dem say variety spice of life."

"Got variety under me own roof."

"Well well well, sound good." Them women joke with Manley because them know there nothing to it. If him tomcatting in bush while Dorothy sad at home, them not joke because friends of Dorothy be quiet about it and them that looking to have some fun with him not say nothing neither. But that Miss Stacia, she forward.

Belle momma there, Manley like her special because Horace like Belle special. "What think 'bout dis, Manley?" she ask. "We talking 'bout animal running free, eating other peoples garden. What to do 'bout it?"

"True problem," him say. If everyone could buy real

strong wire fence, protect them food, that be one thing. But not everyone have money for that, so them try keep them own animal clear of garden. Then one day go to pluck weeds, see peas all gone. Make you see red, grab machete go run around swing at things, but who know what animal eat it? Manley sit down on wall of water collect spot to think about it. Plenty men never sit on wall, that a woman place for woman work, but Manley think such ideas so much bullshit. Besides, him bones ache.

"Animal must be free soometime," him mutter. It old old problem, lead to some bad fights. If only mesh wire fencing not so much money—that the big reason why so few hens and roosters in district too. Come to think, post office bar owner Buster get big roll of mesh a while back from him brother who work on government roads. Him do anything with it? If not, maybe share it in return for something. Two big maybes, whether him do something with it already and whether him willing to trade it. But can ask, no problem in asking. Be down that way today, look for him.

Manley stand up. "Got idea," him say. "Me check it out and tell you later." That please them all, because when Manley set to work on a problem it usually solve somehow. Him move on, but try as him might to be straight and strong, still walking old.

"Stop by me place and get young again, Manley mahn," tease Stacia.

"Must elbow Preacher out dah way first," him call back, make them all laugh and crow at Stacia.

As Manley walk him think about the first time ever him on that road. Him not born there, no no. Born Westmoreland, but keep getting drawn to seaside when him come into manhood. Seeing Kozmo and Horace like they are about fishing make him feel it must be in the blood, because him not raise at seaside but him always want to be there once man juices start to flow. Travel on foot through bush, walk old sugarcane roads and new sugarcane roads, follow railroad tracks sometime, climb up through what now called Marse Martin property to reach ridge of Rose Hill. Then, looking out, no more green fields no more blue smoke no more stone walls no more dirt roads—just sea blue forever spread out below, so blue and free him wish for wings to fly into that blue. Right then him decide to have a house there one day, near top of district road. Land there ripe for plucking because it farthest from seaside. Manley not mind a few extra steps if that be the price for standing at him door with clear sight of that blue blue blue spread out far below, blue no man can cut or change to suit him purpose.

It start then—how old? Horace age, maybe younger. Even fewer people around then and more fish, plenty more fish. Cha, fish and lobster near jump into your boat. No good place to sell them, so eat what you catch and trade fish for garden greens. No money around, but no much needed except for metal and rope and cloth. And block for house. And fare for King Alphanso. And net. And long-line hooks. And . . .

When Dorothy first come into him heart it a real fine time. Him walking road free and easy, see her on porch of her grandmomma house where she raised, she look up at him from under long eyelash so shy, right off them like each other. Dorothy small and sweet and light, so he can pick her up easy, but when time come they love like crazy and work just as hard. She clear bush for house site as hard as any man, plenty days him at seaside she hacking away. Energy of them two together more than either one alone, more than just getting by, so house go up and some money around and that first year a time of stepping forward with big strides. Children soon come, first Koz, then Horace and Sheila and Clifton and Dawn and Jackie and Desiree and Sandy and Olive, year by year one after the other. As they come up them big help around, but early on them pickneys must get everything them can get, take as much as little bodies can take to be strong all the way through life. That what momma and poppa must do, not just momma alone, though at first it all on her. So would be nice if house could grow to cover bigger family, but that take time and money. First pickneys must grow. And meantime house get smaller as family get bigger.

Each year it seem like them just get by, how no one really know, but anyway them do it, until the weight get heaviest just when fish get lightest. Him and Dorothy sit up nights trying to think of how to make it all work out right. Him take gardening job down at tourist attraction Lyman Hall, where white witch live long ago. Not make much, but more steady. And then him hear about signs on walls in MoBay saying men needed for apple picking in Canada. Him go there, check it out, sure enough them need men. Got to go to Kingston, get work permit.

So Manley take half their savings money, get on Kingston train, get there, wait two days, Kingston men say come back next week. Go home, wait, go back again. This time them check him over, stick finger up him asshole, look at sugarcane teeth (before fake ones), most of all them want to know if him have family here in Jamiaca. With family, government figure him not just run away when him get to Canada or States, they figure him come back with wages. So they give him permit. Apple men pay for plane fare, say Manley can work off the price during picking season, and him gone three months, leave Dorothy alone with children, but Koz and Horace just getting big enough to be more help than trouble.

163

Manley learn plenty during that time, more and more things come to him as him see how things work. First thing him learn is that Jamaican men strong strong strong from walking and fishing and eating fresh food. At first them all paid same wage each hour them work, but Manley see himself filling double the baskets of other guys who make same as him. The few Jamaicans get together, talk to foreman about it. Him say, You wanna work by the bushel instead? Them say, Yah mahn. Him hide grin in his sleeve, say, Sure. From then on, apples get pick faster. One night Manley hear foreman, drunk, telling him buddies how stupid them darkies are, giving up a guaranteed hourly wage the government demanded to pick by the bushel. Manley sit thinking about that into the night. In the morning him just go right back out there and pick three times as much as ever, thinking about Dorothy the whole time. Next day three times again, next day three times again, next day three times again. At night him sleep so sound the bugs in the bed don't bother him. At end of picking season foreman show up with less money than Manley expect, point to piece of paper and start telling him about cost of plane and cost of food and cost of bed. Manley look at him once, look at him twice, take out piece of paper from him own pocket. Paper got one mark for each bushel him pick. Paper got how much foreman tell him in beginning it cost to sleep and eat. Paper got plane ticket price. Paper got one more thing—name of government agent for migratory labor (spelled right) and a telephone number. Foreman take one look at that paper, one look at Manley, and him pay full wage without another word. Manley bring home enough money to add onto house with new block plus start tobacco patch near trail to seaside plus bring Dorothy a bright red dress plus a rubber ball for each bwai and girl.

Manley bring home more than just those things too. Him bring home a vision of life in the world. The main thing him realize is that everyone, every single one, born from woman. Every single one have man seed in him to make that birth happen. Every single one want to suck on a nipple, cry when them can't. This what Manley keep in mind when dealing with government man, with white man, with rich woman, with foreman. It not sound like a big thing to say it, but in life it mean plenty to him. With some thought you can see clear what people want, why they do what they do. It never outside you to understand so long as you know what that scene involve. Could be wages for apple picking, could be love quarrel. Could be finger up the asshole, could be man falling down from too much rum. All the world over, people the same, and people have reasons for what they do. Know what you want, know what them want—that all you need to know.

So when Manley come home from three month in Canada with money in him pocket and vision in him brain, it natural that people begin to see him as a man worth respect. Him go overseas and make it back alive—that by itself more than some. Him not preach nothing but him content, that clear, and when people ask what him feeling him say something true, something real. Him make them feel all right because him say that Rose Hill is as good a place as any on earth to live, it not have cars and telephones but it have other things people with cars and telephones wish they had. And it not just words with him—Manley come back with money in him pocket, come back to family and Rose Hill. Could have stayed in Canada, maybe sent for family, but him come home.

From then on, Manley place in district one of clear respect, even though him not born there, just marry there. Certain peoples moving in certain circles turn to him just like certain people moving in certain circles turn to Preacher, or certain peoples turn to Rasta in bush, or certain peoples turn to Miss Pamela at Shire Hall. And them find Manley willing to share more than just to get something good right away for him family, him got a higher idea of how things should be, not just how they are now. It make for cool movement around him.

Not to say that sometimes things don't get bad. How about that time them catch a guy thieving goat up behind the pen? Manley and Kozmo catch him, hold machete to him throat, and tie him up to a tree. Leave him there while them go get police come into district take him away. That take a few days. Man tied to tree few days. Then trial come, no one tell Manley trial come, so him not there, judge say, No one here, so case dismissed. Fookin thief come right back say, Them tie me up two days and me innocent man, me not guilty. Judge say, All right, them owe you damages for that, fifty dollar. When Manley hear that, him say, Just try and make me pay. Thief say, All right, and police come back again, search for Manley, but Manley gone to sea. So police grab bwai of Manley friend, Victor him name, say, If yah want bwai back, tell Manley Wynne come police station and claim him. Manley got no choice, him or Victor. So him show up with life saving from jar under house, plus borrow money from plenty peoples on hill, get Victor out. That thief get that money, but him never able set foot on Rose Hill again long as Manley family or Victor family strong.

And now come this Rooster business. Break a deal one thing, even taking swing at Horace with conch hand one thing, but spear gun? Shoot me bwai with spear gun? A line must be drawn that cannot be crossed, and spear gun cross the line. Rooster know that. Him think Wynnes so weak them cannot take care? Him think we lay water pipe for fun? No, him think nothing when it happen, him brain turn to wood and him act with no thinking at all. Even so, no excuse. All fishmen there all agree how that line get drawn. Him break that line and then move to murder a Wynne. Must be answer to this, must be, otherwise everything break down between peoples. Maybe because him connect to white men with ganja plane Rooster think him above the word of the district. No one who move here above that word, not even Martin.

Manley heart beat very strong for Martin. More than from false teeth, or sharing fence, or anything a hand can touch. It not from so so much time together, but the deep-in feeling very close between them. Martin got a way to be outside himself and inside himself same time, see things from where other man sit as much as where him sit. Manley see this and learn from it. But it go even further than that. It a mystery, but them share a spirit, them tied together in some secret way like way way back them have the same blood. Now that Martin losing touch with this world, Manley not surprised that him feeling so weak too. It not something to say in words, but them two move together, flow together, balance each other—connect in a way just meant to be. And now look what happen. Martinson save Horace, right time right place, make up for that crazy shooting business in bush. Maybe the blood connection pass on? Look like it, if Martinson give it enough time to work. Real in feeling need time like good goat stew, blend everything together, melt all parts to full taste. No one big thing need happen, just settling in.

On down the road Manley walk, take him full time. It a good fishing day, really should be out, but got business to tend to in district. Another time could do both, take care of biz as well as fish, but not today. Too tired, too much ache. Kozmo and Horace take the dugout, Manley favorite boat. That one best because it made from one piece of wood, not plenty plank glued together, so it strong as tree itself. Needing new coat of paint, new seat, new paddle before too long, but them things all second to wood itself, and wood strong. No sponge feeling. Maybe them get enough fish to sell and eat both—good fish always help bad feeling inside. And then later, not at dark dark of night like them got something to hide but after come in from reef, Koz and Horace go dig up Rooster pipe, cut it, and seal it. Him want to do something about it, him can try.

Past Big Turn through shortcut field, near where those guys have fight over what-her-name and just about kill each other, under best banana tree for early fruit, check soursap for Dorothy—none yet—along yard of Rotgut, garden of Longjaw, waterbarrels of Roy and Leroy, through prickers Manley always hate, next to spot of Sil-lygirl who lift her skirt in church one time—Manley not see it because him not go to church, but him hear about it—see half-done house start to rot, see spot marked where someone bury something, step lively through Bingo goat pen him share with half brother of wife cousin, stop for drink and breathing where spring from Black River cut road under arm of red birch worn from pickneys swinging, houses start to get a little closer together and then reach the bar Buster built up beside the post office.

Unusual for bar to see Manley during daylight, most unusual, so men in there call out welcome, stop domino game for short time to see if something big gwan. But when Manley settle in and make clear him on regular business, everything pick up again. As usual, old man One-leg Elrond taking care of biz on domino table. Him sit in special spot: back against bamboo, stump on post, crutch hung on hook near at hand. Lose that leg in big war, plenty Jamaicans go overseas with Brits and fight hard. Elrond come back with stump to show for it. Not much to do but play dominoes and drink rum.

BANG say domino as Elrond slap it on table. Table take so much pounding it all smooth down. Second table Buster must make this year alone, but him never say not to slam dominoes. That like saying don't drink rum in a glass. Just the price of biz, that all.

Seemore look at One-leg Elrond, try see into him mind find out what kind domino him have left. BANG. Seemore slam down two-three. Elrond sneak look at him own domino like him don't know exactly what it say—soon as Manley see that him know Elrond got a winner, just fooling with Seemore. Sure enough, Elrond sudden lean on him stump, rise up into air off seat little bit, bring domino hand crashing down BANG on table with last domino three-one finish that game right off BANG BANG BANG empty hand. Seemore shake him head, give Elrond ten cents.

"Buster," call Elrond, "pour Mister Manley mahn shot ah rum for me. Me pay it."

"Thanks mahn," say Manley. Maybe rum be a pickup after morning droop. Watch Old Elrond, see if him up to same old tricks. Yah, mahn. When him turn over all the dominoes, him put low numbers close to him belly, then move the pile around but not really mix it up so much that low ones push away from belly side. That Elrond good at it, hard to see whagwan. Him do it many many years now, help him win and him good enough so without help him win most times anyway.

"All right, who next?" call old One-leg, and Stickler give it a try.

Buster pour a shot and Manley drink it down quick, like in old days when him and Benjy do plenty rum drinking together. Man oh man, them did like rum. Benjy send son of brother into hills with five dollars, tell him keep one but bring back four dollar worth of bush overproof. Then at night, whooee, fall down sometimes, laugh like crazy, seem like them have answer to every question in all the world. But by morning light it worse than bad, some days miss fishing and then rum show up again at night. Bad pattern, get worse when bush rum come with ganja soaking in it. That stuff, man oh man, best of both and worst of both highs. Manley stop drinking it so much, back off to keep everything around cool, and Benjy move from Shire Hall after him and Pamela fight one day—Pamela say him not taking care of him end in the hall, and she right too. Then Manley and Benjy not as in as before, not bad blood or special thing happen to draw them apart, just a drift like when anchor drag little bit in swells near reef.

BANG—six-four.

"Buster, got a question," say Manley, feeling rum fire in belly.

Buster lean forward. Talking to Manley good thing, better than usual kind of talk come through place middle of day.

"Animal track through gardens, eat up work food meant for peoples."

Buster nod. Him not have a garden, all him money and things come from liquor. But him know about it always being a problem that way.

"So me thinkin, what a solution? Here it is: good fence, real good wire fence. But no one can buy it, too much money. Den me brain remember dat yah got soome fence from your brother." Manley stop there, no need to say more.

BANG—three-two.

BANG—double two, Stickler cannot move.

BANG—two-one.

Buster wipe wood on bar, thinking. Him got wire fence, hide it in special place. No use for it yet, but him not want throw it away. Could say it gone, could say it for sale cheap, could give it to Manley, let Manley spread it around district. Plenty thing him can do. Meantime, no matter what . . .

BANG BANG BANG—One-leg Elrond show empty hand open for ten-cent piece.

. . . pour Manley another shot of rum, free, show no bad feeling for Manley to ask such a thing.

"Thanks." Not throw this one down, take it easy. Manley see Buster must still have wire, otherwise him would say it be gone and talk be over.

"All right, next?" yell Elrond.

"Your brain remember right, mahn," Buster say. "Me got dat fence, not use it yet. But me not sure if me want it for myself, for me own property. If so, den cannot give it or sell it nowhere."

Manley agree. "Do what ya must, Buster, feel no pressure. But think on dis: If yah give me dat fence, or sell it real low for everyone to share, dem word will spread like weed all across Rose Hill 'bout dat good deed of Buster. When peoples got moore food, dem know Buster help dem get it. When dem feelin good, them think go Buster place share dat good feelin wid soome rum. What me try to say is dis, get me clear: Ah good move like dis come back around, mean good ting for your biz later on."

Buster see what Manley saying and it make some sense. After all, him get it free from him brother, why not pass it on? In full truth, liquor biz not need any more good feeling—people come to him whether them feeling bad or good just the same. But Manley got a point, him trying to show a way that doing something good for plenty others

171

also good for Buster. Buster look at Manley, standing straight up at the bar, and Buster just have to smile. That Manley sneaky, but sneaky for good.

"Right now me think it can happen, Manley mahn, me give wire for district. But lemme think 'bout it one night, make sure everything cool. Me send word or tell me bwai just bring wire to your yard if all is well."

BANG—new sucker sit in for Elrond.

"Cool, Buster, cool. If yah change your mind, cool too." Now Manley finish off that second shot of rum, shake him shoulders like it a windy morning on the water.

BANG BANG BANG—another one fall to Elrond.

"Coome play, mahn," Elrond call to Manley.

"No no, yah just beat me if me sit dere." Manley laugh, make ready to leave. Stickler sit in again, try him luck. As Manley step past, the rum make him want to reach down the dominoes and mix up for real, not like Elrond mix them, give Stickler fair chance. But Elrond buy him a shot of rum, that nice move, and anyway Stickler can look after himself. So Manley gone, doing nothing.

Rum put a good feeling inside, make Manley forget about dragging around so much. Now one more thing must happen before him can go sit under tree in yard. Seem like every day got one or two thing must be done even if you don't want to do them. But if them not done today, it just mean that tomorrow got three or four thing must be done instead of one or two. So him cut off road past dead lime tree on weak-hand side and walk that trail down down down not all the way to seaside but pretty far. On the way Manley find nice strong stick to hold in him hand. Could have taken machete from the yard, but Manley feeling that if you got a blade in hand, then hand could use it too quick. Better not to have one, better to trust in eyes and hands and heart and brain and mouth. Even with

someone like Rooster, even at him own home away from
everyone, still better that way because in the end things
have a way of moving to the place you think they might at
the start. If you walk in with machete, then Rooster be
grabbing for him machete, everything just build up. Walk
in with stick just a way of protection if need be. No one
start a fight with a stick. In all this Manley stay calm,
thinking, but mixing up the rum with what him feeling
about Rooster spear gun at Horace—well, hard to stay
clear. What need say to him? Say stay clear, that main
thing. Say water deal over. Even as Manley thinking on it
him see the clearing ahead where Otto build him house,
see water pipe open filling big drums but drums already
fill, so water just flowing over soak up into ground. Cha!
Foolishness. Mosquitoes come, make them pay for it.

"Hoi." Movement in house.

"Who dere?" Woman voice, Nellie.

"Wynne."

"Who Wynne?" Rustle in bush behind house. Someone
leaving.

"Manley."

"Alone?"

"Yah mahn, not here to fight." Enough time pass now
so Rooster sneak away. Foolish man.

Nellie come to door, hold bwai Neal front of her like
shield. "Whagwan?"

"Otto?"

"Not here."

"Where?"

"Seaside."

Manley look at her, she look away. Him know she lying,
she know him know. She all right, but she stand close by
her man even when him not all right.

"Yah know why me here, true?" Him talk loud enough for someone in bush to hear.

She look at him again. "Why yah coome, yes. What your thinkin, no."

Manley lean against tree in yard, bones begin to ache again. "Nice bwai, dat Neal."

She nod, shift him on her hip.

"Right now him small, yah must protect him all de time. But let me tell yah soometing, Nellie. When him get big, God willin, you shall still have same feelin of protection. Him could be moore strong den you, could pick you up in him hand, but still yah shall fear for him."

Nellie eyes gettin wide. Manley see she fear that him make a threat against Neal. That not it, Manley think, but let her have that feeling anyway.

"So just tink on dis, Nellie: Soomeday a mahn sneak up on Neal, try and kill him dead wid ah spear gun, how you feel 'bout dat? Yah feel cool? Yah feel happy? Not care at all?" Manley hear movement in bush behind house. Good, him still hiding there. "No, mahn. Yah feel so strong 'bout it dat yah want to do soometing real rash, real bad."

Manley can see her face twitch, breathing heavy. If him not sure that Rooster hiding, not make Nellie hear this. But that Rooster choice. Him put him woman in front of house while him hide in back. Fookah, just like Horace say.

"Me not gwan do dat, even if it in me blood. Hear dat? If me do dat then bad ting keep coomin coomin coomin. Got to break bad circle." Then Manley do something him got a way of doing. Him take that stick in him two hands, nice thick piece of hardwood, him balance it just so, then him raise a knee and bring that stick smash down on him leg. It a thick stick, but Manley hit it just right, snap that stick clean in two. How him do it, not even he know him-

174

self. But when him real angry or high or need a big thing done, then him just do it.

Manley walk to water pipe where it flow over barrels and shut it off. Then him take both pieces of wood him just break, lay them in a cross over the ground where that pipe come from, ground Manley help dig to lay it. "Tell Otto that water pipe shut," him say very loud. "Tell Otto that if him connect pipe again, MoBay police be cooming to him door wid me leading dem. Tell Otto if him ever, ever, ever raise hand at Wynne family again, him better be ready kill us all and all me friend. Tell Otto it better if him spear gun stay broken, no new one coome. Tell Otto when him act now, him act for all him family too. And tell Otto him can learn soometing from him woman, who know how to show face to ah mahn."

Manley half expect Rooster to come running from bush, but no, him stay in hiding. Him a fool every way around, must be a fool to let things come this far. Manley burn him eyes into Nellie, let her know that him truly serious. Bwai Neal feel it, start crying—can't be helped. Then Manley turn, slow but steady, with him back to Rooster hiding spot like him not have a care in this world, and walk back along the trail. Feel Rooster staring at him back, know Rooster know that Manley full serious, and back prove Manley have no fear of treachery.

Truly, that the case, so much that Manley brain already move on to other things. Got idea for rest of day, now that must-do things over with. Get out carving tool Clinton share, get out piece of wood under house, sit against favorite red birch in front of yard, rest aching bones, and make a little carving. Not so alive like Clinton work, but all right. Make a sphinx, but what it look like? Must look like the elephant him see in picture book about Africa. Bet sphinx and elephant related way back, think Manley Wynne. Like me and Martin.

CHAPTER TWELVE

Dearest Marty,

I received your letter this morning. Let's see, it was written on Sunday, probably mailed the next day, and it arrived here in less than a week. Wonder of wonders, the Jamaican mail system actually worked. I hope this response is as prompt going the other way.

As for gossip and pleasantries: Everyone here is fine. I spoke to Trudy yesterday, she stopped by the office because she was wondering if I'd heard from you. She hasn't, so if you have been writing to her the letters haven't reached their destination. I told her that was probably the case, knowing the vagaries of the mail. She was saying that if only she could take the time off work and had the savings, she would love to fly down and meet you. A wonderful idea, but unfortunately impossible for her. She said everyone in the crowd is wondering when you'll be back, her most of all. But I'm sure none of that surprises you too much. Perhaps I sound too maternally eager to foster a good "match" for you, but she really is a very special person, and obviously she has a very special place in her heart for you. I told her I would send her love along with mine.

In the big scheme of things, the news around here is that the weather has finally turned for the better. That change of season is so remarkably refreshing, such a life-affirming boost—which of course they don't get in the tropics. We had the first of those really warm springtime sunshiny days, the kind that suddenly take about eight inches of snow off the ground and stir up their crocuses underneath. You remember the White Witch in those C. S. Lewis Narnia books which you read over and over when you were younger? It was like when her evil spell had been broken and springtime finally arrived after years of winter. A far cry from the White Witch of Lyman Hall— I'm sure they still fret over her black magic powers down there. That kind of childish silliness really holds the Jamaican culture down.

But there I go, sounding judgmental and negative again. I promised myself I wouldn't fall into that, because if your letter said anything to me it said that you're exploring new ways of thinking about your "roots," as Haley put it, and that this is an important process for you. Yes, absolutely. I don't want to deny you that, and I don't want to be put in the position in your mind of trying to deny you that. It's just that sometimes in life things happen beyond our control, much as we don't like that, and all we're left with is the effort of reacting instead of acting, salvaging instead of creating situations. That's where I was thirteen years ago, and that's why you're feeling a little torn between cultures.

I say all this because, frankly, I'm worried more about the tone of your correspondence than I am by the words themselves. It's almost as though you are accusing me of something evil, of denying you your birthright. That defensiveness scares me right to my core. Please believe me, Marty, nothing I have ever done has had any intent

177

of harming you in the slightest way. I would sooner give up anything of my own than see you hurt or stunted in your life. So why this implicit accusation? Am I being hypersensitive, reading too much into it? Somehow I don't think so, and if I'm not, then I don't think you're being fair.

What I sense partly from this tone and partly from the content of your letter, is that you are indeed falling under the spell of Jamaica which you scoffed about before. Believe me, I know how it can happen, because it happened to me! I've said this before and I'll say it again, from bitter experience: Jamaica is too limiting, culturally and intellectually, for someone with your wide curiosity. You can't have a fulfilling life, a sustained, productive, happy life, by living with a romantic, idyllic notion of rural Third World existence. That's simply not enough to hang your hat on even if it seems very attractive for a while. Day in and day out, week after week, month after month, it is not sustaining.

You wonder why you know so little about Jamaica and your family tree. Quite honestly, you never asked much about it. When you did I tried to answer as best I could, but you seemed much more concerned with the here and now, with life as you found it around you. I admit that, thinking back on those years, particularly the end, was not something I found pleasurable. But when you asked I did the best I could to answer. If you were to say to me that in some way you sensed I didn't want to talk about it and so you avoided the subject, I suppose I would have to say that was certainly possible. But again, keep in mind that I was doing nothing to harm or deprive you in any way. I'll admit to lacking certain things, but not to any sinister motives.

Your questions about background and family tree deserve answering. Of course, your father is better equipped to tell you about all that, although at this point I'm not sure how cogent he is, or verbal. I'll tell you what I know: I met his parents only very late in their lives, but they were good, hardworking people. They had the kind of classic goals for their children which many

178

uneducated poor people have—to send them to good
schools and help them get ahead in life. For the boys, at
any rate. The girls, again in rural and classic fashion,
were expected to work in the cooking shed, to garden,
and to bear good children.

It was hard for me to adopt that kind of persona,
obviously, but to give your father credit, he really didn't
expect me to. His parents, well, in part they saw me as a
foreigner, in part they saw me as a woman out of touch
with what they thought were the important things in a
woman's life, but in part I think they were proud that
their son had found such an unusual wife. It reaffirmed
their sense that he was a very special man. It was
almost, in their scheme, as if their son had married a
white woman, a rich white woman from England. I think
the marriage was symbolic of how far they had come
from slavery, a symbolism I understood, even
sympathized with, but resented as well.

Is that a heritage to be "proud of," as you put it in your
letter? I suppose so, although like the rest of Jamaica it
is easy to romanticize that heritage beyond reality. Your
father's parents, I repeat, were decent, hardworking
people, but certainly they were not literate, or worldly,
and contrary to what you might think, they were not
mysterious or righteous rural folk either. They were
what they were and that was that. They accepted me
formally as their son's wife, but never really accepted me
emotionally as a member of the family. And in all
honesty, I never really accepted them as my in-laws.
They were a part of my husband and his past which at
first I applauded, then I condescended to, and in the end I
came to despise as debilitating to me and my son. There
you have the harsh truth, much as I hate to say it to
you—or myself.

And so the time came when I simply had to leave.
There was no choice for me, because to stay would have
been a kind of prolonged suicide. If you see that, if you
accept that, then you have to see how I could no sooner
have left you behind than leave my heart behind. No
mother could. The memory of you there, alone, with your

father, would have gnawed at me forever. Indeed, it is probably true that your youth was the only thing which kept me in Jamaica for those last few years; I didn't want to separate you from your father at that age, and I hoped for a reconciliation that proved to be an impossibility.

Once we settled here, literally within days, I was convinced I had done the right thing. You took to America, you took to Cambridge, like a fish to water. Would the ordinary Jamaica bush child have been able to do that? Without sounding too superior, I honestly think not. You just had it in you. If I had the decision to make over again today, I still would do exactly the same thing.

Now that you're older, it's only natural that you are trying to round out your sense of self, to learn more about your background and your roots and all that. Of course, such feelings are dramatized, no matter how little you have in common, when your father is nearing the end of his time. I understand that and I sympathize with your position. Believe me, I have many feelings about this moment too. I may sound callous about it—maybe I'm afraid of letting too much out. After all, we were married, we lived together, we were intimate. He is the father of my son. The thought has crossed my mind that I'd like to see him one more time, to try to talk with him and find some resolution, some peace, maybe some mutual understanding before that chance is lost forever. But each day passes, there is so much to do here, and after all this time I suppose whatever understanding there is will have to be something both of us have in our own hearts.

Yet knowing that you're there gnaws at me still, not the way it would have had I left you behind, but still painfully. And it frightens me, too, because I see a progression in your feelings even in the short time between your two letters. Now for the first time I feel compelled to defend myself, to defend life in this country as opposed to rural Jamaica, to remind you that this is your home even if you were born there. You can remember your past, appreciate the mix of your parentage, without going overboard and discounting all the good things about this side of the equation. Perhaps I let the pendulum swing too far one way in my zeal to see you become a part of this country and its diverse culture; don't let the pendulum swing all the way back the other way and lose track of the knowledge and strength of character you have built up by pursuing your education and career. Life is not an all-or-nothing proposition, although sometimes life in Jamaica seems that way. Something about that life implies that it is the only way, the right way, and everything else carries less of the true essence even if it has more trappings of wealth or culture. That is the seduction of Rose Hill, that is the black magic, minus any White Witches, and that enticement is what I sense you're falling into. Don't let it happen, I warn you. You've been raised here and you've had a taste of something more. That taste doesn't get washed away by hiking around mahogany forests every day for the rest of your life. One morning you'll wake up wondering what the latest movie is, or who's playing the hottest music right now, or what's in fashion, or which presidential candidate has a leg up right now. And your ignorance about the world will become like an itch you can never scratch. It will drive you so crazy that you won't be able to appreciate anything else. You'll long for someone to share some simple cultural discussion, someone who will understand what you mean when you refer to a painter or a book. You'll yearn for a woman as a companion, as an equal, not someone to cook for you and hack the bush with a machete. Not only will you not have any of these things, but you won't even have the possibility of having any of them. It's like going back in time, gone from the twentieth century to the nineteenth century. Sounds romantic and fascinating and all that, but day after day? Never an end to it? Not in some game or movie but the real stuff of life? Are you truly ready to live in the nineteenth century? I swear to you, Marty, that is a form of torture worse than slowly dripping water on your skull. I wouldn't wish it on anyone, least of all my only son.

So please don't look at me as the heavy in this scenario, as the insensitive, culturally straitjacketed American parent. I tried to make it work, really I tried. I took the plunge into Jamaica, into your father, with an open heart and an open mind. It didn't work out, and that experience allows me to say certain things to you now. It also makes me very fearful of history repeating itself.

What makes it even more galling to me is that I see so much in your future on this side of the ocean, things you've been aiming toward and working toward for years. I'm not just talking about Trudy and your world of friends, I'm talking about your professional world as well. Charles, "the midget curator," as you used to call him, stopped by a few days ago wondering when you might be home. Apparently the library has just formally accepted a new bequest (I say "apparently" because it's so difficult to know what's going on with Charles) and he is under considerable pressure to get a mountain of material cataloged and shelved. Without you, of course, he hardly knows what to do. But the implication that he gave was that he desperately needed a pair of hands, not necessarily a professional pair even, just someone to help immediately. And as I understand the budget, if he hires someone he'll have to reduce his staff by one— which means you. Maybe I'm being overly dramatic, maybe I'm not, but I fear that if your absence is prolonged much longer, your job will be in jeopardy. Now I know that a concern like that shouldn't dictate your actions, particularly with your father in the shape he's in, but at the same time I feel as though I have to inform you of the facts of the matter. If it seems as though I'm trying to give you an inducement to come home, well, maybe I am. But I'm also telling you the truth.

Meanwhile, just to keep you abreast, my own professional intrigues have deepened considerably in a short time. The professorship I thought might become available has in fact come open. The infighting immediately became fierce—fierce in the way only academicians can be even as they moan about the nation's two-faced, manipulative, and petty politicians. I've been trying to stay above it all and let my character speak for me, but the truth is that I'd very much like to get the chair. Who knows, in this game of musical chairs, when the next one will come open? Who knows when being a black woman will once again become a liability rather than an asset? These professors are notoriously long-lived, what with the easy life-style, and they don't give up their sinecures until they're dragged into the grave head first. So it may be now or never.

At any event, several friends have gone to bat on my behalf, a few with enough weight to make some difference. To them I'll be forever grateful regardless of how things turn out, and the latest news is encouraging: A committee has narrowed the search from a wide field down to four. Your mother, believe it or not, is one of them. So keep your fingers crossed for me.

But more important, please listen to what I'm trying to tell you, without animosity or hostility, without feeling threatened, without adopting your father's stubborn posture. I mean it from the bottom of my heart, with no malice toward anyone and with loads of love for you. When I see the inadvertent ways your speech is changing, when I see some careless grammar or the affectations of Jamaican rude talk, it says more to me than the words on the surface. Be careful, Marty, please be careful with your life and your decisions. Don't get sucked into something you'll deeply regret. You have too much going for you to allow that to happen.

Much love,
Mother

CHAPTER THIRTEEN

BY sun and water and wind it a fine day, but this morning no one stir from Wynne house. Pickneys hide in corners. Horace stay as close to Dorothy as Dorothy stay to Manley, and Manley stay in him bed. Never in year after year after year of them together has she seen this, but Manley so sick him cannot get up.

It just keep coming on and on, slow achy feeling drag him down down down. Then him muscle get tight for no reason, like him all the time trying to drag in big marlin. Body get hot and water pour from him skin. Sometimes body seem to shake like snake wriggling. Then him get quiet again, can talk for a while. But even face get all tight tight, fake teeth clamp together from so tight. Breathing seem a struggle.

Dorothy done all she know how to do, keep face cool make warm tea from different root each one good for different sickness rub body with bay rum and lime keep down fever force goat stew inside keep Manley strength up. But nothing working. Him just get worse and worse and worse. Dorothy search over every little spot on him body see if she can find tick or leech or any sign of sickness like boil or sores. Nothing, mahn, nothing. She sit up all night with him, watch him eyes get dull, see him chest heave, and she pray to anyone she can think of, to Jesus and Jah and spirit of grandmomma and all things anyone ever believe have strength, wood spirit and bee spirit and Jehovah—anything, devil too. No good. All through life them laugh at black magic Obeah talk, but when him face go so tight and twitch run through him body she begin to think maybe someone throw curse on him. She find nutmeg, and sassafras, send for Pamela for tea. Nothing change. Finally, fear in her heart making everything black, she talk with Horace about sending for Dagi with car carry Manley to MoBay hospital.

Manley hear her, groan, and shake him head no no no. Him mouth can hardly move but still him try to talk. She lean close. "No one ever come home from hospital, ever," Manley whisper. "Me not gwan dere."

She know it true, but still, what else to do? Him so sick him like to die, strain every time him try to breathe, weaker man might already give it up. Dorothy just wish she could climb right inside Manley body, climb right in and search out what wrong and take machete to wrong thing and slice it out and throw it away. Or if it too strong, then take that thing, swallow it, and jump out him body, let it eat at her instead of eat at him. And all time him body get more and more stiff like dead stiff, him teeth get lock together more and more like skull teeth. She so scared it all

185

she can do keep little ones from screaming with fright all the time. Thank God Horace there.

Horace search him brain, try to figure what going on, but sickness not something him know much about. When this come? Him remember when Poppa not go seaside two Sundays ago, day police show and Rooster thief and Marty save him. Start then? But nothing wrong with Poppa then, him just feel tired. Bad food? Poison? Some way, some secret way that Rooster gettin revenge for what happen when Horace and brother Koz go to Fookah water line and shut it down? Rooster not strong enough to use black magic, anyway black magic most strong when both sides believe in it. Poppa just laugh it away. It hard to believe that anything, anything in this world, strong enough to take Manley Wynne life away from him. But Poppa right about hospital. No one ever come back from there alive. Some peoples gone there even when them not so so sick, and them never seen again. But can't sit here just keep eye on pickneys. Must do something, help somehow. But what? What? What?

Deep inside Manley Wynne, struggling to get out, be the one thing him can think of to get help. Thought come to him brain now and then, and when him think on it, him try to say it, but mouth just stop working. Or when mouth feel like it can work, then him brain forget that one idea. Manley feel the sickness like it all over him, not one spot or one big thing, it just all over up and down him backbone from head to foot moving up and down him bone, more bone and muscle than blood but not something him can search out. It everywhere and nowhere inside him, overtaking his own self with outside strength like healthy tree get taken over by crawling vine that strangle it dead after a while. Breath get harder and harder to draw, Manley feel like that tree with vine around chest and throat.

Most strange feeling of all, sometimes Manley feel like him step outside, like a hummingbird hover over him own self. Then him look down on heaving chest of Manley Wynne on bed, see Dorothy lovely woman so so worried for him, see Horace hold her up while pickneys so so so scared. Manley get ashamed that him making everyone so worry and him fight to get clear of this sickness so them can all be free from care. Then him lose that feeling of above and get back inside again, fighting fighting fighting to breathe.

In the clear moments him know the one thing that might help, the one person to search out for help. Manley know it because him know what kind of sickness him have—a sickness that spread all over, a small secret thing that get inside him and move everywhere, sneaking up on him like a thief at night. Pamela tea not good for this kind of thing, Pamela tea good for big thing, not sneaky thing. Dorothy teas usually good for this kind of thing, but sickness too too strong, Dorothy tea just lick edge of it. When something so strong and so tiny, it got the two things together that can take a life away.

So Manley hold the idea in him brain long as him can, waiting waiting waiting for moment when him can force words through false teeth. But way of sickness make him face relax only when him brain off in a dream or outside looking down. Manley begin thinking him message over and over again like it the only thing that matter, the only thing him mouth could ever say if it ever get a chance to say anything. And finally, when him doze away, him teeth open up just a little and lines on his neck stop standing out so far and some words murmur out of his mouth over and over again . . .

"Ask Martin, go ask Martin. Seek out Martin, ask Martin. . . ."

Horace and Dorothy both lean close, hear the words, look to each other.

"Think him just crazy?" wonder Horace.

Dorothy search her heart. She wonder if Martin lying on deathbed, Manley lying on deathbed, somehow them connect on the other side, that black magic somehow making Manley seek out Martin beyond life. No, she can't believe that. Martin would not want that and Manley would not want that. "No, mahn," she say urgent. "Do it. Seek him out and hear what him say."

Before she done speaking, Horace already gone. At least now him can do something, anything better than sit there watch Poppa suffer. With as much speed as legs can take him, use every trick and shortcut, Horace run for Marse Martin house. Martin sick as Poppa, sure to be there.

From his father's bedroom Marty could hear the insistent rap on the door. He knew Cora would answer, so he stayed seated in the chair that had become his fixture since that Sunday night when so much came pouring out. Marty especially liked to be there in the morning because then his father was most coherent, although each day he seemed to slip into a deeper haze more and more of the time. His mumbling continued, some of it in the form of instructions, some of it memories of people or places, and some of it incoherent babble. Marty could see his father's face struggle with the pain and the blur of death, and he knew how important it was for the old man to remember specifics because of his feeling that this somehow was the key to keeping something of himself on Rose Hill. There was a repetition to his consciousness, a detail repeated over and over followed by orders about how to handle a similar situation followed by a rambling series of associations that dissolved into mumbled fragments and finally an uneasy doze. After an hour the cycle would start all over again, another spiral spinning away from one lucid moment, reaching farther and farther into space each time. There was still enough gravity in his father's body to bring those spirals back to the center again, but Marty could see how feeble he was and how wide the orbits had become. There was nothing to do but wait, and try to be there during the brief moments when it mattered.

When Marty heard Horace's voice downstairs, and Cora's hesitation about whether it was right for Horace to come into the house, he called down, very glad for the company. "Coome, mahn, follow me voice." An empty chair waited, and Marty turned his attention back to his father, knowing that Horace would prefer to move into conversation slowly.

They sat in silence a short time before Marty looked to his friend and saw tears streaming down his face.

"Laugher, mahn," said Marty, "me father old mahn. It sad but it all right. It all right, mahn." He reached his arm around Horace's shoulder. To see that face, so used to laughing, torn apart by sharing his grief, was hard for Marty to bear.

Horace shake him shoulder, not to take Mooreden arm off but to pull his speech together. "Mooreden, dis bad bad time to ask, but me need your help." Him start shaking again.

"Whagwan, mahn? Tell me."

Horace look to Martin, cheek sunk to teeth, head gray as old rock, eyes shut mouth open, little little breath come in and out, and him almost give up and go home. But him come this far, so him say it:

"It Poppa. Poppa real sick, sick as your poppa."

"Manley's dying? What happened?"

"Me not know. Him get weak, weak, every day pass

189

him weak more. Then him just get stiff, not move him face or neck at all. Breathin real real hard, like him suffocate."

"Have you taken him to a doctor?"

"Him not gwan hospital. Him say no one go dere ever coome home again. But last thing him say, him say coome here seek out Martin, ask him whagwan. Dat last thing him say, so me coome." Horace fall silent; him done what him can do, whatever good may come have to come outside him now.

Marty pulled himself right up against his father's ear. "Father, can you understand me?" Marty couldn't be sure—there might have been a slight nod. "Father, Manley Wynne, Manley Wynne is very sick. It seems like he can't breathe, and he's stiff. Horace is here looking for help. Can you help? Do you know what's wrong?"

Martin Sanders seemed to stir ever so slightly, then slip back into his dreams.

"Father," said Marty louder, sitting on the bed and giving the old man a shake of both shoulders. "Father, Manley Wynne is sick. He's stiff and can't seem to breathe. Can you help? Do you know what it is?"

Martin Sanders was aware that his son, his one and only son, his lifeblood and his connection to his world, was asking something of him. It was important that he know what his son wanted and that he help his son. That was the only important thing left to do. That was the connection. This is the moment. All the struggle up to now, all the years alone and all the pain, comes down to his son's face in his ear trying to get some kind of help. What does he want? He wants something very specific, he wants some information about a person, he wants to know something that I know and he wants it now, before it's too late. What is it? Manley, Manley, Manley Wynne. It has to do with Manley Wynne, my friend. My son wants to know something about my friend Manley Wynne. Ahh, Manley, walking the hill with a string of red snapper on a long line, strong step but always so clear, so smart, so aware. . . . No, my son wants to know something, my son wants to know something about Manley Wynne. What does he want to know? He wants to know why something is wrong with Manley Wynne. He is mistaken, there's nothing wrong with Manley Wynne, Manley Wynne is one of the most right people on the face of this earth. But my son, my son can't be wrong, not now, there is no such thing as wrong now, once there was but here there is no wrong, my son wants to know what's wrong with Manley Wynne, but there is no such thing as wrong. My son can't be wrong, what does that mean? That means there's something wrong with Manley. He can't breathe, Manley can't breathe is what my son says, my son came home before it was too late and now he's here with me when all I need to do is remember something clear, a moment a situation something of Rose Hill to keep me here, hold me here with my son, my son wants to know something from me that has to do with Manley Wynne, something is wrong with Manley Wynne, Manley Wynne can't seem to breathe and he's stiff and that's what's wrong with Manley Wynne, but how can that be? Nothing is wrong with Manley, but my son says something is wrong, so it must be so. Manley my friend, who sees me limping toward Dagi's house and so he limps himself to let me know of his sympathy, and then I tell him he doesn't have to limp just because I limp he says, No mahn, me stab me foot. That is the kind of wrong with Manley Wynne, a caring wrong and a sweet wrong. But no, something my son wants from me. This is the moment. Hold on to something concrete. Hold on to my son and what he wants from me. He wants me to tell him what's wrong with my friend Manley Wynne. He says

Manley can't seem to breathe, he says Manley is stiff. Horace is telling him these things. What could be the matter? He's stiff and he can't breathe. Him stab him foot, we walked up the little path to Dagi's porch limping together, the grapefruit tree laden down and Dagi's chairs set out in a row to welcome us, me with a cane but Manley limping beside me just like me because him stab him foot. Now him stiff and can't seem to breathe. My son wants to know what's wrong with him and I have to tell him before it's too late, this is the moment, this is the connection, this is what the struggle has been all about, I have to tell him what it is, I have to say the word "tetanus," Martin mumbled to his son. "Tetanus. Tell Doc Stephenson. Tetanus."

"Of course!" Marty shouted. "Tetanus. We have to get a shot for him to stop the tetanus. Lockjaw. Him step on a nail, true?"

"Yah mahn," Horace cry, jumping up and down.

"All right, I'll go to MoBay for Doc Stephenson. He knows my father and he'll remember me. Horace mahn, stay here—no, go run tell Dorothy we know what it is and me go get medicine cure it. Everything gonna be all right."

Marty held his father's face in both of his hands, leaned over, and kissed him on his gray lips. "I'll be back, don't worry," he said, and he sprinted past Horace and out the door.

Horace look back one more time before him run home, see Martin's head sag to heart side and a slow smile grow and grow and stretch across him face like crack across a stone. Horace say thanks to that gray stone with all him heart, and then him race for momma and poppa.

CHAPTER
FOURTEEN

MARTY took the trail straight to seaside rather than through Shire Hall. It was steeper and faster but with more danger of slipping; he tried to tell himself that if he fell and twisted an ankle then everything would be lost, but his heart wouldn't stop racing and he couldn't keep his feet from scrambling on. He became like a boulder shaken loose above, a personal avalanche careening down the trail pulled by gravity and haste and fear. Birds flew away as he came and small animals froze in the bush beneath the ancient stone walls. The loud rush of his emergency, the driven purpose of a human who would crush anything if it was in the way, frightened them into silence and flight. Marty tumbled down the mountainside within a moving pocket of stillness that his single-minded haste created, and none of that mattered because all of himself was directed toward Montego Bay, toward the office of this Dr. Stephenson. He had the vaguest memory of a small white house in town but no idea where it might be. The question was not whether he could find it; the question was how fast he could find it.

The trail emptied onto the road between the Neptune and seaside beach, where Marty had the idea that he'd either catch the King Alphanso or try to flag down a ride headed into town. But he couldn't bear to stand still, so he kept walking, sticking his thumb out whenever a car roared by. Before long he realized he had reached Clinton's shop, and sure enough Clinton was there, thunking on some wood. "Hoi," Clinton call. "Whagwan?"

"Gotta get MoBay," called Marty, still walking.

"Cannot walk all de way, mahn."

Marty stopped as another car came by and stuck out his thumb. Nothing.

Clinton watching him. "Yah tryin catch ah ride?"

"Yah mahn, yah mahn," said Marty, impatient.

"Don't stick out your thumb, den, mahn, that make'em think you're mad. Go like dis," and Clinton shake hand fingers pointing down to ground. "Dat mean yah want ride."

"Thanks, Dreamer mahn."

"No problem, Mooreden."

Sure enough, a fast-running van screeched to a halt when the driver saw Marty shaking his hand. Dust flew up as the side door opened and Marty piled into what seemed like a minibus, some kind of public transportation. There were three rows of seats, every inch of them taken up by someone or something, jam-packed so that Marty crouched near the door. Two speakers had been mounted behind the driver's seat and reggae music blasted out.

194

"Who know where Doc Stephenson?" shouted Marty above the music. No one paid him any mind.

"Driver mahn, got question," he shouted again.

Driver wave at him, keep eyes on road. "Soon as song over," him call back. "Me favorite."

A searing guitar line cut through the van and Marty was forced to wait, watching Lyman Hall Holiday Inn fly by and some stray goats jump aside and the first of the MoBay tourists walk along the highway. With speed of the essence Marty had no complaint because this driver roared through the straightaways and veered through the curves as fast as he could push the van. Even some of the passengers used to breakneck speeds among the minibus drivers shouted a few words of warning, but the driver ignored them as he rocked to the guitar solo and stamped his foot on the pedal. When the song slowly faded he let up a bit.

"Love it, mahn, love dat tune," driver yell. "Got tah move wid dat tune."

"Doc Stephenson," Marty shouted. "Who know where him?"

"Got sickness?" ask woman sitting near Marty. She look fearful, like she might catch it.

"No, not me. Who know Doc Stephenson?"

Older man in back call up. "Me know it. Elizabeth Street, straight up from square. Before Chin."

"Before Chin Market?"

"Yah mahn."

"Thanks. Driver, yah drop me dere?"

"Close, but not right dere."

"All right."

It was market day in Montego Bay, so the streets were jammed with even more people than usual moving fruit and vegetables, carvings and coral, T-shirts and cigarettes. Women with straw baskets on their heads full of mango

195

and star apple, tomato and soursop, swayed along. While most of the Jamaicans moved steadily, headed for some specific spot, the tourists seemed to stop and start, disrupting the flow and making it hard for the fruit women to balance through the throng. Stalled in traffic, with the minibus driver leaning on his horn, Marty could see an argument in progress in one corner: A woman's basket full of fresh things had been knocked to the ground, meaning several days of collecting and traveling to make a few dollars in town had been lost in one clumsy instant. The man who obviously had bumped into her so hard that she couldn't keep upright was standing along beside, caught within a ring of Jamaicans who were angrily demanding that he pay for the loss. Although he was protesting, he was also reaching into his pocket.

"Driver, get dere faster on foot?" called Marty.

"Look like it," driver agreed. "Just straight to bank, heart side, dat Elizabeth Street, go up."

"Thanks." Marty jumped out the side door and began racing through the crowd when he heard the driver's voice crying, "Stop, stop dat thief. Two dollar, mahn, two dollar, thief." Policeman hear the cry, bring stick in him hand like to chase Marty down, but Marty realized his mistake and ran back, paid up with an extra dollar as apology, and rushed away.

From many years of practice, Marty could move through a city crowd with the kind of instinct that Horace could use on the trail. Like a broken-field runner, dodging knots of congestion at corners and slipping off sidewalks to follow streams of dirty water running through the gutters, he made up for the time he had lost with his clumsiness on the way down the mountain. Elizabeth Street was just where he understood it to be, and as he turned up into the heart of Montego Bay everything seemed to pulse and throb before him—the beat of the city on a busy morning. He felt it and the rhythm suited him, but theirs was the tempo of a working day, not a crisis. He double-timed, stepping through at a half-run he could maintain despite tangles. People watched him blow by and expected to see a policeman hot on his heels, or an angry storekeeper, or a distraught girlfriend; when none came they figured he had escaped for good.

Marty didn't know exactly what he was looking for, but when he came upon Chin's big supermarket near the top of the street he realized with a curse he had gone too far. Backtracking, jogging more slowly, he found a wrought-iron fence along the sidewalk in front of a large hedge. On the gate a plaque read: "Dr. J. Stephenson, General Medicine. By appointment only." The gate opened onto a stone walkway through a small yard that was full of clustered bushes, small coconut trees, even a banana plant. Cool leaves filtered sunlight as well as exhaust from the street. The effect of such a sanctuary in the middle of the city was calming even for Marty. He slowed to a walk, reached the wooden entry of a whitewashed house, and rang the first doorbell he had seen in a long time.

Nothing happened.

He rang again. It had never even entered his mind that there might be no one home, and his heart started pounding. But all right, there was a sound inside, someone was coming.

Slowly the door withdrew and standing before Marty was a short elderly man, white shirt open at the collar and neatly pressed slacks above bedroom slippers. Half glasses hung off his nose, his skin was light by Jamaican standards, and his features were European. Yet his gray hair was kinky and despite a paunch of age he had a distinctly

Jamaican way of standing, as if he was used to physical activity. He looked at Marty from over his glasses quietly, steadily, and Marty felt obliged to wait despite his haste.

"I delivered you into this world," said Doc Stephenson, "so I guess you can come into my house." The door closed behind them and suddenly Marty had the strange feeling that he was back in Cambridge—rugs and electricity and modern paintings and above all a sense of order and academia seeping out of a floor-to-ceiling collection of books on the far wall.

The doctor padded into his office and sat down behind a large desk. "What does your father need?" he asked.

"It's not my father," said Marty. "There's another man in the village who seems to have contracted tetanus. At least, that's what Father thinks. I came here looking for help."

"Tetanus is very serious. Left untreated, a high percentage of cases result in death. Tell me the symptoms."

"The man had a foot wound several weeks ago. Now he's having trouble breathing, his muscles are stiff, and he can't open his mouth easily."

"Well, that is the classic situation," Doc Stephenson mused. "Except that the incubation period seems a little long. Is he otherwise a very healthy person, strong, and so forth?"

"Very."

"That would explain it, then." He leaned back, watching Marty closely. The blend of father and mother remarkable, the mission extraordinary. The doctor's medical knowledge and personal instincts said that this young man held the fate of two other men in his hands: one physical, the other spiritual. That did not need to be said.

"Tetanus is a bacteria, Martin, which produces a toxin which attacks the spinal cord. Many people think it comes from a rusty nail, but that is not true. It's like saying that sickness comes from bad water. It's the germs thriving on the nail or in the water, not the medium itself. The danger is that rigid muscles constrict breathing to the point where the patient actually suffocates to death."

"How is it treated?"

"Antibiotics, an antitoxin, muscle-relaxant drugs, and an artificial respirator are the usual remedies. If the patient can be reached while he's still breathing, chances of recovery are excellent because the drugs tend to work quickly. . . . And now that you understand, tell me: How is your father?"

Marty groped for words as precise as what he'd just heard. "He's, well, he's dying. Every day he has fewer hours when he's lucid."

"Does he seem to be in pain?"

"Yes, sometimes, but he doesn't want to take drugs, even now."

Dr. Stephenson nodded. "He's a very strong man. I'm sure he feels that taking pain-killers would have been like leaving the country for therapy—leaving the country in his mind. He simply refused to do that." As he spoke he took an orange off his desk and broke the seal of a syringe from the top drawer. "Here; you're going to learn to give an injection."

"Me? Why me?"

"Because speed is of the essence, because you can get there much faster than I could, and because I have other patients who must be attended to today. Is there rubbing alcohol there? Probably not. Take some of that too. Practice on this orange: One sure, clean, forceful move is what's needed, then a slow, steady push. Allow no air to get into the injection. Flinching and twisting are the dangers to avoid. Straight and sure. If you can do it with this orange you can do it with a human buttock; the resistance is very similar. Good. Do it again. Good. Take it out just like you put it in, have someone hold a piece of cotton over the area until there is clotting. Good. I'm going to give you four syringes in case there are problems. Once you break the sterile packaging, work as quickly as possible without getting flustered. Here are two vials: One is TAT, tetanus antitoxin. From what you've said, your man will also need a muscle relaxant. Here it is. This dose should be enough to ease him considerably. Now, once his mouth has relaxed, you can introduce pills. Again, there are two vials. The capsules are antibiotics; the others are muscle relaxants. Make sure he takes all the antibiotics—have him take as few of the muscle relaxants as possible and destroy the rest."

"It's amazing to me that you have all this here at hand."

Doc Stephenson laid down his half glasses. "You shouldn't be so amazed. Tetanus comes from the intestines of grass-eating animals, especially horses. It's often found in cultivated soil. Put that together with a barefoot rural population, and you get high incidence. These drugs are needed often." He folded them all into a small pouch with pockets to keep the vials and syringes apart from one another. Cotton acted as more padding, and rubbing alcohol went in last. A folded flap with leather string tied the package securely.

"Before you go, is there anything I can do for your father?"

Marty felt himself tremble. "No, no, Doctor, I think that doing this, saving Manley, is what he would want."

"I'm sure that's true," said Doc Stephenson, "but even more important, I think your doing it is what would matter to him. Your return probably prolonged his life more than any therapy or drugs I could have arranged. That's why I insisted he write to you."

"You insisted?"

"Yes, strictly on medical terms. I suppose that gave him the excuse to do what he had wanted to do for many years."

They looked at each other evenly. "Did you know my mother?" Marty finally asked.

"Yes. Very well."

"What did you think of her?"

Doc Stephenson ran his stubby fingers through his hair. "I admired her very much. I think she tried very hard to create a successful life here, but in the end she developed a kind of disease. Strangely enough, the symptoms were a lot like tetanus, believe it or not, but emotional. She was suffocating with a form of lockjaw and the antibiotics she needed didn't exist in Jamaica."

"Did you socialize with both of them? How were they together?"

The doctor stood up. "Martinson, the answer is yes, to the first question. The second involves a much more complicated answer—which you do not have time to hear while a life hangs in the balance. There will be another time for that—if you want. Right now you need to get back to Rose Hill, and quickly."

"Yes, of course, thank you," and Marty stood abruptly, embarrassed at his selfishness. "How much do I owe you?"

"Another time we'll talk about that too. God speed."

A look, nothing more, and he was gone. The pouch was just about the size of a football, so Marty held it beside his hip as he resumed his broken-field run through town. "Hoi, runner return! Olympics MoBay dis year!" shouted a drunk from one of the open-air bars.

"Where taxis wait?" Marty shouted back, barely breaking stride.

"Off square beside tourist center," call a young woman.

Sure enough, a line of cabs stood at the curb, drivers hanging around talking and smoking. In the middle of the row was a beat-up familiar-looking Chevy.

"Wallace!" Marty cried as he ran up from the corner.

Wallace, in the middle of an argument about whether schools should be free to all children, looked up just in time to see Marty diving into his taxi.

"Hurry, mahn, hurry, me need ah ride," Marty urged from the backseat.

Wallace left off in mid-sentence and ran around to start the Chevy, but as he did two other cabbies planted themselves in front of the car.

"Cannot take him, mahn, not first in line," one shouted, folding his arms across his chest and standing in the street.

Marty looked up at him. "Me got no time to talk now," him say very quiet but straight into the man's eye. "Me know Wallace, and me need someone me know right now. Clear out, mahn."

The driver did not move, but Wallace turned the key and the Chevy growled to life.

"Don't make me get out of this car," said Marty with the edge in his voice that only comes when someone is willing to do anything necessary to get what he wants.

The cabby looked down, saw Marty fingering a pouch which looked suspiciously like it might hold a gun, heard his tone of voice, and backed away. Money and principle not worth it, mahn. Wallace wheeled away as the cabbie turned to his friend, saying, "Me not know Wallace drug-dealin driver. You know dat?"

The old Chevy was already halfway through town, Wallace leaning on the horn at every corner. "Well well well," him say, checking out Marty in rearview mirror. "Same mahn me pick up at airport, but not same mahn neither. Whagwan, dere—what your name?"

"Martinson."

"Yah mahn, Marty. How papa?"

"Him dying, can't be save. Another man dying, can be save. Dat what dis all about."

"Well, time for dis old engine show it still can kick," and with a screech of tires Wallace tore around the last knot of MoBay traffic and hit the coast road.

"Where dis mahn need savin?" ask Wallace as they cruised at top speed.

"Know Neptune Café?"

"Sure. Him dere?"

"No mahn, him at Rose Hill. But from Neptune I can climb faster than we can drive the road."

Wallace look at Marty again in his mirror. "True, mahn, true. Last time yah cry because yah got to walk from Big Turn. Dis time yah say yah can make it on foot faster den in me car. Things change, mahn, change plenty."

Marty laughed. "Guess so, guess I was kind of a jerk."

"Better den most me get, even den." Wallace shrug, forcing the big old engine into a deep roar and letting the tires whistle.

The landmarks whizzed by, tourist heads turning to watch the speeding taxi, past the turnoff for the old coast road, past the turnoff for the road into the district, past small clusters of shacks, honking wildly to keep animals out of the way, past Clinton's and other familiar shanty shops until the Neptune's white walls gleamed in front of them. Marty had twenty U.S. and two Jamaican dollars already on the front seat as they ground to a halt.

"Too much, mahn," said Wallace.

"Two for Red Stripe in Neptune, rest for speed and trouble back in MoBay."

"All right, den, cool runnin."

"Me need dat," answered Marty. He took a deep

breath, hefted the pouch carefully in one arm, and took off at a jog.

It had taken him a little more than half a day to get into town and back, and because he had gotten an early start the sun was still closer to noon than setting. It was the hot, quiet time, which Marty figured must explain why no one was out and about. Perhaps another time he would have thought about the deep stillness around him, wondered why the middle of the day is so static, maybe thought that the quiet he sensed was unusual even for the tropics, but none of that mattered. All he wanted was to establish a rhythm, breathing and walking in unison so that the gradual inclines would be gobbled up and the steep sections would pass beneath his feet like the ground under an escalator. And through it all he wanted to hold something in reserve, because when he got there he still had a delicate thing to do—jabbing a big needle into someone's ass for the first time should not be done while blacking out or heaving up and down with exhaustion. Two big needles actually, antitoxin and relaxant. Did the order matter? Doc Stephenson didn't say anything about it—antitoxin first, get that in there, then relaxant.

The open fields behind the Neptune were gone and the first section of heavy forest loomed up. This path through Shire Hall was a little longer, but because it had gradual slopes he could do more running and make up the difference. And he felt very strong, sure that now what was left to do was under his own control. He had the medicine and information he needed; he was on foot in his own district; he didn't need to rely on strangers or cars for a damn thing. Now it was only a matter of his hands and his feet and his head.

Pushing on through the forest, he could see the first few

signs of Shire Hall. There was the old brickwork nearly buried under roots and soil. Then the rusted boiler with a huge exploded hole in its side rested under a canopy of tall red birches. From there Marty knew it was only a hundred yards or so until he emerged into the grazing land where he could see Shire Hall itself rising up on the hillside. He counted the steps to take his mind off fatigue . . . eighty-one, eighty-two, eighty-three, eighty-four . . . it was getting lighter ahead. All right, once he hit this stretch he would be a good third of the way home.

He emerged out of the trees at nearly a dead run, thinking he saw something glittering on the open field beside Shire Hall, but in the instant it took him to wonder what it might be a powerful body came flying into his. An arm, a white arm, wrapped around his neck from behind and hurled him to the ground. Marty turned his shoulder to take the brunt of the fall, trying desperately to protect the fragile contents of his pouch. The other body landed on top, and the cool metal barrel of a gun pressed against the side of his face, forcing his head into the dirt.

CHAPTER
FIFTEEN

THE gun stayed exactly where it was, but the body swiveled away into a crouch beside him. The legs were big under army fatigues, but the move had been smooth, very smooth.

"We got ourselves a little problem here, Frankie," called the man.

"Shit. Well, bring him over."

The other hand took the back of his collar with a handful of hair and pulled Marty to his feet. He still had the pouch.

"What's that you're carrying there, boy?"

"For sickness, mahn, dat all. Medicine." For some reason Marty didn't even try to figure, he wanted to sound and act as Jamaican as possible.

"Well, keep your hands free, understand?"

"Yah mahn, me not gwan nowhere."

"Damn right."

In the pasture sat a single-engine plane, gleaming in the sun. All of its doors were open and Marty could see the man with the donkeys, the man he had seen weeks before clearing rocks from this strip, leading his animals toward the site. They moved slowly because they were laden down with ganja.

A second white man, this Frankie, met them at the edge of the homemade airstrip. He studied Marty. "All right," he said finally, "I need some answers from you in a hurry. First of all, who are you?"

"Marse Martin son, Martinson."

"Don't give me that bullshit Jamaican accent. You're wearing good sneakers and expensive eyeglasses and a top-shelf button-down shirt. Who are you—and I won't ask again."

"Me tell yah clear, mahn: me Martinson Sanders. Me family got plenty bees and plenty land other side Rose Hill." Don't let it drop, thought Marty, don't give it up no matter what.

"Frankie, I think he's government," said muscleman.

"Could be, Gino, could be."

"Then why take a risk? Finish him and get back to work."

"But if we do that and he turns out to be local, we've fucked ourselves. They'll never let us back in here again without taking revenge." His eyes never left Marty. "Why are you here? Don't you know no one comes through here on ganja loading day?"

"Sickness on Rose Hill. Medicine for it need go dere right away. Me bring it. Check it out, mahn, look in dere." Marty held up the pouch, but quick as he did muscleman had locked his elbows, forcing his hand down. It was all Marty could do to keep from dropping the precious package.

"Don't you point at no one, asshole," growled Gino as Frankie the pilot took the pouch and untied its leather strings.

"Checks out," he said. "On the other hand, it's fucking good cover too." He retied it but held on to the pouch. "Hey, Mover, you know this guy?"

The man with the donkeys looked up from his loading. "Seen him one or two times recent, dat all."

"Frankie, I tell ya he's been staking us out."

"Could be, could be. Mover, we bury this guy, anyone gonna care?"

The donkey man barely looked up. "Him move wid someone from hill, me tink. But not sure, mahn, not sure. Do it right and no wahn know."

If I make a run for it I'm dead—and Manley's dead, thought Marty. Shit, I can't even break free from this guy, let alone run. "Peoples up dere know only one thing keep me from getting dis medicine to dem," said Marty. "Dat if me dead. You do it, dem know, mahn, guarantee dem know."

The pilot remained poised, indecisive. "Otto, what you say?" he called.

From the far side of the plane Rooster stepped around. When him see what going on, slow smile spread over him face.

"Never seen him," said Otto, nice and slow.

"Think he's government?" asked Gino the muscleman.

"Look like it. What else him doing here sneakin up on ganj day?"

That was too much for Marty to take. "Otto mahn, dat pouch dere need get Rose Hill so Manley Wynne can live. If it not get dere, him gwan die."

208

"Who?" say Otto. "Who him talkin 'bout?"

"Manley, mahn. Manley Wynne."

Otto shake him head, smile. "Dis guy smart, but him liar. Me know no such mahn as dat."

"Me ah liar!" Marty exploded, no longer caring about the gun in his back. "You dah liar, Otto. How me know your name be Otto if me not know yah?"

"White man say it first," say Otto.

"Well, him not say your nickname. First nickname Rooster, but new nickname better den Rooster. New nickname Fookah. True, Fookah mahn? Reason for Fookah nickname is from yah doing thing just like dis one right here."

The pilot showed a hint of a smile, but Otto's eyes bulged in anger. "Kill him, mahn, me you partner all along and me say kill him."

"Know why him say it?" Marty demanded. "Him say it because me snap him spear gun when him try shoot me friend. And know who me friend? Bwai of mahn needin dis medicine. You kill me, mahn, and if you ever show your face Rose Hill again, you dead. Fookah not protect yah from Rose Hill."

Even muscleman began to back off a bit. Marty sensed he had the edge and he wanted to keep it. On impulse he called out, "Hoi, Pamela. You dere?"

From inside Shire Hall on the hillside above the landing strip they could hear Pamela's voice answer, "Who dere?"

"Martinson."

She stuck her big face out one of the windowframes long ago empty of glass. "Whagwan? How poppa?"

"All right. Me want say thanks for offer of tea, but him not need it."

"All right, cool," and she was gone.

"Him sneaky," Otto shouted. "Dat womahn him partner. Him set her up dere. Doan let him go or we fooked, mahn, fooked."

There was movement in the trees. They all wheeled around to see the brother of the donkey man, the Rasta who sat in his small house on the coast road, come striding into the pasture with his collection of ganja for the plane. Jim's small packet was among the stash in two burlap bags.

"Rastaman, you know this guy?" asked the pilot.

Rasta strode over. "Seen him, true. Not know him good."

"Maybe only seen me once," said Marty, "but yah know me, mahn. Yah give me nickname dat stick."

The Rasta smiled. "Mooreden, dat me name for him. Mooreden meet de eye, moore gwan den him let on."

"See?" yelled Otto. "Him got secret. Him undercoover goovernment mahn."

"You think so?" asked the pilot to Rasta.

Marty and Rasta looked at each other straight in the eye, holding nothing back. Finally Rasta shook his head. "One time long ago, maybe him doing soomething like dat. But not now, no mahn."

"Once an agent, always an agent," muttered muscleman.

Fuck it, thought Marty. I didn't come all this way to get caught up with these assholes and let Manley suffocate to death. He turned to the pilot, obviously the brains of the operation. "Listen here, mahn. Me gwan take dat pouch and me gwan to Rose Hill. You want shoot me now, den do it. But friend up dere need me, or him die."

Marty took his pouch out of the pilot's hands, shook free from muscleman, and started walking straight for the old plantation road that led through the forest to the top of the hill. It was all he could do to keep moving, to keep his knees going up and down instead of buckling under, to keep himself from looking back. Each step means one less I have to take, he thought. Each step makes me smaller. Each step brings me closer to the trees. Don't look back. Don't make Orpheus' mistake. Each step brings me closer to the Overworld—and freedom.

From behind he heard a sudden movement, the pilot crying, "No, Otto," and the sound of a shot. He broke into a run, wondering if he should be feeling anything. He had to look back—he couldn't stand it anymore. But unlike Orpheus, Marty's overwhelming temptation cost him nothing: Otto was on the ground, covered by muscleman, the gun still in his hand.

Marty needed to see nothing more. He reached the ancient stone wall that marked the end of the field, the end of the Underworld, ran his hands all over his body just to make sure there wasn't any hole anywhere, and then leaped into the bush. A laugh start in him belly, growing and bursting into a wild, high-pitched howl. He'd made it.

CHAPTER
SIXTEEN

S H A D O W S getting longer breath by breath. Dorothy watch them crawl across rock and across little banana tree she try raise up in thin dirt back of house. Manley laugh at her, tell her it never come up, but she try anyway, and sure enough here come little sprout. Even if it make no banana, least it come to the sun. That nice because she can see it from window inside the house, window by the bed, window where she sit with one hand on Manley shoulder and other hand against wall to hold her up.

Idea of another night like this make tears roll down her face, even though little ones staring at her full of fright because them never see her cry before. Another night be a night of death. Dorothy live through other nights of death, her grandmomma and her momma. Her papa gone too, but him go quick and quiet. Grandmomma specially go with big struggle all night, moan and cry and make rattle noise in her throat and then at dark dark time just before first sign of sun she near to rise up straight out of bed lying on her back, then drop down slump into mattress and it over. But she ripe, she ready to get pick by the Lord. Manley, God no, him still got plenty left to do right here on Rose Hill, children raise fish catch time with Dorothy him wife whether gold ring or no. Him got right to see oldest boys grow to man, laugh at grandchild, remember older times and tell people near them wisdom to keep same mistakes from happening over and over.

Her hand on him shoulder feel muscles tight as tight can be, like straining against biggest fish in ocean. Even in tightness shudder pass through like ripple on water, like someone throw a stone right in Manley and waves pass all over him body. Shadows get longer, ripples come more and more, Manley get stiffer and stiffer, eyes bulge out more, breathing even more hard than ever. And what can she do? Just sit. Just wonder if Horace right when him say that Martinson be back in time with medicine from MoBay. Soon as Horace come back in morning from Marse Martin house him seem to ease up, feeling like it gwan be all right, but not Dorothy. Horace go to yard and be there all day doing some thing or other, banging around with wood and old mallet him friend Clinton give him, once in while stick head inside see whagwan, but not just sit there. Might as well work, him say. Just sit there no help. But Manley maybe say something, need something, so this where she belong. Him give so much, him care so much over so many times; now when him need her she can do so little, only keep touching and holding him here, pray that help come in time.

Dorothy think her touch not helping, but it her touch

keeping Manley Wynne on Rose Hill. More and more it seem to him like him perch on top inside the house, like a bat in the roof, looking down on Dorothy and him body stretch out in bed. Sometimes get a feeling like him spirit could fly all over Rose Hill, visit all over check it all out swoop down seaside out to the ocean and barthes. Just like him want to do first time him come to Rose Hill. But Dorothy hand on him shoulder like string on kite. Only let him go so far, then bring him back. And her tears, tears him never see her cry in daylight, them goddamn tears make him fight so she can stop them and feel all right. Is their time come to this, her tears and him stiff as ripsaw piece of lignum vitae? Pickneys huddle in corner? No way, mahn, no way. Spirit can be selfish thing, wanting to fly like a hawk. But that not right, not yet. Body might not want to, but body must still breathe on.

From up above, looking down on him own body fighting to be alive, that Manley realize someone else come into room, bursting in full of smell and sweat. Dorothy say nothing, just turn away long enough to wipe tears off cheeks so him not see them. She look at him with eye bright as electric light bulb, feeling hope.

"Me got it," say Martinson, untying little pouch in him hand. Careful he remove the vials—everything survive his fall intact only not one syringe, where needle pierce the packaging. Marty put that one aside, drew several deep breaths to compose himself, to force his mind to slow down, to listen to the thunk thunk in the yard and catch that rhythm, to watch Dorothy's face and the little ones scared half to death—finally to look at Manley, mouth drawn back like a death smile, eyes bulging, every part of him stiff as, as a corpse, but wheeze and rattle of hard breathing still moving his chest up and down. Seeing him made Marty decide to go with the relaxant first; the immediate danger was that Manley would harden up like concrete and suffocate. Get the relaxant into his body first, then the antitoxin.

"Need to turn him over," said Martinson.

"Afraid him cannot breathe face down," worry Dorothy.

"Hold him head, den."

Together they turned him belly down with the sheet back to expose his buttocks. Dorothy hold him head. Manley spirit see them move that foolish body so clumsy, him wish him could help them, but no way.

Martinson opened the first syringe and held it needle up like he'd seen in all the doctor shows on TV. No air, so let's see, get the plunger in all the way, then draw it out for the fluid. The top of the vial seemed to have some kind of waxy plug in it, not something he could unscrew. He could pierce it, though. He jabbed the needle too hard in his worry not to get through the wax, almost knocking over the vial as the syringe tapped against the glass. But it was all right. As he drew the plunger back out, the entire vial filled the syringe.

"Dorothy, yah must rub one spot wid dat alcohol and cotton."

She let go of Manley's head, not wanting to but with no choice. Quick as she can she pour little drop on him, rub with cotton, get back to him head. Even in short time she can feel him breathing harder. Marty, thinking thinking thinking, pushed the plunger just a bit to force out whatever little air bubbles might have snuck in. A patch of Manley's ass glistened from the alcohol and it was tensed, the big muscles back there standing out. Straight and sure, Marty thought, quick and straight and sure. In the yard he could still hear the thunk thunk of someone at work. He poised the needle, waited for the rhythm of the hammering to make sense again, and on the next beat jammed the needle under the skin.

From him perch above, Manley watch them get ready, watch them show him ass, watch them hover around, breathing and staring. Him see the needle, big needle too, but even so him not put it all together and realize them gwan stick that thing into him deep deep worse than any bee sting ever. It hurt and spirit feel like Fook it, mahn, leave it, just fly away and leave all dat boolshit and pain behind. But leavin dat behind mean leave it all to Dorothy, leave burden for her to bear. Dat not de way to live, dat not de way to die. Spirit can be selfish, but Manley not selfish. He fight himself down down down, string getting shorter shorter shorter, and Manley force him full self inside him body again. Not leaving it. Not yet.

"Already me think him ease," say Dorothy.

"Doc Stephenson say these work fast, but not that fast," said Martinson. He pulled the syringe straight out, covered the spot with another piece of cotton. Dorothy come back to do same thing again with second needle, make skin patch ready for it. This time Martinson move surer, faster, needle jab clean and quick, serum into blood and needle out no time at all. Martinson hold little piece of cotton over second spot with one hand, with other hand hold up two little bottles with pills in them. She listen good because it important but now she know, sure as sun going down, that Manley gwan be all right. She look at Martinson in in in, her way of pouring out all the feelings she have for him, as him tell her what need be done with the pills until him talking slow down to nothing. Them just look at each other. Never, he thought, never have I seen as beautiful a face as that.

"Where Horace?" ask Martinson when them let each other see enough.

216

"Dat him in yard wid hammer," say Dorothy.

"Should of known." Him smile, and walk out.

"Hoi," call Horace.

"Where yah been, mahn? Risk me life get medicine for your papa, yah not even coome see when me return."

Horace look up at him, eyes smiling but rest of face quiet. "Here all de time." Him turn back to work with wood in yard.

"Well, mahn, it nip and tuck, as them say in States, but Manley gwan be all right. Your papa gwan be all right."

"Yah mahn," say Horace, smile again, still working.

"I'd of thought you would be jumping up and down," Marty cried, exasperated at not receiving a hero's welcome.

"No, mahn," say Horace. "Me just know you gwan do it. Me know it sure sure sure. Your name is Mooreden—mooreden meet de eye, mooreden anyone expect, so yah can do it. Mooreden, mahn, you truly dat and yah show it again. But now yah got new nickname: Lifesaver."

The air filled with the loud roar of a small engine firing up in the twilight. "Ganja plane take off," say Horace, not looking up.

Martinson could see the plane, barely higher than the treetops, struggling to climb over the highest point of the ridge of Rose Hill. "Look like him gwan crash," he muttered.

Horace look up. "Him greedy, mahn, too too greedy. Him take too much ganja. Plane not big enough." Just as Horace spoke the side door opened and several burlap bags were thrown out. The plane circled into the valley and began the climb again. This time they just barely cleared the summit and were gone, the sound of engines dying away in the night.

Thunk thunk thunk—even as the light failed, Horace

217

kept hammering away. "What you doing anyway?" asked Marty.

Horace say nothing for little bit, then: "Got to finish dis cedar."

"But what is it, mahn? Look like big box."

"True. It big box."

"But what it for?" ask Marty. Horace just look at him. "If me not know better," Marty continued, "me think it ah coffin."

Horace look at him with look meaning True.

"But forget it, mahn," Marty cry. "Manley gwan be all right, I say."

"Not for Manley," say Horace quiet. "Never meant for Manley."

"Oh no." Marty stumbled, but Horace caught him and made him sit on the backyard wall. "Am I too late?"

"Not too late, mahn," say Horace in him ear, "but it over for your papa."

CHAPTER
SEVENTEEN

THE night passed, so much like so many of the nights before, Marty sitting at the side of his father's bed while a kerosene lamp played tricks with the old man's profile on the far wall, that it was hard to believe he was dead. Through the still, dark hours it even seemed as if his father responded in his subtle ways—the cruel tricks of rigor mortis and slow slow decay. Cora had turned his head face up, eyes staring at the cracks in the ceiling he knew like the lines in his hand. Long past midnight Marty leaned over, telling his father that he had meant to be there at the bitter end, that he wished he had been there for more of the sweet times, that only a matter of life could have drawn him away from the matter of death, that he hoped his father could understand, that there were still a few things he needed to know that only his father could tell him. As Marty whispered through his tears Martin's head suddenly fell to the side, pulled by gravity and by its wish to be where it had finally come to rest. Martinson screamed and jumped away, dead unblinking eyes watching his horror. But even after death the small smile remained, the final expression, as if to say, The crucial moment came and I knew, I remembered the moment and it was my anchor. My son saved a life and a part of me remains here on Rose Hill my home. That was why I held on. That answered many questions, and became the meaning of many things. I trusted my life and its own reality before I trusted the Church and its hocus pocus, or the doctor and his drugs, and I was right. Martinson saw the smile for what it was, recovered from his horror, closed the eyes before they could never close again, and left the head facing him where it wanted to be. He dozed fitfully, lamp sputtering, until the first signs of dawn appeared even before light; a change in the wind, birds restless, an early rooster crow. Marty went to the balcony to watch the light come, everything gray until the earth spun far enough to let the sun bring color to his world. And just as Martinson's eyes were following the walking trail from home through the fields into the mahogany forest, the trail his father's feet had created from decade after decade of passage, he saw Horace emerge from the trees with the coffin hoisted on his shoulder, Horace in a white shirt and long pants and shoes. Martinson took a deep breath, wondering what this day had in store for him. Funeral day coome.

He listened to murmurings and movement downstairs, knew he should rouse himself to prepare, so when the soft padding of Cora's feet in the hallway brought her to him and her calm look of concern told him that it was time to begin, he was already dressed in a white shirt and tan slacks that had belonged to his father, composed and ready for formality. Alone with this empty shell, he had made his peace as best he could and said his good-byes. Cora called downstairs, and it was Horace and Dagi who came into the bedroom—Horace standing in for his father, who could not take his rightful place. "How papa?" ask Martinson. Horace nod him head: All right, mahn. The three of them grasped the corpse, Dagi at the feet and Horace and Marty each at a shoulder. It had fallen to Dagi to do this many times before, but still he never could get used to it, dead skin and stiff muscles, smell of death, empty empty feeling of a body with no spirit. From his spot he looked down the length of the corpse, belly bloated like never in life, and there at one shoulder Martinson looking more and more like his father every day, and there at other shoulder Horace, plenty Manley in him too. Dagi never have children—it just not meant for him and Lilly. Sometime the ache of that come into his heart—watching them lift him dead friend Martin Sanders make ache return. Bomba have son, that close enough. Time of a new generation soon come, time of a new generation begin right here, two sons lift a dead man into a box.

They lowered him into Horace's coffin and the clean, menthol scent of cedar seemed to take away the stink of death. Marty admired the work and saw how nicely the hue of cedar matched his father's skin, even in death. "Clinton be proud dis box, mahn," and they smiled. Marty picked out one of his father's favorite blankets, a cotton bedspread with bright stripes of color streaming through it, an old old present from a seamstress in Falmouth, and covered the body but left the head exposed. The playful smile was fading, drooping into the folds of his neck, melting into the neutral expressions of death, but still it was there.

"Coffin open or close?" ask Horace. Him have cover if need be for now or for moment when stick in ground.

Martinson paused. "Open. Dis last time Papa see Rose Hill. Dat all right with you, Dagi?"

"Your decision, Martinson."

Slowly they carried the heavy coffin down the stairs and set it in the foyer, morning light streaming in from the open door. Outside Marty could see Bomba sitting on top of an old wagon with metal wheels and an open wooden bed. It was hitched to a donkey. Bomba couldn't help but look comical up there, as solemn as he meant to be, wearing his cleanest clothes and a tweed cap that was a family heirloom even though a goat once took a nibble on it, holding a riding crop to keep the donkey from getting too stubborn. Marty thought of the ferryman in those Greek myths who took dead people across the river. What was his name? Didn't matter. Bomba was a Jamaican version and just as good.

They stood in the hallway, looking at one another, taking a few deep breaths. There was a feeling that once they walked through the front door the funeral would truly begin. For a moment they paused over this dead man, letting whatever was left of him rest in the place he had maintained for so many years, and then they bent down together and hoisted the coffin. Cora held the door as they carried their weight to the cart and slid him, headfirst so he could see the procession about to unfold, into the wagon behind Bomba's driving chair. Bomba made ready to move his donkey, Horace and Dagi fell in behind Martinson, and all was set when Marty looked up to see Cora standing under the awning of the porch. "Cora," he called, "will you walk with me?"

Her mouth trembled and tears came to her eyes. She had been the old man's sole companion for more than a decade and at the same time a stranger, a member of the family and a hired hand, always there but never completely there. She didn't know her place, what she really had meant to this man. Now she knew. She stepped in beside Marty, the comfort of Dagi behind her just as Marty felt the support of Horace behind him, and when Bomba flicked the donkey into motion they began the slow walk through Rose Hill to the cemetery.

The gate at the end of the long driveway creaked open. "Leave it," called Marty as Horace moved to close the latch behind them. "We soon coome back." The way he said it made Horace feel good; Martinson care about here, him not just come and go and stop caring now that him papa gone.

On this day the gate should be open, thought Marty. On this day the gate and the doors and the windows should all be open to let his spirit come and go. That way there won't be a ghost in the house and there will be a clean sweep of feeling. When that has happened and everything has gotten as free of the past as it can be, then I can decide what to do and what not to do. But all I have to do now is open up, open up everything, open coffin and open gate and open heart.

A hum filled the air, a hum they all would have ignored except that something strange was happening. The bees had come to the coffin. Scores of them settled on the colorful spread over Martin Sanders, crawling over him as if he was a giant flower.

"Bees like color," say Dagi, but that didn't explain why so many searched out his face, covering it as though it was their hive. Their low hum filled the air and Marty couldn't tell whether it felt angry or contented. He wanted to brush them away but there were too many. The donkey shuddered, nervous about them swarming around, and picked up the pace despite Bomba's tight rein.

"Marse Martin plenty good luck for where him gwan," say Horace. As they moved farther from the old boxes that Martin had raided for honey so many times in his lifetime the bees thinned out, returning to their homes. Marty could see that several had stung his father about the mouth and eyes and then fallen away into the coffin with him, wriggling into death, his fitting companions.

Marty was still thinking about the bees when he felt something falling on him, like hard rain or hail from a perfectly blue morning sky. He looked up, and standing at the side of the road in front of her little store was Miss Ethel. Her old stringy hair was pulled back under a black skullcap. She wore a print dress that reached all the way to her feet, and her sagging breasts were covered by flowers which she had collected that morning and pinned to herself. She had even found some white cardboard or tape and fashioned it into a makeshift denture so that her face lost some of its shrunken age. The store was all boarded up and she had been waiting since early morning to make sure she didn't miss them. Now that they had arrived she reached into her brown bag, grabbed another handful, and threw more rice on Martinson and into the coffin. Once they had passed she fell in at a respectful distance, trying to keep up despite her weary feet and tight shoes, clutching her bag so that when they laid Martin to rest she could throw more rice into his grave.

The old road rolled out before them through a line of tall coconut trees. Martinson could see children from the district who had shimmied up to the coconut crowns to get a good view of the procession, twittering and whispering ahead, then falling silent and somber as the coffin drew near. Little monkeys, he thought, little monkeys like me.

As soon as the donkey passed they scurried down and scampered through their shortcuts to see the funeral again farther along the road, shouting and laughing the moment they were out of sight.

Big Turn appeared, and when Marty looked up he saw a strange pair waiting to join the procession. Large, very black except for the shine of gold chains about her neck, sweat draining off her face despite constant mopping with a white handkerchief, exhausted from her first climb up Rose Hill in many years because it was the first time in many years that no one else could take care of this business for her, Miss Ella stood in the sunlight paying her respects. She would rather have been in her little wooden booth in the dark coolness of the Neptune, but Martin Sanders was more than a business associate; he was a man worthy of respect and friendship. It would be an insult to his memory not to attend his funeral—it wouldn't look too good with Martin's son either, and hard hearts have a way of turning into hard heads in business matters. Maybe the young man wasn't going to stick around, but then again maybe he was.

And with her, taking pains to mention to her more than once as they climbed the trail together that if she wanted to live a long happy life she had better take off twenty pounds, himself more winded than he wanted to admit despite their slow pace, his seersucker suit jacket slung over one shoulder because it was getting damn hot and he knew Martin would have cared less whether he wore it or not, holding a sliver of aloe in his hand that he had used to soothe a mosquito bite on the back of his neck, stood Doc Stephenson. "How did you hear?" asked Marty, shaking his hand warmly.

"Miss Ella sent me word yesterday, not too long after

you left," he said. Quietly they shared the irony. "I hear your patient is recovering quite nicely."

"You know more than me," said Marty.

"Perhaps. By the way," and Doc Stephenson paused, as if considering something. "No no, I'll speak to you later."

Miss Ella reached into a pouch at her belt, produced a small handful of ten-sided half-dollars that she had collected the night before, and threw them one by one at the slowly moving coffin. A few fell in with Martin's body, a few came to rest in the bed of the wagon, and some fell to the ground, gleaming in the dirt, as a score of pickney eyes watched them, just waiting for the first possible instant when their parents would be far enough along not to cuff them on the side of the head for interrupting this solemn moment to dive for one.

"Hoi, Denise," said Marty quietly. She looked at him to say she was sad, but he could also see she was happy he remembered her name, and she joined the growing line of people keeping Martin Sanders company on his last climb to the top of Rose Hill.

At the big water collect spot where women tended to meet and sit no matter what day it was, the funeral added many people to its line. Standing just below the concrete slope in a spot he had chosen to ensure best possible exposure was Preacher, already rumbling in his throat, which meant he would soon burst into loud exhortation. Martinson skewered him with a look to say, No, mahn, not at my father's funeral. But if Preacher was in the habit of being stopped by looks, then he wouldn't have been what he was. This was a Death, and he had a Mission.

"Funeral day SAD day," him chant, "funeral day ah day of de LAWD. . . ."

"Dat what you say to Miss Stacia, mahn?" call a voice nearby.

Marty knew that voice—who? Of course, standing there with her eyes flashing like she had swallowed sparks of a fire, was Pamela. If anybody was going to josh Preacher, Pamela was the one to do it.

Preacher look at her angry. "Pamela, yah blasPHEMer, doan bring your SIN to Marse Martin funeral."

"Hoi, Pamela," call Martinson loud enough so all can hear him, all know him glad she there.

"In de DARKest hour before de DAWN," Preacher continue, "when it seem like de world STOP its turnin, when it seem like dere NO hope for mornin, NO hope for the sweet LIGHT of DAWN, it is in DAT hour dat yah must beLIEVE in JEsus CHRIST . . ."

"Now I KNOW him say dat Miss Stacia," chuckle Pamela.

". . . the SAvior, the reDEEMer, for as surely as the LAWD giveth, so too does de Lawd TAKEth aWAY."

Marty touched Preacher above the elbow, making him jump. "Enough, mahn," he said without anger but straight into his eyes. Preacher have respect for the dead—him back off and join the line.

Pamela meanwhile bring up a wreath of the brightest bright red hibiscus flowers she can find, tied together real careful with young green shoots. It not a full ring, just a string, but when she lay it on Martin's chest it look like him wearing it around him neck. She step back to admire her work and so did Marty, thanking her for such thought and care. The white teeth of her smile show and her eyes light up in a flash. "Yah mahn," she say, "me door always open for Sanders, young or old."

The road was steep but still the strong old donkey plodded along, drawing people into the procession house by house, yard by yard. Buster from the post office bar there, even One-leg Elrond make the trip. Every once in a while

Marty seemed to see some rustling in the bush off the road, but he never saw anyone come out of there to join. Finally he turned back to Horace. "Soomeone in bush?" him ask.

"Yah mahn," say Horace, jerking his head toward the spot Martinson mean.

"Who dere?"

"Take one guess."

Martinson thought for a second. "Fookah," him say. Horace nod, true.

"Whagwan happen wid him?" Martinson wonder.

"Not know, mahn, not know."

"Dis not right day think 'bout it, but soon," say Marty, "soon we sit down wid your papa, maybe Dagi, and talk about dis. Cannot stay like it is now."

Horace nod again, think, Yah, mahn, me like what me hear, just like him say leave gate open.

Marty had been so preoccupied thinking about Rooster that he hadn't noticed a small girl running alongside, trying to keep up and catch his attention. Finally he realized she wanted to give him something. It was a piece of paper and he could see there was a word written in careful, childish script: Carla.

"Yah learn your name." He smiled, rubbing her head.

Carla have big eyes, fingers-in-mouth look. Then she point to the coffin. "In dere," she say. Marty took her name and placed it in the folds of his father's colorful bedspread. For the first time that morning since leaving the bedroom, he cried.

Up the road the donkey walk, Bomba urging him on with a flick of the whip every now and then. It the biggest funeral anyone could remember, big as biggest Sunday gathering at seaside. And while people feeling serious and sad, Martinson's tone keep things lighter. He look about with a smile as much as a tear, and the way him walk behind his papa say that he proud to be there, that his father live a full life and now him gone, that this the way of everything and it not all sad. When pickneys jump about calling to each other, him not look at them and hush them up. Their running about a part of things. Them alive even if Marse Martin dead and it a good thing them alive, not a bad thing. Tonight if people want drink rum in honor of Marse Martin, the feeling all around is that it all right with Martinson. Mix glad with sad, that the way of life and death. That the way of best funerals too.

Almost at the top of the road Martinson looked ahead to see a cluster of people waiting to join the procession. In the middle was a welcome figure—Manley Wynne still stiff but upright, head and shoulders above Dorothy, who stayed at his side so he could put his arm around her shoulder. Circling around them like little planets were the smallest of their brood, while Kozmo and his woman, Joanne, stood behind. This day Dorothy let none of the little ones hide in the folds of her dress, the white one she wear only for best weddings and most important funerals.

Her inside feelings torn, ripped in two between sadness for friend and neighbor Sanders and deepest deep deep happiness to feel Manley arm around her shoulder. Him still leaning on her kind of heavy, but him up, that what count. Him alive, that what count. Marse Martin pass on and it sad for Martinson, but everything Martinson do that day not in vain because Manley live on. She feel a deep meaning to this, a meaning about Martinson and him place on Rose Hill, the way life play tricks with people, feeling like a Big Hand move them around sometimes to be in right place at right time. Everybody think they can just decide what to do next, but sometimes they don't have so much choice as them think. These are true funeral thoughts, think Dorothy, different than birth thoughts or wedding thoughts or Church thoughts. Funeral thoughts travel a long way here and there, connect things together.

Manley stand feeling sore, but different kind of sore than before. Healing sore. Him stand thinking about all the things him want to ask Martinson. Like how him know what to do to save Manley life. Like how him papa know what wrong with Manley. Like if a sphinx really look like elephant, sort of. And Manley feel like him got plenty things to tell Martinson too. Like what it mean for him to be here on Rose Hill, two-way meaning for him and us and both ways good. Sure, if Martinson leave, then Dagi and Manley get plenty things could never get any other way, maybe even get rich from it, but over time it would get bad, something go wrong, things get sick on Marse Martin land. No, Martinson should stay, make things better for himself and all of us. Come and go, if that what him need, go to States see momma when him need it. But dis him home. Him prove it to them all but himself. Him thrive here like plant with just right sun and just right water. Him as in now with Wynnes as if him born in. And look at Martin lying there—smiling even as him rot away. Him die, me live on, but in me there some of Martin because him save me at end of him time. Can never forget that. Honor him now, honor him later, honor him through him son.

"How feelin?" Manley ask when Martinson get close.

"All right. Dat my question to you too."

Manley smile, rub his ass. "Yah jab me good, mahn, feelin sore. Whagwan after dis over?"

Marty shrugged; no idea.

"Coome me yard, mahn, me cannot walk your house as yet. Coome sit and drink soome rum."

Martinson looked at Dorothy and the children staring

up and Manley resting on her. "Not a place in this world I would rather be than in your yard after funeral," he said. For the first time Martinson wondered what it would be like to be in the big house alone.

Belle standing just little bit off Wynne family but with them just the same, waiting for Horace. She look in coffin and see bedspread her momma make for Martin Sanders long long time ago now going with him into the earth. Me make another one, she think, make one for Mooreden, become him own thing in house so not everything left over from him papa. Too much of old man might make him feel strange. Maybe me and Horace come stay one night like him ask us before. Now be a good time do that. She slip into line behind Horace while rest of Wynnes wait because Manley be slow and them not want hold everyone up.

As the people pass by, Manley look down the road and see one lone person trying to catch up. Him nudge Koz, who got better farseeing eyes, and ask if Koz know that walk. Koz shake head no. Martin have plenty distant friends, must be someone from MoBay or even Kingston. With Dorothy as a cane, Manley move him aching joints up Rose Hill.

Not long past Wynne yard the Rose Hill road come to its end. Bomba stop the donkey, tie him up at old stone posts marking a trail Marty never walk. Resting on top of posts everyone can see two big carvings, one post a hawk perching like him ready to pounce on mouse, other post a lion sitting up like him smelling the breeze and sensing danger. The wood been rubbed so it gleam with shadows and sun playing on it like animals truly alive and moving little bit here and there. Clinton work, think Marty, and as him think it Clinton and Vernica step out. Clinton holding small carving in him hand, give it to Martinson. "Dis one me carve when me hear sad news," him say. It fit in one hand, all mahogany, a big honey bee with wings and feet just right crawling on an open flower. "Dat for you, mahn, for de living," Clinton say.

"Coome help carry the coffin," said Martinson.

So it was Dagi, Horace, and Clinton who took three corners to help Marty along cemetery trail. It not a long trail but it climb a little bit. Soon as word of a death pass through the district people walk the trail with machetes, hack back the bush, and that way it keep clear wide enough for a few people side by side but not for donkey cart. At trail end find very very highest point of Rose Hill, very top of the ridge. For as long as anyone can remember or even know about from old stories this place open land and a spot for burial. Crumbling stone graves show it used for hundreds of years, early plantation time to now, for same thing. From the spot look to one side and see the blue sea going out forever to the sky, then look to other side and see green green valley deep into countryside where even in morning blue smoke from burning sugarcane rise up. And then next mountain ridge, and then next even higher. In all his boyhood years on Rose Hill Marty had never been there, another fact of his youth that didn't make sense thinking back on it now.

An ancient stone wall held back the forest, and near the back of the field Martinson could see where old man Winston and him son Coomfy been busy digging. A mound of dark earth rise up beside a deep hole; the hole sink in beside two clusters of rock next to each other. Martinson wait until Manley come up, pointing to the other graves. "My grandparents?"

"Yah mahn." Lone person still not catch up, think Manley. Hope him make it in time.

They set the coffin down beside the hole and everyone gather in close, just standing quiet. It like that for a while, young ones begin shuffling their feet around, until Martinson realized that they were waiting for him to say something, do something, whatever. He move him feet from side to side and everyone could see him ready to start.

"It only six weeks ago that I coome back to Rose Hill, see me papa before him die. Seem like lot longer, lot lot longer."

"Mooch has happened, mahn," cry out Miss Ethel.

"True. I coome to see me father, but soon I see meself. I was thinkin me purpose to ease him to death, but I coome to find that there moore den one reason for my cooming here, moore den one purpose to it."

"Mooreden," whisper Horace.

"My father, him Jamaican through and through. Even now, sittin in him coffin, him look Jamaican. His skin same color as the cedar around him, same color as the dirt soon throw on top of him. Plenty things in dis world make no sense, but seeing him at rest here at top of Rose Hill, dat make sense because here is where him heart want to rest, and dis him home."

"Your home too, Martinson," say Manley.

"True," call Pamela.

"It my home, true, but same time it not my home. I got two homes now, and that can make me real strong or real weak. My father wanted me here to show me dis home before it too late. That him have to be near to death before it can happen is a sadness that will be inside me always." Marty stopped, fighting back tears.

"De LAWD work in mySTERious ways," Preacher announce, "and de LAWD'S will be DONE."

"JAH Rastafari need no church or preacher," call Clinton.

Marty held up his hands. "My father had little need for any kind of god, but to me him ah religious mahn. Religion for him to do with the land and animals and most of all him friends and all the people of Rose Hill. He was alone many years, but so long as him here he could never be truly alone. He cared too much for whagwan to be alone."

"Him bring post office so no one alone on Rose Hill," cry Bomba.

"Boy, I remember that fight." Doc Stephenson laughed. "He pulled every string in the book."

"Year of ah fire, most dah bees in me box get burned," remember Dagi. "Him stand by me, not try drive me out so him can make moore profit. Dat doings of religious mahn."

"When me CHURCH in need of MUsic, and the CALL go OUT, who reSPOND?" ask Preacher. "MARtin reSPOND. Him want his doNAtion be PRIvate, but when we listen to the guiTAR Sunday MORNings, it MARTIN'S generOSity bring that sound. Praise JEsus."

That news to most people on Rose Hill, because Marse Martin never go to church. Some dem wonder whether Preacher making that up, but no good reason for him to do that, so it probably true.

"I'm sure dere are plenty good memory for me father, plenty good things to say about him. I know in me heart dat him want people to carry a memory of him with them, to keep his spirit here on Rose Hill him home. Dat moore important than anything. Dat moore important than money or goat or honey to him. To keep him spirit among us, keep him spirit alive."

"Dat for you, mahn," say Manley, "dat part your purpose."

A rustling in the bush by the trail tell Manley that the person him see down the road finally come.

"Soome of you may know this, and soome may not, but Martin Sanders have a nickname, a real name . . ."

"Keeper," whisper Manley.

". . . and dat name mean as much now as it ever mean

while him living. 'Keeper' was dat name. Keeper of many things here on Rose Hill, Keeper of him family here and friends and good feelings. So we can close dat box and bury the body of Martin Sanders, because the real feeling of him keep on inside, and what in dat box just like seashell dat wash ashore empty."

Horace take coffin cover and set it on, hammer it down as Miss Ethel shower him with rice. As him do it Dorothy call out, "Martinson, coome look by stone wall."

They walked to the far corner of the cemetery together, the highest of the highest point, and clinging to the ancient wall, gnarled and sprawling and old and wild, was the one thing he had always expected to see but never had seen in his travels around the district—a rose bush.

"It bloom," she whisper, "it bloom for your papa."

One small flower, delicate but stubborn, had forced its way out of the thicket. It was as though the entire hill, its rock and road and forest and bush and clearings and gardens and homes and goats and donkeys and people and squabbles and spirit, had all come to a point at the very top and there, the sum of it all, was a single wild red rose.

Dorothy reach down to pluck it and put it with Martin, but Martinson stop her hand. "Leave it," him say gentle, "it better here den underground."

She nod yes, and when the two of them walk back to the burial site the shovels of old man Winston and Coomfy already covering the coffin. The dirt was warm and dark, and Martinson's words hung in people's minds—dirt like the old man's skin, same color and feeling. That be something people remember when them work their yards and gardens.

Marty took a shovel and filled the grave, working alone and quickly. It's enough now, he was thinking, it's time to get on with it. He was so intent on the feeling of the worn wooden handle, the heft of the rich dirt and the sound it

235

made as it fell into the hole, the sense of beginning and end as one, that he didn't notice how the crowd around him had parted to allow a latecomer to reach the grave. There was no sound except the shovel biting the earth—the midday sun beat down on the people of Rose Hill all gathered together, suspended, waiting for Martinson to rise from his work. But he did not. On and on he shoveled until the raw mound of earth over his father's body was complete. Only then did he look up, realizing that everyone around him had become statues. He leaned against the shovel's handle, not recognizing that it was exactly the way his father had leaned against the barrel of his rifle during those last long walks, and he took a deep breath.

"Hello, Mother."

CHAPTER
EIGHTEEN

THEY sat on the porch under the blue light of the awning in unspoken agreement that it would be much easier to talk there than inside the house. The old wicker rockers had been repaired more than once and each had a peculiar squeak and chirp that added a syncopated music to the moment—at least for Marty. His mother's cadence was much faster, so there were three squeaks from her rocker for every chirp of his. He enjoyed the combination of sounds and he wanted to tell her about it and laugh together and then get themselves into a good rhythm—but he could not. Clearly she was far from pleasantries, in no mood to linger over small talk and small pleasure. He saw her preoccupied, uncomfortable, wishing she was somewhere else, anywhere else, and her way felt very familiar because it had been his way just a short time ago. He sat silently waiting for her to speak, knowing they had time, knowing that the moment would come quickly because she needed it to come quickly. He was full of things to say, but her restlessness was like a barrier between them. He felt he had no choice but to adopt a patient, hopefully compassionate silence—which felt very familiar, too, because just a short time ago it was that same silence which had exasperated him so much.

In the normal turning of the calendar little time had passed since they last saw each other, no more than any of the summers he had spent at camps or traveling around. But so much had happened that he looked at her as though they hadn't met in ages. Her black hair closely cropped in that short, almost masculine way of professional American women, gold hoop earrings, a practical and neatly pressed blouse, new dungaree skirt over white running shoes—everything spoke of a responsible and mature person, straightforward, secure, without the need of pretentiousness. She looked the part of a university professor at rest, for whom a flashy and flamboyant appearance is frowned upon in favor of conservatism. She had always maintained that in the important, internal, intellectual matters the academic community encouraged freedom, and the external conformity was inconsequential. Marty had not been so sure; that was one of their long-running discussions.

Yet what her appearance suggested in Cambridge was far different from what her appearance suggested in the bush, and Marty found himself regarding her with a Jamaican eye. Earrings and white sneakers, clean bright clothing, all spoke of wealth and ease. Skin a light tan, the color of preference within the racial caste of old-style Jamaicans, the color that proved the luxury of not having to toil under a beating sun year after year, the color that proved a mixture of ancestry. Full lips clearly from Africa, but a sharp nose more Roman. And behind her gold-rimmed glasses, so much like her son's glasses, were gray and troubled eyes, frightened eyes. Long tapered fingers strummed and fluttered in her lap as she searched for a starting point, betraying nervousness bordering on a panic beyond anything she felt facing hundreds of strangers with pens poised to make note of her every word. Here she was, doing nothing more than trying to begin a conversation with her son, which should be the most natural and enjoyable thing in the world, and she was dry-mouthed with fear. Marty certainly knew this and wished he could help her, hoped he could satisfy her, but first he had to know just what she needed. And then he had to decide what he needed, and wanted.

"It was Jerry, I mean Dr. Stephenson, who sent the telegram," she finally began.

"I'd guessed as much," said Marty eagerly, glad to break the tension on a note of agreement and neutrality. "He started to say something to me this morning on the walk up, but I guess he wanted to wait to see if you'd arrive. I'll tell you, for a place with no formal communication it sure is incredible how quickly the word gets around here."

She felt the ice breaking, and smiled. "Yes, like the beat of jungle drums."

He stiffened, then tried not to stiffen. She noticed him stiffen, then tried not to notice him stiffen. Is it my hypersensitivity, he wondered, or is there a constant undercurrent in every little thing she says that belittles any aspect of here? Is it my imagination, she wondered, or does he feel like he has to defend every little thing about Jamaica?

"No, mahn, not like dat," him soon say, real quiet. "Just peoples talking one to another, dat all."

The dialect and the quietness, resurrections of the man who had brought them both to this point, were like red flags in her face. "You're not an uneducated rural Jamaican boy, Marty, and there's nothing romantic in trying to sound like one."

He shrugged, pulling back even further. "It ah language, got own rules and words and beat. Gwan Paris, speak soome French. Coome Jamaica, speak Jamaican. Cool, no problem," and him feel a Horace giggle in him belly.

Louise took a deep breath. This was all wrong, they were speaking about the wrong things, emphasizing a difference that had grown up like a weed between them instead of seeking their common ground of mutual respect and love which was underneath it all. What could bring them back to that?

"Oh yes, before I forget, I have a note for you. I'm sure you can imagine who it's from." She gave him a sealed, scented blue envelope. For an instant it crossed his mind that it would be better not to open it until later, but clearly she wanted him to read it then and there, so he slit open the top. Inside was a photograph that made him shiver with déjà vu: He was walking down the street in Harvard Square, Christmas package under one arm, Trudy at the other, kicking some dirty snow with his boot. On the back was a note:

Dearest Marty,
Your mother says it's the Jamaican mail system that is holding up your letters, but I don't think so. Are you all right? What's going on? I thought I was ready for this as a short separation, but not hearing from you is making me feel really hurt and kind of scared. I'm not getting any feelings from you at all. Are you still in love with me? Is it over between us? I feel like I'm in limbo. I still love you, but are you going to stay there much longer or come home? Your mother says you're coming home with her, and I hope that's true, but I've been

having these terrible dreams over and over again where we're reaching for each other in the night but the distance between us keeps stretching more and more, like we're drowning or getting pulled apart. Then I wake up, and think I'm just being silly, that your thoughts must be with your father, that's all. That would explain the absence I feel . . . but I don't know. I just don't know. Oh hell, almost out of room—hope you're okay. I do love you,

T.

He felt the tug of the letter, the warmth and sincerity, but he did not feel free to experience it because his mother was watching him so avidly—observing his every gesture and change of expression. She's using this to draw me back to her life, he thought bitterly, she's trying to seduce me emotionally, and Trudy is a co-conspirator. "Dearest Marty . . ." There was a level of guilt injected into the letter, unintentional, he knew, magnified by his mother's posture. Yet Trudy's fears were well founded; she had drifted out of his thoughts, he had been preoccupied with other people, the absence she sensed was real.

He has become so silent, thought Louise, so noncommittal, as though every emotion has to be weighed and measured before it can be released. He never used to be like that, he used to be relaxed and open. No doubt this environment does that, no doubt the influence of his father was even more profound than I had feared it might be.

"Marty, I know I wrote this to you, but I'll say it again now: I think your coming here to be with your father in his last days was really an honorable, loving gesture on your part. Courageous, too. I'm sure it meant more to him than we can even imagine."

Martinson nod.

That's all, she thought, a nod. "How do you feel about it, about the experience of it?" she asked, an edge of impatience creeping into the question, turning it into a near demand.

Isn't it obvious? thought Marty. "Well, I agree with you. But I don't see it in altruistic terms, or as a one-way street. I think he gave me a great deal, certainly as much as I gave him in those final days. He gave me a father I could love and respect, and that is a big thing." Suddenly Marty wanted to defend that memory. "You know what his final words were to me? His very last words? They were words that saved another man's life. On his deathbed, when there would be every reason in the world to be self-centered, he thought clearly enough to save another man's life. I think that's pretty incredible, don't you?" It was his turn to demand an answer.

"Yes," she said, trying to summon up all the respect she could, trying not to let fear and petty feelings get in the way. "That's the stuff of great men, and the stuff of myths that survive great men." He listened for sarcasm, and instead softened to hear her agreement come from the heart. She used the thaw to push on. "And you know, this is sort of amazing, but I had already bought my plane tickets to come here before Jerry called with the news. I didn't come for the funeral—I thought I was coming to try and make some peace with him."

"Really? What made you change your mind about seeing him?"

"What made me change my mind? Well, you, I suppose, your example . . ."

"And your fear that I was sinking into the horror movie quicksand of the Jamaican bush."

"Well, yes," she managed to admit with a smile. "You are the one thing he and I had in common, after all, and I was hoping to talk to him about you. Maybe to have the talk we should have had thirteen years ago."

"Better late than never, eh?"

It was a low blow, a mean comment that he regretted the instant it left his mouth. She said nothing, but her shoulders began to shake and she reached up to take off her glasses, shielding her eyes until the tears stopped.

"I'm sorry, Mother, I didn't mean that."

She nodded. "I know, you're under a lot of pressure right now."

Squeak squeak squeak chirp, squeak squeak squeak chirp. That's true, he thought, but it's you who seem pressured. This is a funeral day, for God's sake. On a funeral day people stop and mourn, reflect, take it easy, cool out, doesn't matter if it's Jamaica or America. You're taking the grief time and turning it into something else. Squeak squeak squeak chirp, squeak squeak squeak chirp. But as you said, it's like he's been dead for all these years, while for me he only came alive these last few weeks. Shit, that's not fair. I wanted to know him better, I want more time with him NOW. . . .

The sound of footsteps interrupted Marty's thoughts. Horace appear from around corner of house, moving easy, expect everyone to be inside. When him see them on porch him stop—freeze, like Martinson say.

"Hoi."

"Hoi, Horace mahn, coome. Meet me mother, Louise Sanders."

Horace nod to her, mouth shut tight to hide no teeth. She turn sour, Papa say. She sweet before she sour, say Momma. She big part of what make Mooreden moore den, think Horace.

"Whagwan?" ask Martinson, sensing his mother tense at the dialect, not caring if she did.

"Dorothy wonder if yah want coome eat at me yard dis evening. Cook ah goat, get soome rum. She ask for both you."

Martinson smile. "Dat real nice, mahn, real nice—"

"But really we have some things to resolve here," said Louise quickly, tensely. "I think it would be best for us to have supper here."

Papa say expect this, think Horace, Papa say not feel bad if them not come.

Marty stood up, wanting to go, thinking there was no place he would rather be right then than drinking some rum quietly in the backyard with Manley and Dorothy, watching their family scamper about, little ones staring up at him with knuckles in their mouths, Dorothy eyes so in in in . . . but he did not want to make a family scene in front of Horace.

"Horace tell your momma many many thanks, but not tonight."

"All right." Horace turn to go.

"Say, Horace. Can you go ask Dagi, see if we can meet on him porch tomorrow?"

"Sure thing. Who be there?"

"You, me, Dagi, Manley."

Horace smile, show him empty space. Who care? Him coome meetings now. Big thing. Him big man now, teeth or no.

"All right, until," Horace say, and as him turn to go him put up third finger of both hands to say good-bye and cool runnings in the way Martinson show him from States. Him point it more for the mother to show everything cool, no problem she not want come to yard for goat. And then Horace gone, tell Dagi whagwan.

"My God, the rudeness of these people," Louise exploded the moment Horace disappeared, the floodgate breaking.

"You mean him giving you the finger?" Marty asked, having his best laugh in days. "Oh no, it's not what you think—"

"Why do you have to justify every single solitary stupidity in this bush?" she cried. "Not what I think? I can see with my own eyes, I can hear with my own ears. These people never liked me because I'd rather sit in a chair than squat in their yard, because I have my own way of life and don't have to play Jane to someone else's Tarzan. Toothless, rude, uneducated lout."

"No, Mother, that's not true."

"No? No? You've been here less than two months and you think you know so much. I was here fourteen years, Marty, fourteen years. Can you imagine that? If you could, you wouldn't even be here now, we'd both be camped out at the airport waiting for the first available plane back home. Fourteen years in this bush, do you have any *idea* what that means? And here you sit as though you have the slightest notion of what's going on around here, of the horror of it, the slow death, vines that would strangle you if you let them creep into the house, devious people thieving behind your back. Oh God, oh God, and you talk about a meeting tomorrow. Marty, we should be going *home* tomorrow. You've fulfilled your obligation, you've done more than anyone could have expected. It's a chapter in your life you should end now, while you can. Look," and hurriedly she produced two envelopes, as though they were a tetanus antidote. "Here's your ticket, here's my ticket. We're both booked on the same flight, leaving tomorrow at noon. It's as simple as that, all right? Why make it so difficult? It's over now, so let's go home, all right?"

The pressure between them had risen to such a level that Marty had to break away. There was nothing he could say to all that, they were too far apart to bridge right now. So he stood up suddenly, silently, startling his mother at his abruptness. "Too much pressure right now," him say. "Take a walk, clear out me brain, wait for the sun to cool a little bit, and then we can talk."

The dogs, as if on cue, scrambled to their feet, ready to keep him company, a little confused, sniffing the brown pants and white shirt that smelled of their master wrapped around the body of the other one their master loved. They followed as Marty stalked off the porch, taking the same worn path in the same way—even for the same reason— that she had known too too well for too too long not too many years ago. She watched him go in horror, unable to take her eyes off this reenactment, this cruelest of life's tricks, this transmigration of souls, his final revenge on her. "Oh my God," she murmured, trembling uncontrollably. "This is my worst nightmare come true."

They spent the afternoon apart, closer in thought than either of them realized, anguished in their own ways. Marty expected to take an aimless walk, but his hike turned into a methodical examination of the cedar posts that marked the boundaries of the land, and his mind turned to questions of upkeep, pasturing, and bee cultivation. Then he would return to his father in the ground, then to his mother on the porch, then to Trudy's letter in his pocket, and then he would once again alight on a cedar post. Clear decisions aren't made during times of mourning, he thought. I mean really, could I truly have changed so much during these weeks that I would want to rearrange my life completely? Completely turn my back on everything that has meant anything to me, my profession, my friends, my lover, my mother? For what? For guilt about not knowing my father better? Then he would see where the barbed wire of the goat pen needed mending, and he would think maybe he could scarf up some of the fencing off a cedar post section, but then he would remember that there would be no barbed wire around the cedar posts because that fence only to mark land, mahn, not keep anyone in or out, not hurt anyone. And then he would sit on the stump of a mahogany tree recently cut down and cry for the dead, while at the same time hoping that Clinton was keeping his promise to take care of the forest. He closed his eyes, tried to place himself back there, back "home," as his mother said, to remember how much she loved him and that she meant only the best for him. He tried to resurrect the richness of his life, but when he saw himself in Cambridge it was as a character in a silent movie, dimly projected, jerky in black and white. Then he opened his eyes to the overwhelming green, the bruises of red clay earth, the tawny bark that would forever be his father's skin. Reality and mirage, oasis and Oz, past and future, all hopelessly gnarled together like bamboo roots and shoots. When the tears came again, he decided they were meant for the living.

Louise, desperately trying to collect her thoughts and emotions, fending off near-supernatural fears, expected to take an aimless walk through the house, but her amble turned into a methodical, traumatic journey through the past. So many things that she had forgotten about remained just where they had been, symbolic objects left almost as altars to their long-dead marriage. She was forced into a reverie of memory at almost every turn. There, on the mantel, a hand mirror he had bought for her during a rare trip to Kingston; the corner had chipped on the ride home and he was upset but she hadn't cared. Here, on the table, place mats she had stitched with her own hands, still intact, made of grasses twisted into rope. There, in the cupboard, the little toy they had found in MoBay for Martinson: shells of small nuts connected into the shape of an ingenious little man with a string through them all that could make him dance and jump about. And here, dustless, spotless, yellowed behind a cracked glass frame, their wedding picture with a snapshot of a baby boy slipped into the bottom corner of the same rectangle. I was so scared of this man exerting control on my son that I made a huge mistake, she thought. I tried to deny a boy his father, I tried to deny the past. I made something mundane, sad, but ordinary seem exotic and mysterious, forbidden fruit, so of course I made it seem very attractive. But how can I bring him through this? Must he waste a decade of his life, as I did, coming to terms with the truth of it? Is there no shortcut a mother can offer her son, a helping hand a little farther up the ladder? Must mistakes be repeated generation after generation? Yet her intellectual honesty forced her to admit that an element of competition for her son's affection, even now that the competitor was gone, clung to her heart. Her victory had been so complete for these thirteen years that she thought the game was over. But this is no game and it never ends, certainly not even in death. She was hard on herself, too hard, and so saw that her own insecurity, her own fear that Marty would forsake her, had been the seeds that finally had flowered after such a long dormancy. A fear has a way of making itself come true, she thought, and what's worse, now I've put my son into a terrible quandary. Maybe I should just back off? Maybe any amount of pressure, like pulling on the ends of a knot, will only bind him tighter? But all ego aside, all the stupid mistakes past, every maternal instinct told her she was right, that this was a rescue mission. She could not ignore her responsibility, or her love. She could not be passive with so much at stake. "I did love you," she cried, looking at the yellowed snapshot again, "I did try."

When the cool breath of evening accompanied the return of long blue shadows, they met again on the porch. The silence between them was more tender, more compassionate. The chirp and squeak of the rocking chairs seemed more harmonious. Yet still, neither of them knew where to begin.

"You must feel as though you have a very difficult decision to make," she finally said.

"Yes I do," and try as he might, Marty could not avoid emphasizing the word "I," as a child might enforce his right.

"Yes you do," Louise repeated, so he knew that she heard. "But before we, I mean you, reach any conclusions, I have to add one more ingredient to the stew. I must admit that part of the reason I decided to come here now is because your boss Charlie contacted me. It seems that this bequest of books I had written you about really has pushed him to the limit. One minute he talks about being overworked and understaffed, while the next minute he talks about retiring because it simply isn't worth it anymore. It's hard to know with him, Marty, that's for certain, but he as much as said that he wanted to step aside within six months, as soon as his pension package coalesces. And he desperately needs you on hand to help now, to make that transition, and, he all but said, to become the new curator." She paused, watching to see how this big news might sink in. At his young age, curator of a prestigious collection, it was exactly what he had been aiming for professionally since graduation. And here he was, considering jeopardizing all he had worked toward—for what? "Well, that's pretty great news, isn't it?"

"I suppose so," his mouth said, but obviously his heart wasn't in it. Why does all that seem so superfluous to me? Why does it feel like she's turning the screws one by one?

"But Charles also said he needed to get some kind of commitment from you about returning," she pushed on. "Otherwise, he's going to have to fill your position. He simply has too much to do, too few hands to do it, he feels as though he's seriously falling behind, and he needs an overlap period with a new curator."

To her deep, deep disappointment, there was no urgency in his response, no pleasure, no quickening of the beat. He simply nodded. That was all. A nod.

"Marty," she pleaded, "look at yourself. You've got no job to stimulate you here, no way to meet people who can provide you good friendship, no culture, no contemporaries, no movies to see or bookstores to browse through, no newspapers, not even a car to do some traveling and sightseeing. Your range has shrunk to nothing, and now you can hardly even talk to me, for God's sake. You're as close to catatonic as I've ever seen you in my life."

"Perhaps you forget that I buried my father today," he answered bitterly. "That's not an everyday occurrence."

She leaned back. "I'm sorry. Forgive me, and believe me, I don't discount that. But to recover, to resume your own life as best you can, you *should* come home. Marty, this isn't your home. It's a part of your past and it has many good things to be said for it, but it isn't your home. It isn't your life. It was your father's life and it made sense for him, but that doesn't mean you have to step into his shoes now that he's gone. That's not the way to mourn his passing. You've got to move on, pick up the pieces of your own life again, be productive and healthy in his memory."

"You're right about that. But do you really think I should let the homestead rot away, let it just sink into the past and out of the family? Do you think that makes good sense?"

The pragmatism of the question gave her hope, represented the possibility of compromise that would get him out of there, that would let his other world have its chance to work its own brand of magical attraction. "Let someone manage it for you down here," she urged. "Keep the house in the family, certainly, but to do that you don't have to move in personally, year round. You don't have to revert to the past, to your father's past, simply because the house exists. That's a form of materialism you would normally disdain, letting a possession dictate your actions."

Again, she was right. But the house was not simply an

250

object, it was a symbol. The house was not dictating his action, it was providing him with an alternative. Silently, he toyed with such radically different ways of seeing the same situation. Louise, concentrating intently, could feel she was making inroads.

"Try to be clear about what is past and what is future," she pleaded.

Hearing so much talk about the past made something snap inside him. "You know," he interrupted, "we were talking about the language here earlier today. I've noticed something about Jamaica. When people talk, they always talk in the present tense. They may not be so sophisticated about the past and the future, but then again maybe they're really very smart that way. Dem think about now, here, whagwan dis moment, and that helps make decisions clearer."

"Simpler," she argued, "but not necessarily right."

"Both. How can you say that being preoccupied with the past and the future and what might happen if you do this, and what might not happen if you do that, makes for better decisions? Tell you true, me not believe it. Each moment builds on the next moment, and if each moment you do what seems right to you, then you're building in a good direction. If you deny what's in front of your face because you have some fixed idea of the future, then today doesn't exist anymore. And then down the road, when the future turns out to be something much different than you expected, you feel cheated, like you wasted your time. No, mahn, present, present, present, as much here and now as possible."

"Yes, that is the philosophy of Jamaica, the philosophy of the tropics in general. But it's such a dangerous, seductive attitude! What does it lead to? Nothing but a kind of self-indulgence. In a year, or a decade even, when you look back and wonder what you've accomplished, there's nothing there. There's nothing to show for your time."

"What should there be, a skyscraper?"

"No, but maybe something more than a bottle of honey or a fence post. I mean, seriously, Marty, would that be enough to hold your attention for the next fifty years?"

"I don't know." But again, hearing "fifty years" thrown around like a chunk of something, like a block of wood he had to set in a certain place right now, seemed wrong. "Look, let's not talk about fifty years from now, let's talk about tomorrow morning. All right, cool. You are going back to the States, that seems plain. The question is, am I going with you or am I staying here?"

She shook her head violently, past the point of emotional composure. "You're trying to reduce a life decision to something as simple as what time to get up in the morning, which is really a way of avoiding the issue. The truth is, if you don't make a commitment to go home you're letting your career go up in smoke. My suspicion is that your personal life at home also is rapidly deteriorating, judging from the tears I saw on Trudy's face not more than a day ago. And you talk about day by day, being in the moment? It's a 1960s drug mentality translated into the Jamaican bush, and I think it's an incredible mistake on your part. God, every time I consider it I feel so frustrated I could just scream! Good friends, fantastic job opportunity, great place to live in the intellectual hub of the world, and you are seriously sitting here talking about retreating into—into a form of nothingness. Even a month ago this would have been unthinkable to you, but now I feel as though if I walk out of here tomorrow without you, that you're gone to me, you're lost in this bush, in this *Heart of Darkness* scenario. Please tell me I'm wrong! Please tell me my fears are making me exaggerate everything way out of proportion!"

252

He said nothing. A long minute passed and silence settled between them. This was the thing Louise feared most of all. As long as they were still talking, still arguing, then there was a chance. But that shell of silence, that nonverbal wall, was too thick to pierce. She knew that silence all too well; the silence of that house had been the most bitter experience of her life.

Into that quiet Cora arrived from indoors, bringing plates of akee and salt cod for them. Marty noticed that the two women did not communicate, as though there was bad feeling there—bad feeling or no feeling? He wasn't sure. Perhaps there was some event from the dark past, some kind of jealousy, unspoken recriminations. . . . On the other hand, he might well be exaggerating what was simply the customary noninteraction between a housekeeper and the missus, a class division, a menial relationship, a modern holdover of slavery, sustained between these two despite a decade of separation. Maybe he had been the same way himself, maybe he hadn't changed much even now, but there was no way in hell he was going to leave Cora sitting in the house alone on funeral day. She and his father weren't married, true, but few people on Rose Hill married. His father paid her a wage, true, but it was just a more formal way of doing what most couples did—him work the land and bees, her work the house, them split the money. The only way they weren't common-law husband and wife was that they didn't sleep together, and who knows about that? Maybe there were times, in the long years of loneliness, when he'd sought her out. Would she have refused him? Probably not, probably not. Maybe that's what the friction is about, two wives of the same man in the same place. He wished he could ask his father about that, and realized how many times he had already had that same wish on this, only the first day. . . .

"Thank you, Cora," said his mother. He looked at her, she look at him, that enough.

Maybe maybe maybe, all his thoughts began with maybe, while she seemed so sure, so clear. Maybe he should go back with her, take care of Cambridge business, put Cora in charge of the house, and return as soon as possible. Or maybe he should plan a vacation every year, three weeks if possible, keep a hand in while Dagi and Manley run the place day to day—could be the best of both worlds. Then maybe when he got older, got his career together, he could quasi-retire, or retire early. There were so many maybes, so many rational maybes, yet the nature of this life seemed to demand a commitment, not a compromise. The bush was not a place you could strike a deal with, the bush would not meet you halfway. You had to be there completely or it was pointless, even dangerous. He sat on the porch eating, not tasting the food, knowing that when all his rationalizing was done, he was caught in an all-or-nothing proposition. On that point, at least, it seemed he and his mother were in agreement.

Louise watched him, so glum and withdrawn, and she searched for an emotional fulcrum big enough to move him off his stuck position. She was detached enough to watch herself and realize that she shouldn't be pushing him so hard, yet she did not have the iron control of her emotions that would have been required to avoid pushing, to play him like a fish and give him his head for now, only to reel hard later. Like any mother anywhere in nature who believes she is fighting for the survival of her offspring, she was fierce. Yes, the shrinks could tell her about transference and Oedipal triangles and fear of loss of her baby and competition with the father for the son's affection. They could say all that shit but goddamnit she also felt certain, in her womanly heart, that she had to pry him free of this morass.

"Look at it this way," she began again. "If you stay here

now, you're destroying your options—by staying here you lose your job back home, for starters. But if you leave, the house still remains. The world here still remains. You can always decide to come back in whatever capacity is most comfortable. But by insisting on it right now, you're burning your bridges back to Boston, back to the real world."

He felt like a defensive debater, refusing to acknowledge the gist of her argument as true, focusing instead on one small point which rubbed him the wrong way. "This world is as real as that world, you know."

She sighed. "For the people here, yes, absolutely. In some kind of philosophical abstraction, yes, absolutely. But not for *you*, Marty. For good or ill, whether it's my fault or not, you've moved beyond this world. You can't simply step back into it like you don't know what you'll be missing. This is not the real world for you, just as this is not the real world for me."

And there it is, he thought, there it is in a nutshell. Her and me, him and me. Am I going to live the life my mother has laid out for me, or am I going to live the life my father, more subtly, but just as certainly, suggested for me? As if that's all my life should be, an expression of one of them, a continuation of one of their ideas, an affirmation that one of them made the right decision years ago. My life should be something other than that, something beyond that.

He stood up with sudden decision. "Today I buried my father, and tomorrow there's a meeting on Dagi's porch that I announced, and I have to attend. It's absolutely important that I be there, and because I can't be in two places at the same time, that means I can't go back to the States with you tomorrow—"

"Marty, you're talking like a robot, like a child—"

"No, I don't think so. If you want to stay here for another couple of days while I get things in order, then perhaps it will become clear that I should head back. But right now, I simply cannot leave. If I left now, my heart and thoughts would remain here and I'd feel torn in two. Simple as that."

"You're hiding behind that simplicity," she murmured. "I'll say it again: Understand that it will only be harder to leave the longer you stay."

"Like pulling out of quicksand?"

"Yes," she shouted, "like pulling out of deadly quicksand. You think you can toy with this place, these people. But once you sink into it, once you're seduced by it and become a part of its suspiciousness and slowness, you're no good elsewhere."

He thought of the people he would see tomorrow—Horace, Manley, Dagi, Bomba, Miss Ethel at the shop, Dorothy in her yard—and to think of them as suspicious, slow, and seductive seemed the height of absurdity. In spite of his mother's anguish he had to turn away to keep a Horace giggle from splattering like an insulting spit in her face.

He's lost, Louise thought, and silent tears began rolling down her cheeks. One last time she said, "You came here to be with your father in his last days. You did that. Now it's over. You don't have to become him just because you've realized some good things about his life here. You don't have to turn into him."

"True, not him. But"—he tried to say it as gently as possible—"not you either, Mother. You'll have to have faith that the future for me won't necessarily be the same as the past for you, and all I can do is try to find my own brightest trail."

She was exhausted, beyond argument, beyond even upbraiding him for the foolish bush analogy about his life and career. But she was not beyond her love of him, never that. "Marty, I truly wish that I could stay on with you for a couple of days, to help put things in order, maybe to lighten the load. But I just can't"—she began to tremble—"I can't stay here, Marty, I just couldn't hold on to my sense of myself. . . ." And walk by the black hole of the deep well, and see the green vines crawling over everything, and be numbed by the beating glare of the sun. . . .

Whatever ice remained in his heart melted. He reached across the barrier of space between their chairs and touched her arm, took her trembling hand and kissed it. "Nothing we're doing here is cast in stone," he whispered. "If you're right, and I'm making a mistake, it can be corrected. I'm still your son, you're still my mother. We still love each other. I'm not commiting suicide."

A form of it, her mind answered, but she only nodded, gulping for breath. The moment she had been dreading ever since she walked into the travel agent's office in Harvard Square had now arrived: It would require the last shred of her courage and self-respect simply to stand up, turn around, walk into the dark abyss of the hallway, ascend the stairs into the black gaping mouth of that place, and pretend to sleep through a blind, silent night with nothing but memories and ghosts filling the air—vengeful, gloating spirits.

"I'll sleep in the guest room," she said, trying to keep her voice even, wondering with a shiver whether he would sleep in the master bedroom this very night, or wait until she had left.

"You need some help getting set up?"

"Marty, I believe I can find my own way around this house," she answered, unable to keep the cold, protective irony out of her voice. Summoning herself, she began to climb. "You didn't ask," she called out as much to her husband as her son, using her voice as a weapon, "but I'll tell you anyway. I got the professorship."

"Congratulations," said Martinson. But she had already disappeared into the night.

CHAPTER
NINETEEN

In the mornings's first light they were both already moving with exaggerated energy, neither able to sleep, as though they had so much to do they couldn't find time to talk to each other. Louise's small handbag was zippered shut and sat waiting at the front door before Martinson was fully dressed—she was anxious to get off Rose Hill as soon as possible. The night had been terrifying and full of recrimination, and now if there was time to kill she would rather kill it at the neutral, impersonal airport.

"We'll walk to Dagi's and ask Bomba to give you a ride to the bottom of the hill," said Martinson.

She nodded, relieved. She had spent hours in the darkness trying to re-create the jungle trail down, trying to remember the turnoffs, trying to fight back her fears of walking it alone. She didn't want her son to go down with her. She wanted to leave him here, alone, to make the break cleanly, to drive the point home one more time that this was the choice he was making—isolation, more now than even in her time. The district road was so battered that there wasn't even occasional Jeep traffic anymore to catch a lift to the bus stop, necessitating the long walk down. The taxi driver yesterday had abandoned her below, forcing her to make a hike on foot, delaying her arrival just long enough to miss the funeral procession. And of course there was no more little truck to drive down, to sit in and wait for the King Alphanso bus. . . .

Yet Marty remains, she mused, still incredulous, watching him amble about the cracked, crumbling house. For him to choose to stay here in spite of everything, with the equation of pluses and minuses so obviously skewed against the decision, despite so many advantages on the horizon back home, was such folly—she bit her tongue. More argument would only lead to a deeper rift. More argument would only make it harder for his pride to accept the mistake in a month or two and come home.

All was ready. A look to Cora sufficed Louise for a good-bye, and then mother and son, widow and heir, lecturer and curator, professor and bush gentleman, Missus and Mooreden, Louise and Marty, walked through the old gate. He left an oil can resting on it to remind him to take care of the hinges. She felt like crying to see his mind occupied with such trivialities. Within a hundred yards he realized he had made a mistake—it looked like rain today and the oil can would rust. Oh well, he would learn. Within a hundred yards the weight of leaving him behind became so heavy that she had to say something. "Marty, it's not too late. . . ."

He held up one finger to shush her, shaking his head no no no.

There was a quietness on the road, as though everything had turned away from their passage. The bees did not swarm out to investigate, staying quiet near their boxes. Miss Ethel's was closed—she must be off to market. It was as though the flowers themselves had turned their colorful faces away, as though the bush had parted and they walked through it on the sterile dry land of the road. Not in it, through it. Marty would have thought it all a projection of his mind except that his mother, looking about as they walked, seemed to see it as well. "This country never liked me," she said. A matter of commitment, he thought, a matter of chicken and egg. Which made him wonder: Why not have some chickens? He'd have to ask Manley whether it a good idea.

They rounded Big Turn and up ahead they could see Dagi and Bomba, both wearing their white bee suits with their tent hats under their arms, walking their donkey home. After yesterday's burden, the donkey was happy to haul a morning's load of honey. I wonder if my father's suit will fit me, Martinson mused. Thank God they have their hats off, thought Louise, or it would look like Martin risen from the grave walking toward me.

The four of them met at Dagi's gate. Dagi see from the handbag that Missus not staying. And him see from way them both standing that she not happy Martinson staying. Same things have a way to repeat, him think. This life a matter of over and over again, little things like gather honey day by day inside of big things like people come and go year by year, son pick up from father in the wheel.

"Bomba mahn," say Martinson, "think you can give me mother ride tah bus stop?"

"Sure thing," him say. "Whether me get back up, dat another question."

Marty smiled at the joke. He knew that the truck moved a short time ago to take Papa home, but still it looked like the bush was about to swallow it up from no use in years.

"That's all right, really, I don't want to strand you down there," Louise said. "I'm sure I can get down. . . ."

"No no no," say Dagi. "Dat just Bomba way ah foolin. Soometime me call him Fooler because him fool all de time." Bomba already open hood of car, connect battery, and jiggle starter motor get engine ready to fire up. It crank once, twice, then come alive like always.

When Dagi open the gate it serve two purposes—make ready let car out, plus let Horace and Manley in. Even since yesterday Manley feel much better, walking easy and looking around free from pain. Dorothy say him must take all them pills, so him keep on with them even though everything all right. It a miracle, no hospital-disappear-forever sadness. A stay-home miracle.

Horace wearing him PNP button as well as a watch him find one time down by the Neptune. It broke, always say same time, but that all right, it still a watch. Him big now, good to wear watch and pin, walk tall. Seem like the right moment, meeting time, to start in.

Manley see what Dagi see and in him heart he rejoice. Just as sure as Louise felt it was wrong and unnatural for her son to remain behind, so Manley sure it right for Mooreden-Lifesaver to stay. Him alone in big house, true, but not for long if Denise have anything to say about it. And if it not Denise, it be someone else, because soon as him settle in word go out around district that best catch ever, better than ten Preachers, just ripe for love-plucking. Maybe that why him momma feelin bad, maybe she not want let go. Them two still got cord between them. Cord in heart and cord in brain not cut clean like cord in belly. But not too harsh on her—like Dorothy say, she sweet before she sour.

Louise looked at Manley and Horace, knowing that somehow they were responsible for her son staying here. For that reason she hated them, and as they stood before her with their version of politeness she felt that they were like everything else on Rose Hill—closed, turned away, withdrawn, their deference to her family's position only a thin veneer over their hostility. She knew that they represented something profound here, that they had some kind of authority and moral force. They had snared her son with it, whether they had meant to or not. She knew there was no evil in their hearts, but it was what they had done that counted. A part of her wanted to curse them for depriving her son of his future, for depriving her of a piece of her own future, but that was pointless. They were people made strong by their world, that was all, and their attraction was rooted in their world, not themselves.

"Coome, Horace, sit on porch wid me so me rest me bones," say Manley, meaning, Leave Martinson and Missus alone to say good-bye.

"Shall coome as well," say Dagi.

The Sanderses walked to the passenger side of Bomba's little truck. "It's important to stay in touch," said Louise, "not just with me, but with things in general. With the Real World, if you'll pardon the expression."

"I agree, really I do. I think there's a very good chance you'll see me in Cambridge before long."

She had a vision of an uncomfortable, quiet man standing at intersections in khaki trousers, willing to hunt a wild boar alone but afraid to cross the street without an escort. "Don't wait too long," she said, trying to smile. "Is there anything you want me to say—to anyone?"

"Oh yes. As for Charles, he'll just have to carry on without me for the moment. But most important, I'd like you to deliver this letter, all right?" It was a message to Trudy, trying to explain, telling her that he felt as though he had no choice but to remain, understanding that she would feel the need to be open to other men, hoping that she wasn't hurt, offering as one consolation the feeling that life sometimes is out of control and beyond anyone to predict, making sure she heard that it was nothing she did wrong and no lack on her part that was making this happen. He hoped it didn't come across as a lame "Dear Jane" letter, as stupid and senseless and condescending and impersonal. But it was better than nothing, it was better than having his mother say whatever she would say, and despite some sentiment at the end about perhaps returning there at some point in the future, it had the tone of finality that was the only right note to strike.

She put the letter in her bag, knowing she would take it out more than once during the long trip home yearning to rip it open and devour the contents, but knowing just as surely that she could do no such thing.

And then all that was left was to say good-bye. He kissed her with much more than politeness and she hugged him with much more than sorrow. She held him at arm's length to look at him one more time. "Oh, Marty," she said, trembling.

"This isn't Good-bye—dis just Until," him say, giving her one more squeeze.

She pulled him close, and whispered, "I left your airplane ticket on the mantel in the dining room. It's there in case you have a change of heart, and it's good for a year."

"Thank you," he said. Good, him think. Cash it in, get money for fence wire.

Then she was in the truck, sitting just as his father had sat so long ago yet so recently, and Bomba let go of the hand brake to begin the long coast downhill. Marty walked up to Dagi's porch where he could see better and wave good-bye, and so many things were happening at once:

Waving waving waving, while Dagi pluck grapefruit with strange contraption—what it? Manley and Horace sitting in the middle of four chairs, Manley whispering, "Maybe in MoBay dem got picture of dis sphinx," while fast-moving low clouds from the east blotted out the sun at just the moment the old truck temporarily passed behind a tree. Thoughts racing through him head, so much to talk about: chickens, where to buy fencing, bees and taking care, Fookah that fookah, ask Manley the story of Cora, ask Horace best way to get sewing machine for Belle so she feel good about taking it. Waving waving waving, his mother's face leaning out the window, her bright-colored arm waving her hand that was dark brown on one side and pink on the other like some leaves that are green on top and silver on the bottom. Sun appearing one last time before the rain, catching a shiny glint on her face which he thought was her eyeglass but which really was a tear, both of them waving waving waving until the truck reached Big Turn and passed out of sight, Martinson still waving, paying no mind to the pain in him shoulder. Only after all four of them were sitting, when a hard drumming on the porch awning began and they were spitting grapefruit seeds into the raindrops, when each in his own way felt grateful to be alive and allowed to sit in this place to talk through the hours of a gray wet day, only then did them all see Martinson knock away that dying bee from his shoulder and pluck out that stinger. That just the kind of joke no one need say a thing about, but make Horace giggle all the way from him belly out.